"I don't really give a damn what they say,"

Kate said. "And they can take their narrow-mindedness and stuff it." Regaining control, she met his gaze. "This is your home, Tanner. And if people are that small-minded, they're going to twist my being here into whatever they want, whether you're sleeping in the bunkhouse or not."

"You don't know these people, Kate," Tanner said.

"Don't do this, Tanner. Please. I don't want you to leave because of me. Please, don't do it."

He held her gaze for a long, tense moment, then looked away, his face haggard with strain. "I'm afraid you'll live to regret it if I don't."

Kate looked at him, her voice steady. "No," she said with quiet certainty. "I won't."

Dear Reader,

The holiday season is here, and as our gift to you, we've got an especially wonderful lineup of books. Just look at our American Hero title, another "Conard County" book from Rachel Lee. *Lost Warriors* is the story of a heart that returns from the brink of oblivion and learns to love again. That heart belongs to rugged Billy Joe Yuma, and the saving hand belongs to nurse Wendy Tate. To learn more, you'll just have to read the book. Believe me, you won't regret it.

And here's another special treat: Judith Duncan is back with *Beyond All Reason,* the first of a special new miniseries called "Wide Open Spaces." It's set in the ranch country of Alberta, Canada, and will introduce you to the McCall family, a set of siblings you won't soon forget. More miniseries news: Marie Ferrarella completes her trilogy about the Sinclair family with *Christmas Every Day,* Nik's story. And the month is rounded out with books by Christine Flynn, a bestseller for Special Edition, Alexandra Sellers, and a second book from Julia Quinn called *Birthright.*

So from all of us to all of you, Happy Holidays—and Happy Reading!

Yours,

Leslie Wainger
Senior Editor and Editorial Coordinator

BEYOND
ALL REASON

Judith
Duncan

Silhouette®

INTIMATE ✦ MOMENTS®

Published by Silhouette Books

America's Publisher of Contemporary Romance

SILHOUETTE BOOKS

ISBN 0-373-07536-7

BEYOND ALL REASON

Copyright © 1993 by Judith Mulholland

Books by Judith Duncan

Silhouette Intimate Moments

A Risk Worth Taking #400
Better Than Before #421
*Beyond All Reason #536

*Wide Open Spaces

Silhouette Books

To Mother with Love 1993
"A Special Request"

JUDITH DUNCAN

is married and lives, along with two of her five children and her husband, in Calgary, Alberta, Canada. A staunch supporter of anyone wishing to become a published writer, she has lectured at several workshops for Alberta's Department of Culture and has participated in conventions in both British Columbia and Oregon. After having served a term as 2nd Vice President for the Canadian Authors' Association, she is currently working with the Alberta Romance Writers' Association, which she helped to found.

To Leslie Wainger—the best there is!

Chapter 1

Harsh fluorescent overheads added to the bleakness of the nearly deserted truck stop café, the blue-white light washing out the colors of the orange vinyl upholstery and turning the plastic plants an unnatural shade of green. The steady hum of the neon sign over the pie case filled the emptiness, and the flashing images on the muted TV reflected in the offside windows.

Outside, thick flakes of snow drifted down, forming eerie halos around the mercury vapor lamps that arched over the service islands. A semi, headed for the border crossing into Montana, rolled past the last set of pumps, its diesel engine rattling the windows as it turned toward the highway approach, its wheels sending up a wild flurry of white. Brake lights flashed, and the sound of shifting gears ground through the darkness as the rig pulled onto the highway and disappeared in the swirling snow, leaving an eerie stillness behind.

Kate Quinn watched the snow settle into wavering lines at the side of the road, her expression lined with tension, the chill of fearful anxiety draining her of any warmth. Alone—God, she'd never felt so alone, or so trapped. She didn't know what to do, and her options were limited, at best. The next Greyhound headed for Calgary was due past just before midnight. If Mr. McCall hadn't shown up by then, she would have no choice but to move on. That hard cold reality settled in her stomach like a deadweight.

Determined not to fall victim to the panic that hovered just below the surface, she dragged her attention away from the empty highway and looked down at her five-year-old son. He lay with his head in her lap, his thick lashes creating dark crescents against his pale face. Gently tucking her coat around him, she smoothed back his blond curly hair, worry gripping her as she felt the heat radiating from him. He was definitely running a temperature.

She had been concerned when they'd made their last bus connection in the interior of British Columbia—glassy eyes, the bright spots of color in his cheeks. But she had assured herself it was nothing more than exhaustion. She couldn't afford for it to be anything more than that. Only her concern had nothing to do with money. She had four thousand dollars in a money belt around her middle, and another three hundred in her purse. What she couldn't afford was the risk; she couldn't take the chance of leaving a trail that could be followed. And now she was stuck here in a truckers' rest stop, miles from the nearest town, with no means of transportation, and Scotty burning up in her lap. With a big sign posted in the window noting that the café closed at midnight, she had to face the fact that her only remaining option was the Greyhound headed north.

Trying to quell the swell of panic, she looked under the table at her nine-year-old son sleeping in the opposite seat. Mark was stretched out flat on his stomach, his head resting on his folded arms, his face turned away from her. God, he had been so terrific through all of this. Such a little man. Tears welled up, and she looked back out the window and swallowed hard, desperation moving in hard against her breastbone. It had seemed like a gift from God, the ad in the paper. A job and a place to live that was isolated and untraceable. A place for her to collect herself, to think things through without fear of Roger finding her and throwing her life into another crisis.

But fate had stepped in in the form of a mechanical break-down and a two-hour wait on the highway for a second bus to be brought out from Calgary—which put her two hours late for the prearranged rendezvous with her new boss. In the space of those two hours, all her plans had gone up in smoke. And there was nothing she could do about it but hope to God that she could contact him and explain what had happened.

Wearily tipping her head back to release the tension in her shoulders, Kate tried to control the expanding panic in her abdomen. She wouldn't be in the quandary she was in if the truck stop was a scheduled stop—but it wasn't. Following the instructions that Tanner McCall had sent her, she'd asked the driver to let her off here. Unless Mr. McCall checked with the depot in Lethbridge, which was the bus's next scheduled stop, he wouldn't know what had happened; he would just as-sume that she'd backed out. Experiencing another surge of desperation, she rubbed her burning eyes. She would give it another ten minutes, then try his number again. Ten more minutes. And if she couldn't reach him then, she was going to have to face the fact that she was at an absolute dead end, that she had no choice but to get the gas jockey to flag down the midnight bus.

"You like a refill?"

Kate dropped her hand and gazed up at the woman stand-ing by her table. Her name tag identified her as Rita, and she was obviously either the manager or the proprietor. She'd shown up about half an hour earlier and had let the waitress and the short-order cook go, then had dragged out a ledger and a bag of receipts. She had spent the remaining time at the front table doing books. Somewhere in her middle to late for-ties, she was a squat, flat-faced woman with mousy brown hair and blunt square hands, her plainness softened by deep-set intelligent eyes. Almost masculine in build, she wore blue jeans and a plaid Western shirt with pearl snaps up the front. Kate could imagine her comfortably handling the big rig that had just rolled out.

Easing the cramp in her back, she dredged up a polite smile. "No, thanks. I'm fine."

The older woman rested the coffee carafe on the edge of the table, giving Kate a penetrating stare, a glimmer of something reassuring in her eyes. "You meeting someone? Or are you waiting for the midnight bus?"

Kate wrapped her cold hands around her empty mug, despair cramping her throat. Easing the sudden contraction, she finally spoke, her tone uneven. "I—I was waiting for somebody, but the bus got in late, so I must have missed him." Looking down, she touched Scotty's hot face. Her voice broke a little when she continued. "I'll have to catch the midnight bus back to Calgary."

Disregarding Kate's response, Rita filled her mug, the rising steam carrying the aroma of freshly brewed coffee. Dropping some small containers of cream on the table, Rita reached across and picked up the empty containers Kate had stacked on a saucer. "Well, now," the waitress said, resting the pot back on the table, "I don't figure that's a good idea. The boy's looking a little peaked, and maybe you should try to let your party know you've made it this far."

Her eyes smarting, Kate looked down and began shedding the paper napkin by her cup. "I've tried to call him, but there's no answer—I was hoping at least he would have an answering machine."

"Who were you waiting for? I know most folks in these parts—maybe I can give you a hand."

Struggling against the desolation wedged in her throat, Kate glanced up and tried to smile but faltered badly. "His name is Tanner McCall—he's a rancher from around here."

There was a short pause, then Rita spoke, a funny undercurrent in her voice. "Tanner McCall."

Kate looked up, meeting the waitress's eyes, trying not to acknowledge the sudden flutter of hope. "Yes. Do you know him?"

Rita was watching her, an odd look in her eyes, then the corner of her mouth lifted. "Indeed I do. In fact, I met his big black Bronco about two hours ago—heading toward Lethbridge, he was, and at a pretty good lick."

Kate tried to dampen the wash of relief that shot through her. Maybe. Oh, God, just maybe. Before she had time to think, Rita spoke again. "Tell you what. Just give me a minute and I'll see if I can raise him. He carries one of those cellular phones with him. I'm pretty sure I got the number here somewhere—he stops in pretty regular for my homemade pie."

Rita disappeared, and Kate tipped her head back. The surge of hope was so strong that she was almost sick, and she closed her eyes, sending up a fervent prayer. *Please, God, please.* She waited for the awful tightness in her chest to ease; then she looked down at her son. "It's going to be okay," she whispered unevenly. "Everything's going to be okay, sweetheart." The boy stirred, rolling onto his side, the movement dragging the cover off him. Kate drew her jacket back over him, letting her hand rest on his shoulder, the worry lines reappearing. She should get some aspirin into him, but Lord, she hated to wake him. It was the first decent sleep he'd had in two days.

She closed her eyes, the awful stress and her own lack of sleep catching up with her. She was so tired—so damned tired. There was a movement beside her, and she opened her eyes to find the older woman bending over Mark, her awkward actions indicating an unfamiliarity with children as she tucked his jacket more firmly around him. She peered out the window at the freak springtime flurry, then dragged a chair over from an adjacent table.

Unaccountably touched by the small act of kindness, but sensing it would embarrass the woman if she acknowledged it, Kate spoke, her voice unsteady. "I'm sorry to put you to so much bother."

Rita waved off her concern. "Don't fret about it. Just one of those things." She met Kate's gaze with an uncanny directness, then stretched out her hand. "Rita Johnson. Been watching over this stretch of road for twenty-five years."

Kate took her hand. "Kate Quinn."

Rita tipped her head in acknowledgment. "Well, Kate Quinn. You can rest easy. I just talked to Tanner—he'll be here in about twenty minutes. He left a message with Karen—that's my waitress—that he was going on to Lethbridge. Which was a mistake, leaving a message with her. Anyhow, he figured the bus driver forgot to let you off, so he headed on into Lethbridge."

Kate closed her eyes against the sudden sting of tears, the release from the panic nearly disabling her. It was going to be okay. Thank God, it was going to be okay.

"Now, don't you worry there. Tanner's a man of his word. You won't have any worries with him, I can tell you that."

Keeping her eyes closed, Kate swallowed hard, her insides roiling with a mixture of relief and an over-load of tension. She hadn't realized how scared she was until just now. Swallowing again, she opened her eyes, managing a wobbly smile. "Thank heaven that's straightened out. I wasn't sure what to do."

Rita tipped her head and pursed her lips in an expression of acceptance. "You look like you could use some shut-eye." She motioned to Scotty. "Why don't you lay the boy down and stretch out in the next booth? You look like you're running on empty yourself."

Kate sighed and raked her hair back off her face with one hand, then caressed her son's face with the backs of her fingers. "I better just keep him here. He'll wake up if I try to move him, and it's the first decent sleep he's had all day."

Rita stood. "Then I'll turn out the lights over here and just let you be. I've got to finish cashing out, anyhow."

Kate's voice was husky when she spoke. "Thanks, Rita."

Rita nodded in acceptance. "No problem. Now, you just put your head down and get some rest. Tanner'll be here in no time at all."

It was the sound of the bell over the door that brought Kate out of the gray reaches of sleep, but a deep male voice that brought her fully awake. Automatically tightening her hold on Scott, she opened her eyes, feeling almost disoriented. Every other row of fluorescent lights had been turned off, leaving the restaurant in an eerie half-light, the incandescent spot located over the cash register creating one circle of brightness. Kate straightened, her stomach giving a funny little lurch when she saw him.

She didn't know what she'd been expecting, but this man wasn't it. Big, wide shouldered, he stood framed in the light, his black broad-brimmed Stetson casting his face in shadows, his shearling coat pulled back as he stood with his thumb hooked in the front pocket of his jeans. His hands were long and well shaped, and there was something almost deceptively casual about his stance, about the way his fingers splayed out against his thigh. Something lethal and a little too careless, as though he had small regard for danger.

Experiencing a strange flutter at that unexpected thought, Kate clenched and unclenched her hands, recognizing the flutter as an extreme case of nervousness. Tanner McCall was *not* what she had expected. When she had responded to the ad looking for someone to take care of an invalid on an isolated ranch, she had, for some reason, expected the patient to be a woman. But when Tanner McCall had responded, he had informed her that the invalid was an eighty-year old man by the name of Burt Shaw, who was his partner. There had been several letters, but she had only talked to him once on the phone—and for some reason she had assumed Tanner McCall was older. Much older.

As if sensing her gaze on him, he turned and stared back at her, and Kate's heart nearly stalled out. There was something about the way he turned his head, the way he looked at her, that made her insides knot up. Something cool and hawklike.

He made one final comment to Rita, then slapped his hand against the counter and started toward her. Kate closed her eyes, trying to quell the sudden frenzy in her chest. Lord, she hoped she hadn't made a mistake. Taking a fortifying breath, she watched him come toward her, trying to reassure herself. She had checked with Burt Shaw's personal doctor, she had checked with Mr. McCall's banker and she had talked to the therapist who had worked with the patient while he was in the hospital. All of them had given this man unqualified recommendations. She had not made a mistake. She had *not*.

Feeling as if her heart were going to come right through her chest, she watched him approach, her heartbeat stopping completely when he took off his hat and she could see his face. Stern and unsmiling, he met her gaze with an unreadable expression, his bronze skin and black collar-length hair revealing his native ancestry, his features chiseled by both heritage and time. This was a man who, in another time, would have been a warrior, who would have hunted and survived in these hills. Kate had been around enough reservations as a kid to realize that he was not a full-blooded Indian—another, equally strong bloodline was stamped in his face. And it was a face that gave nothing away, the hard line of his mouth a warning to anyone who dared to challenge him. This was a solitary man, a man who was never a part of a herd, a man who knew how to fight his own fights, and God help any man who crossed him.

"Mrs. Quinn." He stretched out his hand, more in a business manner than in welcome. "I'm sorry about the mix-up. I should have checked with the depot in Lethbridge before I drove in."

There was something about the sound of his voice, something about that quiet, slightly husky tone, that instantly eased the burst of anxiety. Meeting his gaze, Kate took his extended hand, her pulse stumbling. A different kind of nervousness made her voice waver. "It's okay. It's just that it was so inconvenient for you."

He released her hand, then motioned to Mark with his hat. "I'll get your luggage loaded, then we'll get the two of them settled. We have another forty-five miles to go, and with the roads like they are, it won't be a quick trip."

Kate started to ease Scott off her lap. "If you just give me a second, I'll—"

"No." He held up his hand, stopping her. "It'll only take me a minute. You just stay here with your boys."

For some reason Kate wanted to put her head down on the table and weep. She was so damned tired, and for the first time since she started down this road she was on, she felt as if she could let her guard down. That sensation was almost too much for her to handle.

Struggling against an overwhelming fatigue, she eased Scotty onto the padded seat. He whimpered, his hand twitching, and Kate stoked his head, soothing him. "Shh, love," she whispered. "It's okay. Just go back to sleep." Worried, she watched him for a minute, then slid out of the booth, her cramped muscles protesting as she straightened. Lord, every bone in her body ached. Tipping her head back to relieve the tension in her shoulders, she exhaled tiredly, then reached over and gently shook Mark's shoulder. "Mark, honey. Come on, it's time to wake up."

The boy stirred, turning his head to the other side. She shook him again. "I need you to wake up, Mark."

He made a sound of protest, but he opened his eyes and looked at her. She combed back his hair, her touch gentle. "I have to go to the bathroom. Will you watch Scotty for me?"

He stared across the space under the table at his sleeping brother, then nodded. "Okay," he responded, his voice hoarse with sleep.

Kate took her mug to the bathroom, bringing back a cup of water when she returned. She managed to get half an aspirin down Scott, but he wasn't happy about it and went immediately back to sleep. Mark managed to make it to the bathroom and back, and was sitting at the table, his head on his folded arms, when Tanner McCall came back in. His hat was beaded with water from the melting snow, the scent of cold and leather clinging to him as he stuffed his gloves in his coat pocket. "Rita lives out back in a trailer, so I borrowed an extra sleeping bag from her. We've fixed a bed in the back for the boys."

Nearly overcome with gratitude, Kate felt like crying all over again. She honestly didn't think she had enough energy left to hold Scotty for another long drive. She wasn't sure she had the energy to get herself to the vehicle. She avoided his gaze as she pulled up the collar on Mark's jacket. "That will be wonderful," she said, her voice on the verge of breaking. "Thank you."

There was an odd little pause, and Kate knew he was staring at her. His own voice was gruff when he responded. "You're more than welcome."

Even though Tanner had pulled the truck right up to the door, by the time they got the boys tucked into the back of the Bronco, Kate was shivering from a combination of cold and the kind of exhaustion that comes from going days without enough sleep. She had been on the move for the past five days, her only means of transportation either by bus or taxi. And in that five days she'd had maybe twenty hours of sleep and experienced so many terror attacks, she'd lost count.

It had been a nerve-racking journey. She didn't dare use airlines or rented cars. That was how he'd traced her the first time, when he found out she'd moved back to Alberta. With a safe, secure job waiting for her here, it had been imperative that she cover her tracks as well as she could. She had to be sure that there was absolutely nothing to lead him here. If she'd covered her trail well, and she was sure she had, there would be no way he would ever look for her in the ranching country of southwestern Alberta.

Nor would he ever find her here even if he looked, providing she was very careful, providing she never left any kind of paper trail. So, in the past five days, she had traveled across two provinces, leaving the northern part of Alberta by one route, entering the southern part of the province by another, and God, she was so tired. And now Scotty was coming down with something. The very last time Roger had tracked them down, he had managed to trace them through their Medicare number and Mark's school records. She leaned back against the headrest and closed her eyes. This time she had to be more careful. Much more careful.

The driver's door swung open, and Tanner climbed in, the cold draft making her skin shrink even more. Too drained to even turn her head or open her eyes, she huddled in her jacket. She didn't think she would ever get warm.

Something fleecy and heavy was draped over her lap. "Here. Cover up with this. It'll warm you up."

Struggling against exhaustion, she opened her eyes. The fleecy weight was his sheepskin coat. For some reason, it struck her as a monumental gift. The gift of warmth. A large lump formed in her throat, and she had to swallow twice before she could ease it. "Thank you," she said, her voice wavering. "But you'll get cold."

"No," he answered, his voice gruff. "I won't get cold."

Adjusting the heater controls on the console, Tanner turned on the windshield wipers, then put the truck in gear, making an automatic check in his side mirror before pulling away from the café. It was the habit, she recognized, of a man who was used to pulling a horse trailer.

The falling snow created a swirling white kaleidoscope effect under the bright mercury vapor lamps, and Kate squinted, her bloodshot eyes oversensitive to the brightness. The hypnotic effect became even more mesmerizing as they pulled onto the highway, the sweep of the headlights turning the swirling flakes into a tunnel of brightness surrounded by pitch-black.

Cocooned in the semidarkness of the cab and warmed by Tanner's coat, Kate snuggled down, her weariness fading into a kind of drifting lethargy. About five miles down the main highway, Tanner made a right-hand turn onto a secondary road. A green, snow-spattered road sign listed the different designations, and she recognized the town of Bolton. It was to a box number in Bolton that she'd sent all her correspondence, and although the mileage was obliterated by snow, she knew from checking it out on a map that the small town was about sixty miles north. From his letters, she knew that the Circle S Ranch was about twenty miles this side of Bolton. On a night like tonight, it was going to be a long drive.

Resting her head against the back of the seat, she turned to look at him, again drawn to the long masculine elegance of his hands on the wheel. He still wore his hat low over his eyes, but he had exchanged his coat for a dark green quilted vest that she'd seen in the back of the truck when she'd covered up the boys. He seemed to fill up the whole cab with his presence, his size. As she watched him, he picked up the cellular phone from the console and hit the redial button with his thumb, then put the unit to his ear.

Driving one-handed, he checked the rearview mirror, then guided the vehicle into the middle of the road, where the blacktop was clear. Repositioning his hand on the wheel, he lifted the receiver to his mouth. "Cyrus. Is everything okay there?" There was a brief pause, then he glanced out the side window and spoke again. "We should be home by twelve-thirty. There was a breakdown on the bus so it was late getting to the crossroads." There was another short pause; then he spoke again. "That's fine. Just leave the outside light on by the back door."

He shut off the phone, then slid it back into the case on the console and glanced at her. "You may as well catch some shut-eye—we have a ways to go."

Drawing his sheepskin coat up over her shoulders, she folded her arms beneath it. "Would you mind telling me a bit more about Mr. Shaw? You mentioned in the first letter that he'd had a stroke two months ago, and that he was pretty much paralyzed on his right side. But you didn't say much else."

Tanner made an adjustment to the speed of the windshield wipers, then leaned back in his seat, his profile taut. He didn't say anything for a moment; then he glanced at her, the set of his jaw indicating his reluctance to answer. He held her gaze briefly, then turned and stared out the windshield, his tone clipped when he finally answered. "He had the stroke when we were at a horse sale just west of Calgary. We got him to the Foothills Hospital right away, which was fortunate, or he'd be in worse shape than he is." Shifting his position, Tanner kept his gaze fixed on the road ahead. There was something remote and unapproachable in his whole demeanor, and Kate got the feeling that Tanner McCall rarely, if ever, answered questions that infringed on his privacy, or the privacy of those around him. People would not be comfortable around this man, she realized; he would be able to make them squirm with one look—one of those cold, dark leveling stares that could make any man think twice. No one with a shred of intelligence would ever mess with this man; his size alone was intimidating enough, but it was what she'd glimpsed in his expression and the way he'd stood at the cash register that made her aware of where the real danger lay. Still waters. Still, deep, dangerous waters—surrounded by high granite walls. She wondered what color his eyes were.

Jarred wide-awake by that stray thought, she pulled his coat more snugly around her, considering her next question, speculating on why she had no instinctive reservations about this man. Fingering the spare button that was sewn inside the coat, she studied him. All things considered, she should be scared to death. She wasn't exactly sure why she wasn't. Finally she spoke, her tone quiet. "If he was left with such an extensive disability, I'm surprised they let him out so soon. Usually they like to do fairly extensive therapy with stroke victims."

He shot her a sharp look, then turned his attention back to his driving. Kate got the distinct impression that he did not like her pressing the issue, and the only reason he was talking about it at all was because she had to know.

His clipped tone confirmed her suspicion. "One of Burt's biggest fears was of dying in the hospital—he didn't much like the idea of strangers handling him after he was dead. It upset him so much that he got hard to manage, and the only time he'd sleep was if someone from the Circle S was there." Tanner paused, and Kate watched his hands tighten on the wheel. When he finally continued, his voice was gruff. "After four weeks of that, even the doctor could see that keeping him there was doing more harm than good, so I brought him home."

Kate experienced a sudden tightness in her chest, and she looked away, afraid that in the dim light from the dashboard he might see too much. It made her hurt to think of the old man's panic and fear; old age should never be like that. It should be kinder, gentler. She would be willing to guess that Tanner McCall's decision had met with considerable resistance from the medical staff at the hospital, but she could understand why he had done what he had. She would have done the same for her grandfather if she'd been in the position to make that decision.

"You never said why you quit nursing."

Jarred from her sobering thoughts, Kate looked at him. "I didn't really quit. I got married shortly after I graduated and went to work in a doctor's office." She wasn't prepared to go into the details about Roger's opposition to her doing shift work—or to her working with young doctors. She should have realized then what he was like, but she had honestly thought it was out of concern than out of unreasonable jealousy. It had taken her years to figure out that it all had to do with power and control.

Tanner McCall's quiet voice broke the silence, the flatness of his tone catching her off guard. "You said you were in the process of getting a divorce. Is that going to be a problem?"

Kate's stomach clenched into a hard, tight ball. As long as Roger didn't track her down, it wouldn't be a problem. Trying to keep the sudden tension out of her voice, she answered. "No," she said quietly. "It won't be a problem."

He shot her another penetrating look. It seemed like a lifetime before he looked back at the road. She wasn't prepared for any response, and certainly not for the one he made.

"I'm sorry about your grandfather," he said gruffly. "It must have been tough to see him go through that."

Kate's eyes suddenly burned. "Yes," she whispered, "it was."

She had written him about her grandfather—not written, exactly; detailed, would be more like it. Because she'd spent so much time at the hospital with him during those last two years, because she'd done routine nursing care, like changed his catheter bag, given him back rubs and changed his position to prevent pneumonia and bedsores. She had fed him and bathed him, had changed his bed when he'd soiled himself, and she had inwardly raged at her grandmother because she wouldn't halt the medical intervention that had kept him alive and in terrible pain for the last nine months of his life.

She had included the care regime in the list of qualifications when she'd first answered the ad. She felt that the caregiving was appropriate information. It caught her off guard that Tanner McCall had seen through that straightforward information to her sorrow. She had been devastated when her grandfather had died; she had been overcome by a terrible rending grief. Grandpa had understood—he'd seen beneath the veneer of her life and had known what it was really like. And he had given her the means to get out. Just before he died, he'd signed over a small, forty-year-old insurance policy that Grandma knew nothing about, and when the agent came to inform her about it, he brought with him a letter from her grandfather telling her not to tell the rest of the family and to use it do whatever she had to. It had been a little over a year ago that she'd received the ten thousand dollars. The four thousand in her money belt was what was left.

Needing something to distract her, she undid her seat belt and turned around, stretching across the space between the two bucket seats to check the boys in the back. She couldn't reach Mark, but she could reach Scotty, and she experienced a wash of relief when she found that his face wasn't nearly as hot as before. Brushing back his hair from his forehead, she pulled the sleeping bag up over his shoulders, hoping, *hoping,* that he wasn't heading for another bout of tonsillitis. That would mean a doctor and prescriptions. And problems.

Determined not to think about it, and equally determined not to cross any bridges until she got to them, she settled back down in her seat and pulled the sheepskin coat back up over her arms.

Tanner glanced at her. "If you're still cold, I can turn up the heat."

She shook her head. She wasn't cold. She just liked the feeling of being wrapped up in his coat. "No, I'm fine." She studied his profile, oddly reassured by the sincerity he had expressed. "I'd like to hear about your ranch."

He cast another look at her, only this time she caught a trace of amusement around his mouth. "What do you want to know?"

She shrugged. "How big it is, where it is, what kind of cattle you run." She smiled. "You know, ranch stuff."

The corner of his mouth quirked again. "Ranch stuff," he responded, his tone dry. "Well, let's see. It's about twenty-five-thousand acres, and we run about fifteen hundred black Angus crosses. Most of the deeded land is typical rangeland—rolling grassland, deep ravines—a little too bleak and barren for most people. The leased land west of here is more scenic. The home place is located right along the mountains—nice country, but fairly isolated. You're twenty miles from Bolton, with no neighbors to speak of. You and your boys might find it pretty lonely."

Kate allowed herself a tight smile. She was more than ready for a little isolation. She would be happy if she didn't see another soul for the next three or four months. She had to get her head back together so she would stop jumping at shadows. Forcing a strained smile, she tried to make light of his comment. "If you have a dog, mud and wide-open spaces, the boys will love it."

A touch of dry humor was in his voice. "I think we can accommodate them on all counts."

By the time they reached Circle S land, there was almost a blizzard, except that the snow was melting almost as soon as it hit the ground. Because of the weather conditions, Kate could make out very little when they turned off the graveled county road onto the lane leading to the ranch buildings; she only knew that they seemed to be driving through pastureland that was fairly heavily treed. But she saw enough to know it was going to be beautiful. That feeling was reinforced when they came over a small rise and she saw a wooden bridge spanning a creek, the headlights sweeping across the black tumbling water, its course defined by the light covering of snow along the banks.

They rounded a huge clump of spruce trees, then climbed another small rise, and the ranch buildings came into view. Two yard lights illuminated the spread, large halos forming around them, their spheres of brightness filled with heavily falling snow. For some reason, those halos encompassing falling snow made her acutely homesick for her childhood.

Experiencing a sudden rush of apprehension and an equally chilling rush of self-doubt, she clasped her hands between her thighs, aware of the frantic pulse in her neck. Lord, she hoped she hadn't made a terrible mistake. If things weren't what they seemed, she could have brought the boys into serious danger. It made her stomach churn just thinking about it.

There was such a flurry of panic breaking loose in her chest, that she hadn't realized Tanner had parked the truck until he turned to stare at her. He didn't say anything for a long time; then he reached down and took the keys out of the ignition and extended them to her. "This vehicle is yours for as long as you're here. I'll give you the other set of keys when we get into the house, and your rooms all have locks on the doors." He gave her a humorless smile. "In spite of what you might already have heard, you don't have anything to worry about here."

Her face burning, she stared at him, stunned by his perception, stunned by the hint of bitterness in his voice. And something rose up in her, a perception of her own that was so strong it left her a little dazed. She had nothing to fear here. She didn't know why she knew that, but she did. Feeling suddenly very foolish and very small, she eased a breath past the funny sensation behind her breastbone, then shook her head. Her words were not quite steady when she responded. "You don't have to give me a set. I imagine you normally just leave them in the truck."

Turning to face her, Tanner McCall draped his arm across the wheel with his hand hanging inches from her, the light from outside slanting through the windshield and exposing his eyes beneath the brim of his hat. There was something oddly disconcerting about the way he scrutinized her, as if he was peeling away layer upon layer, looking for the person within. Kate didn't move a muscle, her heart suddenly laboring, her breath stuck in her chest. Awareness churned through her, making her heart labor even harder, and she was struck by a nearly paralyzing fascination with his hand, making her wonder what it would be like to be touched by him. A disabling weakness pumped through her, and it was all she could do to keep her eyes from drifting shut as need—need so strong, so overwhelming, that she felt suffocated by it—coursed through her. More than her next breath, she wanted to reach out and smooth her hand across the back of his, to feel the texture of his skin, to experience his strength and his warmth. More than anything, she wanted to experience his warmth.

His expression suddenly grew shuttered, and he jerked his gaze away from hers, shoving open his door, his jaw bunched. "Don't wake the boys. I'll carry them in."

Closing her eyes, Kate clenched her hands into tight fists, her nails scoring her palms. Oh, God, what was happening to her? And what had she gotten herself into?

Chapter 2

Feeling groggy and disoriented, Kate awoke the next morning, buried so far under the quilt that her head was totally covered. It was the smells that brought her fully awake; the scent of sheets dried in sunlight, the aroma of bacon frying.

The strangeness sent a start of alarm through her, and she rolled over onto her back and abruptly shoved the quilt down, her gaze connecting with an unfamiliar ceiling fixture. Her stomach gave a funny lurch, and she closed her eyes in a wash of recollection.

The Circle S Ranch. Tanner McCall. She winced, a rush of embarrassment climbing up her face. Tanner McCall. Lord, she didn't know what had happened to her in the truck last night—she didn't normally react to men that way. But what made it worse was that she'd had the unnerving feeling that he'd known exactly what had been going through her mind. Raking her hair back with both hands, she stared at the old-fashioned light fixture, a funny ache settling deep in her chest. Well, it had happened, and she had to deal with it; somehow she had to face him. She experienced another flush of embarrassment. Maybe she had reacted that way because she'd been so exhausted. Maybe it was because she'd felt safe for the first

time in weeks. And maybe, some wayward little voice interjected, she was lying to herself.

Startled by that thought, she threw back the quilt and sat up.
She had to get a grip. She needed this job, and she couldn't
afford to screw it up. The welfare of her kids depended on it.
Sobered by that thought, she got out of bed, keeping her
movements as silent as possible as she glanced across at them.
Tanner had indicated this was to be Mark and Scott's room—
a big, white room with dark, varnished woodwork and a gabled ceiling, no curtains on the windows and chipped gray linoleum on the floor. It was sparsely furnished: two double
beds that looked brand-new; an old, scarred walnut dresser
with brass-and-glass handles; an equally old oak wardrobe; an
old gray chrome kitchen table with two chairs, and a TV. There
were empty built-in shelves along one of the low gabled walls,
and the alcove for the windows had a wide seat built in. It was
a wonderful room. And for some reason it made Kate feel
empty inside.

Tiptoeing across the floor, she checked the boys, releasing
her breath when she touched Scotty's forehead. Cool. Blessedly cool.

He opened his eyes and looked at her, his gaze out of focus
and groggy. She bent and kissed him, then rolled him onto his
stomach and tucked the covers over him. If she could block
out the light, both of them would sleep until midmorning.
Glancing at the casement windows, she saw the blinds above
the darkly varnished woodwork, then eased each of them
down, careful not to disturb the boys. Satisfied that all was
quiet, she picked up her clothes and the carryall that was on
top of their stack of luggage, then crept out of the room, closing the door softly behind her.

The bathroom next to the boys' bedroom was cold, and Kate
shivered in the warmth of her flannel pajamas, eyeing the deep
old-fashioned claw-footed tub with longing. Lord, it would be
wonderful to be able to take a long, hot soak. The sink was
equally old and stained with rust, but the water was blessedly
hot, and Kate found towels in the Federal-style closet by the
door. It was obvious by the emptiness of both the closet and
the medicine cabinet, by the lack of curtains on the window

over the tub, that this bathroom was rarely, if ever, used. The same white paint covered the walls, trimmed with the same wide, darkly varnished oak woodwork, and the floor was covered with the same gray linoleum, with a worn spot in front of the sink and a large crack in front of the toilet. The same feeling of emptiness rose in Kate's chest, and she avoided her own gaze in the mirror as she brushed her teeth. She didn't know why, but that emptiness upset her.

The upstairs hallway was long and wide, with the stairs at a right angle. The door at the head of the stairs was closed, and Kate's heart gave a lurch. She knew that was Tanner's room; she'd heard the door close after she'd gone to bed last night. She had her hand on the top newel post before she noticed the recent restoration of the oak steps, risers and banister. Everything had been stripped down and sanded, and finished in a natural matte finish, the beautiful grain of the wood showcased in the elaborately turned spindles of the railing. The restoration was flawless and precise, indicating hours and hours of patient, painstaking work. It was absolutely beautiful.

Caught off guard by the staircase, Kate paid careful attention as she descended the stairs, absorbing the details of her new home for the first time. She'd been so out of it last night that the kitchen was the only thing that had made any impression, and it had been stark and functional.

But now, with the early-morning light streaming in through the living room windows, what she saw made her go dead still. The room was huge, running the full length of the house, with four tall narrow windows and a leaded glass and oak door opening onto the veranda along the east side of the house, and another set of French doors leading to a large sun room on the south end. Floor-to-ceiling oak bookshelves had been installed along the north wall and all along the east side of the room, framing the windows and housing not only an impressive collection of books but a state-of-the-art sound system. The floors were pegged oak, and in the slanting light she was able to tell that the off-white walls were finished in lath and plaster. Here, too, all the the oak moldings and woodwork had been painstakingly refinished, and the French doors leading into the empty sun room looked as if they had had new brass fittings. The living room was sparsely furnished—two dark, forest-green leather sofas, a black leather recliner, two chrome-and-glass end tables and a large oblong coffee table that looked as if it had been made out of a 1940s pedestal dining table. There were some magazines on the coffee table, and a shirt was draped across the back of the recliner, but those were the only traces of anyone having ever been in the room.

Unsettled by both the simple uncluttered beauty of the room and the unlived-in look, Kate wiped her hands against her thighs and stepped off the last stair, feeling as though she were invading Tanner McCall's private sanctum. The place was spotlessly clean, with not a trace of dust, and even the windows gleamed. It wasn't until she stepped farther into the room that Kate saw the U-shaped computer center built along the stairs. A large modern desk flanked by a side-pull file cabinet stood adjacent to the computer setup, the high-back swivel chair behind it showing extensive use. The desk was cluttered with papers, and an empty coffee mug and an open telephone book sat on the file cabinet. But what finally relaxed the funny tightness in her midriff was the Post-It note stuck on the telephone. She found that very human reminder somehow reassuring.

Experiencing a sudden attack of nerves, Kate closed her eyes and pressed her hands hard against her abdomen, trying to quell the flutter in her stomach. This was silly. Really silly. He was just a man, after all. Dark and stern, but just a man. Gathering up her courage, she took a deep breath and started to turn.

"Good morning."

Her stomach, which had been in an uproar anyway, shot directly to her shoes, the rush leaving an unnerving hollow in her belly. She whirled, feeling as if he'd just caught her snooping through his desk. Determined to brazen it out, she forced herself to meet his gaze, aware that her pulse was going a mile a minute. Sticking her hands behind her back, she dredged up a smile. "Good morning."

Tanner looked at her, his steady, unsmiling stare unnerving her, his perusal making her want to squirm. He stood in the archway leading to the kitchen, dressed in blue jeans and a navy and burgundy plaid shirt, his left hand braced high on the frame, his other hand stuck in the back pocket of his jeans. It was the first really good look Kate had had of him, in daylight and without his hat. He was a big man—wide-shouldered and heavily muscled, and with his boots on, had to be at least six-three. He lounged in the doorway, having the relaxed attitude of a man aware of his own strength. His black, collar-length hair was brushed back from his face, his chiseled features more defined in daylight. There were fine lines around his eyes and deep grooves around his full mouth, his high cheekbones accentuating his high, straight nose. He was at least forty, she realized, but there wasn't a trace of gray in his thick, black hair. His face gave little away, except his native ancestry, and his eyes even less—guarded, unwavering, inscrutable. They were, she realized with a funny flutter in her abdomen, a deep, dark, bottomless hazel—impenetrable and mesmerizing.

Realizing that she was staring, Kate shifted uncomfortably and stuck her hands in the pockets of her jeans, then withdrew one and made a nervous gesture toward the kitchen. "Um—would you like me to finish making breakfast?"

Tanner stared at her for a moment longer, then straightened, his expression hardening. "That's pretty well taken care of." He straightened and motioned to her with a jerk of his head. "Come on. I'll introduce you to Burt."

Burt's room was situated at the northwest corner of the house, behind the kitchen. It was a large room, also spotlessly clean, with windows facing north and west, and it was clear the room had been recently renovated. A bathroom that was wheelchair accessible had been built in what, Kate guessed, had once been a large pantry off the kitchen. The bedroom floor was covered in top-of-the-line linoleum, and the door had been widened to accommodate a wheelchair. Venetian blinds covered the windows, their slats partially closed, but the window by the head of the bed was open a few inches. Sounds from outside drifted in, and the minute Kate and Tanner entered the room, the form in the hospital bed stirred. Tanner opened the blinds, then released the safety railing on the bed. The old man opened his eyes and looked up, a disoriented expression in his eyes. "Tanner?"

"Yeah. How are you doing?"

"Okay. Okay, I guess."

Tanner reached for the controls clipped to the head of the bed, holding Burt in place as he began raising the bed. "Let's sit you up. There's someone here I want you to meet."

Clasping her hands together in front of her, Kate stuck a smile on her face and held it, an ache of compassion filling her chest. His body wasted by age and illness, Burt Shaw closed his eyes and curled his gnarled, yellow fingers around the top of the quilt, the stubble of white on his sagging skin making him seem more vulnerable. Age spots marked his scalp, the part at the side indicating that he wore his hair combed over his bald spot. Kate tightened her hands, the thickness in her chest expanding. Just like Grandpa.

Tanner rearranged the pillows to support the old man's head; then, bracing his hand beside Burt's shoulder, he leaned over him. "Burt."

The old man opened his eyes, and suddenly the tightness in Kate's chest disappeared. Burt Shaw was staring up at Tanner with the shrewdest, bluest eyes Kate had ever seen. He glared. "What?"

Kate caught the twitch of amusement around Tanner's mouth. "I said there's someone here I want you to meet."

"I don't want no damned strangers hangin' around here," Burt said, his tone querulous.

The glint in Tanner's eyes intensified as he stared back at his partner. "Well, I'll guarantee you won't want to throw this one out." He straightened so Burt could see Kate standing beside him. "This is Kate Quinn. She and her two boys will be staying with us for a while."

Burt glared up at her. "Did he hire you to baby-sit me?"

Kate suddenly grinned. "No, he hired me to ride shotgun on you. There's a difference."

The old man continued to glare at her, a shrewd, assessing glint in his eyes. "You a good cook?"

Kate stared right back at him. "Yes."

"You make good pies?"

"I do."

Burt gave her a fierce look, his yellowed fingers fumbling with the bedding. "Damned well better. That damn Cyrus can't cook worth spit." He shot Tanner a disgusted look, then turned his attention back to Kate. "Where did you get all that whiskey-colored hair?"

Much to her discomfort, Kate found herself blushing. Her hair was just plain old light brown with blond highlights, but she did have a lot of it, and it was naturally curly. Whiskey-colored hair seemed—well, it seemed so sensual, somehow. Clearing her throat, she brazened out her embarrassment with a bit of cheek. "I got it from my mother. Where did you get yours?"

A wicked twinkle appeared in Burt Shaw's eyes. "Got a streak of sass in you, don't you, missy? I suppose you've got a streak of ornery, too."

She grinned down at him, covering one of his gnarled hands with her own, giving it a light squeeze. "Yes I do. But I'll let you win once in a while."

Unexpected feelings stirred in Kate's chest when the old man awkwardly folded his fingers around hers, the trembling in his hand transmitting itself to her. "Well, you'd better go get that slop you feed me, boy. Your young lady can feed me breakfast."

Kate did feed him his breakfast, then bathed and shaved him, ignoring his crotchety barbs while teasing him about his own orneriness. She could see pressure marks on his back and knew he was headed for bedsores.

When she was finished with Burt, she found Tanner at his desk, the phone clamped to his ear, idly sketching shapes on the margin of an invoice. He shifted the instrument away from his mouth, motioning her to sit in a nearby chair. "How did it go?"

She indicated the phone. "I can talk to you after you're finished there."

He dismissed her concern. "It doesn't matter. I'm on hold."

Leaning back in the chair, she hooked her thumbs through the belt loops of her jeans and stretched out her legs, a small frown appearing. "With the paralysis as extensive as it is, it's amazing that his speech wasn't affected more.'' Meeting his gaze, she made what observations she could after such a short time. ''It looks like he's lost considerable weight, and I can see the beginnings of pressure sores on his back. I'd like to get a sheepskin for him, if at all possible. It would help keep him from getting bedsores.''

Tanner studied her, a twinkle appearing in his eyes. ''Burt's been a hard-nosed cattleman since he cut his first tooth. You could be in for a real battle if you try to get a sheepskin under him.''

Certain he was putting her on, she gave him a cautious look. ''You're pulling my leg, right?''

Tanner shook his head. ''Nope. Burt hates sheep with a passion. Says they destroy good grazing land and that every one of them should be drawn and quartered.''

Kate chuckled. ''Since the one I want *will* be drawn and quartered, it shouldn't be a problem.''

Tanner's call went through right then, and Kate removed herself from his conversation, slipping out to the sun porch to enjoy the view. The snow had all but disappeared, only traces remained beneath the stands of trees that peppered the valley. The valley itself opened to a spectacular view of the Rocky Mountains, their rugged gray peaks still capped by snow, while the bronzes and browns from the preceding autumn rolled out, broken only by thick clumps of spruce and aspen and dark green copses of towering fir trees. Wild shrubs and silver willow lined the ravine to the east, and huge cottonwood trees followed the course of the creek. In another two weeks, when the trees were leafed out and the grass was green, it would be absolutely beautiful. It was beautiful now. She could fall in love with this country. Very easily.

''Quite a view, isn't it?''

She turned to find Tanner at the door, his expression impassive, but what unnerved Kate was the absolute bleakness in his eyes. It made her think of a wild animal entangled in a net, unable to get free. Badly unsettled by that impression, she turned back to the row of windows, folding her arms in front of her. Her voice had a funny catch in it when she answered. ''It's fantastic.''

There was a strained hesitation, then he spoke again, his voice brusque. "I'm going to have to head out pretty soon, so I'd like to go over everything with you now, if that's okay with you."

Sensing his sudden withdrawal, as if walls had suddenly gone up, Kate avoided his gaze, her voice not quite even when she said, "Now would be fine."

By the time Tanner finished, Kate had been thoroughly briefed about what was going on where. She knew where everything was, she knew who everyone was, she had a detailed schedule taped to the fridge, and she had a phone list of everyone from the vet to the man who delivered alfalfa cubes for the horses. And it was clear to her that the key to her survival was clearly going to be Cyrus Brewster. Cyrus not only cooked for the hands but was also the general handyman. Kate was curious about him—not because of what he did, or the fact that he'd helped look after Burt until she got there, but because of the softening in Tanner's expression whenever he mentioned him. This man was also significant in Tanner McCall's life, and that made her curious.

But something else became equally obvious. Tanner McCall left nothing to chance. He made certain she understood what was entailed in the operation of a ranch this size, who was responsible for what and what the chain of command was— and he also made it very clear that the chain of command ultimately ended up at him.

He sat sideways to the table, one arm across the back of the chair, his other hand around his mug, his thoughts apparently sidetracked. He exhaled heavily, then took a drink of coffee. Setting the mug back down, he met her gaze. "There's a cold room in the cook house and a couple of freezers, so if you need anything, go down and get it, or have Cyrus bring it up. If we don't have what you need, tell Cyrus, and he'll get it for you when he goes into town. As for Burt...there are some things you'll need to know." Leaning back in his chair, he went over her duties, making it absolutely clear what her responsibilities were and how he wanted them carried out.

Kate made some notes about Burt's medication, but for the most part she just listened, growing increasingly discomfited as it became clear that he didn't expect her to do much else other than care for Burt. Kate had expected to have at least casual housekeeping duties to do, especially when Tanner was providing room and board for her sons. She was prepared to work—she *needed* to work. The last thing she needed was idle time. And besides, she just didn't feel right about it. She didn't want to make an issue of it, at least not the first day on the job, but it looked like she was going to have to.

Oblivious to Kate's reaction, Tanner continued. "There's a Hutterite colony a few miles from here—we get some of our supplies from them, and every couple of months we hire some of the women to come over and clean the bunkhouse, the cook house and here. If you want to have them come more often, tell Cyrus. He'll make the arrangements."

More often? She didn't want them at all. Resting her arms on the table, she clasped her hands together, considering how to broach the subject with him. She suspected that Tanner McCall was used to having his orders followed without question, but she also knew that this was something that she had to deal with right up front. She had skirted too many other issues with him already; she didn't want to add this to the pile.

Rubbing one thumb over the back of the other, she tried to ignore the twist of guilt that made her insides knot. Finally she looked at him, her voice quiet when she spoke. "Burt's care isn't going to take up that much time. Some days he'll require more attention than others, but I came here expecting to work." She thought about the two boys still sleeping upstairs, and her throat got all tight. She stared back down at her hands, not sure if her voice was going to hold or not. "Not many people would have hired me knowing I had two kids, and I really appreciate that." She kept her gaze focused on the table until she was certain she had her emotions under control, then she looked up at him, needing to make him understand. "I want to do my share here, Tanner. And I want my kids to pull their weight, as well. This is going to be their home for a little while, and I want them to know there are no free rides in life."

He was sitting across the table from her, his long legs stretched out in front of him, his mood darkly introspective as he rubbed an imperfection on the handle of his mug. His expression was fixed and shuttered, but there was a grimness around his mouth that made her stomach drop.

Finally he lifted his head and looked at her, nothing, nothing in his eyes. "Then by all means make a home for you and your boys, Mrs. Quinn," he said flatly. "Whatever chores you give them or how you decide to handle that is your business. Just make sure they don't interfere with my men or the operation of this ranch."

The sinking feeling in Kate's middle expanded, and she shifted her gaze, feeling as though she had somehow jeopardized the boys' position here. As if, by her comments, they had been somehow singled out.

Tanner stared at her for an instant longer, then rose, something controlled and menacing in his movements as he swept up his black Stetson and turned toward the door. Kate watched him go, feeling as if every drop of color had drained out of her face. She wondered what had put that edge of bitterness in his voice.

Kate had always used physical work as a means to keep her own ghosts at bay. If she kept busy, she wouldn't think about how totally stupid she'd felt after Tanner had walked out. She hadn't meant to seem like she was lecturing him, as if her kids' moral values were his responsibility. That had not been her intent—but she suspected that was how it had sounded, and she wasn't going to forget her blunder for a long, long time. Just thinking about it made her squirm.

And if she kept busy, she wasn't going to have time to think about the awful unknown ahead of her, or the grim history behind her. There was no real distance between the two for her yet—one seemed to be almost a reproduction of the other. Her insides were still too knotted up, but she was not going to fall victim to the nearly paralyzing fear that had shadowed her for months.

She was going to give herself some time to get her balance back, to get some perspective back, to learn how to take deep, cleansing breaths and enjoy the sunsets again. Then she was going to get her life in order. She could do that here. Providing she learned to deal with Tanner McCall.

Having scoured out every bathroom except Tanner's, even though they didn't need it, she started in on the large porch at the back of the house. It was basically a utility room that also served as a mudroom, with a washer and dryer and large utility sink along one wall. And here the floor truly did need a scrubbing. There was also another bathroom built at one end, with a shower enclosure that looked almost new. Coat hooks lined the wall separating the bathroom and utility room, with boot racks built beneath. After checking on Burt and finding him still asleep, she set all the boots on the steps, threw the hemp floor mats on the patch of gravel by the back door, sorted through all the coats, jackets and slickers and put them back on the hooks. The whole time she tried not to think about the look on Tanner McCall's face when he'd walked out that morning—it was as if he'd stared right through her.

She had the utility room spotless by the time the boys woke up, and she cleaned out the fridge as they ate breakfast, keeping a list of what she needed for groceries. Tanner had told her that Burt had difficulty chewing and swallowing, so she wanted to make him some easy-to-swallow foods like custards and puddings, and some puréed homemade soups. He was too thin—far too thin—and she was going to do her best to get some weight back on him.

Scotty came over to stand beside her, folding his arms on the counter and resting his chin on them as he watched her wash out containers she'd taken from the fridge. "When do we get to see that man, Mom? The one you're going to look after?"

Kate stacked the last plastic container on the drain board, rinsed the soap suds off her hands, then reached for a towel. "He's sleeping. You can meet him when he wakes up."

"Do you think he'll yell at us?"

A painful contraction clutched at Kate's heart. She wanted to get down on her knees in front of her small son and give him a thousand reassurances. But Scott wasn't asking for reassurance right then. It was a straightforward question; that was all. She pulled the plug on the sink and started drying the containers she'd washed, keeping her tone noncommittal. "He might, but I don't think so—providing you and your brother don't bug him."

Scott gave a little grunt, trailing his fingers through the islands of bubbles collecting by the drain. Kate watched him, amused by his lack of comment. "Where are your dirty dishes?"

"On the table."

"Where are they supposed to be?"

Scotty heaved a heavy sigh and reluctantly dragged himself away. "In the dishwasher," he answered with another put-upon sigh.

"Mom?"

Kate turned to look at Mark, her stomach nose-diving when she saw the anxiety on her eldest son's face. It broke her heart to see what the past few months had done to him.

"Should we unpack our stuff?"

Kate set the dried containers on the counter, not sure how to answer. Mark understood far more than a child his age should, and the last thing she wanted was to put any more pressure on him. She wanted him to know that he had some control over the situation, that there would be other options if this didn't work out. That was one reason she'd brought the books and toys. Limiting each of them to one suitcase, she had packed the fourth, a huge duffel bag, with as many books and toys as she could get into it. She didn't want them to feel as if they had lost everything, that they had nothing of their own.

Making sure none of her own anxiety showed on her face, she tried to make her smile reassuring. "Whatever you want, Mark. It's up to you. If you want to leave things packed until we're sure we like it here, that's fine."

Mark stared at her for an instant, then gave an uncertain little shrug, rubbing his palms against his jeans. "Would it be okay if we brought down the Legos and played with them at the table?"

Experiencing a rush of maternal guilt for the seriousness in her little boy's face, Kate ruffled his hair, wanting to cry. She dredged up another smile instead. "Sure. You're just not going to be able to scatter toys and books all over the house like you used to, though."

"I know," he replied softly. He shot a look at his little brother. "Come on, Scotty. Let's go get 'em."

Scotty didn't hear him. Abruptly scrambling up on a chair in front of the window, he pressed his face against the glass. "He's got dogs, Mark! Three of 'em! Come look!"

Mark shoved in behind his brother, suddenly coming to life, his face lighting up with excitement. "Mom! Look! He's got *three* dogs. Three!" He whirled and looked up at her, his eyes bright and full of sparkle. "Can we go out and see them? Can we?"

It was the first animation she'd seen in Mark in days, and Kate felt a rush of gratitude. Hunching down to see past the open cupboard door, she saw three dogs rollicking around Tanner as he crossed to a horse trailer in front of the barn, recognizing two as Border collies.

"Can we, Mom? Please?"

Experiencing an uncomfortable flutter in her middle, Kate straightened, remembering how she had trespassed across some invisible line with Tanner earlier. She didn't want to make the same mistake twice. Feeling like a traitor for the disappointment she was going to lay on them, she turned back to the boys, her expression impassive. "I don't think so, guys. Mr. McCall is busy, and he's not going to want you two underfoot."

"Just to see the dogs, that's all," pleaded Scotty.

Trying to maintain an offhand manner, she looked at them, a huge ache forming in her chest when she saw the somber stoicism on Mark's face. God, when had his soul got so old, so knowing? Unsettled by that thought, Kate turned back to the sink. Sprinkling it with cleanser, she began scrubbing it, her vision blurring. Somehow she managed to keep the wobble out of her voice when she answered, "No, Scotty. Maybe the dogs will come up to the house later. Then you can go out to see them if you like."

"Aw, Mom," Scotty whined. "Why not? Why—"

"Come on, Scotty," Mark interjected quietly. "Let's go get the Legos, and I'll help you build a helicopter."

Trying not to give in to the awful pressure in her chest as she watched her sons leave the kitchen, Kate savagely scrubbed the sink, feeling mean and hateful and unkind. Surely the dogs would come up to the house sometime, and when they did, she couldn't see any harm in the boys going out to play with them. Surely, petting a dog wasn't out of line, was it? Wiping her cheek with her shoulder, she scrubbed the taps, angrily collecting her determination. Damn it, if she was going to fall apart over every little thing, she wasn't going to be doing her kids any favors. They would work it out. She just had to take things one step at a time.

"Have you got anything planned for the next half hour?"

Alarm shot through Kate, and she froze, feeling very exposed. The last thing—the absolute last thing—she wanted was for him to see that she'd been crying. Trying to clear her throat, she turned on the tap and began rinsing the sink. "No. Is there something you wanted me to do?"

There was a brief pause, then he answered, his tone clipped. "Yes, there is."

She waited for him to continue, but he said nothing, and she got the uncomfortable feeling that he wasn't going to elaborate until she turned around and faced him. Praying he wouldn't notice that her eyes were red, she folded the dishcloth and hung it over the divider in the double sink, then turned. Steeling herself, she stuck a smile on her face and made herself meet his gaze.

Her smile wavered and her stomach did a funny little barrel roll when she saw how intently he was watching her, his eyes narrowed in thoughtful speculation. Feeling oddly exposed, she stuffed her hands in her pockets, determined not to let her smile slip. It seemed like forever before he finally spoke. "Ross is coming up to the house to make some phone calls. I thought it would be a good time to take you down to the cook house to meet Cyrus."

Kate stared at Tanner, rubbing her palms against the side seams on her jeans, wanting to go, but not quite knowing what to do about the boys. She knew that Ross was the foreman, but she couldn't very well ask him to watch them for a few minutes. A nervous flutter climbing up her throat, she shoved her hands back in her pockets. "I'll have to get the boys ready to go," she said, her voice uneven with apprehension. "It'll only take a minute."

Bracing his hand near the top of the door frame, he continued to stare at her, his face revealing nothing. Finally he responded. "I'll wait."

Feeling as if she was damned if she did and damned if she didn't, she gave him an uncertain look and turned to call the boys. They were standing in the archway, bags of Legos clutched in their arms, looking uncertain and a little guilty, as if they'd been caught doing something they knew they shouldn't.

Kate fabricated a bright smile. "You two run back upstairs and get your boots and play jackets, okay? Mr. McCall is going to take us down to meet Mr. Brewster and show us around."

Scotty looked from his mother to Tanner, then back at his mother, a sudden flash of hope lighting up his eyes. "Can we get to see the dogs? Can we, Mom?"

Feeling as if she were on thin ice, Kate tried to reassure her sons with another smile. "I'm sure they'll be around. Now go get your coats and boots—and take the toys back upstairs."

Both boys' faces lit up with excitement, and they turned toward the stairs. Mark, his eyes bright with expectation, shot her a glance over his shoulder. "Where are our boots and jackets?"

"In the bottom of the duffel bag."

There was the thunder of small feet on the stairs and a clamor of voices, and Kate turned back to face Tanner, feeling acutely self-conscious and compelled to make an explanation. "They're both crazy about dogs, and they saw yours out the window. They're all excited."

Tanner watched her, his expression contained, that same undercurrent of somberness in his eyes. He didn't respond for a moment, just continued to watch her, his gaze dark and unwavering. Finally he spoke, his quiet tone giving nothing away. "Yeah. I noticed."

A loud thump and clatter sounded directly overhead, shattering the odd tension that had sprung up between them, and Kate closed her eyes and gritted her teeth. She knew what that meant; her two little angels had just dumped the entire bag of toys and books on the floor in their haste to get to their boots

and jackets. She knew, as sure as she was born, that there were
going to be marbles and Dinky cars from one end of that room
to the other. And she suspected that Tanner knew it, too.

There was more thundering on the stairs, and then the boys
came racing into the kitchen, boots and jackets clutched in
their arms. His socks half off his feet, Scotty started to ram his
boot on, not even checking to see if he had it on the right foot.
Kate pulled him up short and plucked it out of his hand. "Put
your socks on properly, Scott, and don't put your boots on in
the kitchen. Do it in the utility room."

Rolling his eyes in exasperation, Scott picked up his jacket
from the floor and followed Mark out to the utility room.
Tanner moved aside, hooking his thumbs in the pockets of his
jeans. Sitting on the doorsill at his feet, Scotty looked up at
him, tugging haphazardly on his sock. "How come you have
so many dogs? My dad wouldn't even let us have one."

Jerked back by that piece of disturbing history, Kate fixed
her gaze on her son's hands, feeling oddly embarrassed. There
was a slight pause, then Tanner answered, his tone unreadable. "They're working dogs. We use them when we're moving cattle."

His boots on, Mark got to his feet, glancing up at Tanner as
he dragged his jacket over his shoulders. "I saw that on TV.
Only they used them to herd sheep."

Worried that the boys were getting on Tanner's nerves, Kate
helped Mark get his jacket on, trying to hurry him along. Mark
didn't get the message. "Will we get to see them do that?" he
asked.

"Very likely." Stuffing a pair of doeskin gloves in his back
pocket, Tanner lifted a jacket off a hook and handed it to her.
"This jacket of Burt's should fit you."

Scott, who had been getting dressed behind Tanner, jumped
to his feet, all ready to hit the road. Kate exhaled heavily. He
had his boots on the wrong feet, and she didn't know how, but
he'd managed to get his jacket on inside out. Right then she
would have given anything if she could have gone upstairs,
locked herself in her bedroom and stuck her head under her
pillow. Trying to will away the ache in her chest, she slipped
into Burt's jacket. "Help Scotty get his coat on right, please,

Mark," she said, her voice uneven. "I want to check on Burt before we go."

Tanner shifted, and she could feel his gaze on her. He didn't say anything for a minute, then he spoke, an odd edge to his voice. "I'll check on Burt. You can wait for me outside."

The dogs were waiting on the patch of grass by the back door, and they got up, their tails wagging, their eyes bright with interest at this bunch of strangers. Kate knew that, as far as her sons were concerned, it was love at first sight. The collies came in low to the ground, their ears flat, not in a hostile pose but one of care and caution. The other dog, a German shepherd and retriever mix, was more exuberant, knocking Scotty over in an overpowering welcome, then proceeding to wash his face with his tongue. Giggling and trying to fend off the long pink tongue, Scotty rolled on the ground, while Mark knelt with his arms around the other two dogs' necks, giving them idle scratches as he watched his brother.

The instant they heard the back door, the boys scrambled to their feet, keeping their eyes averted as they went to stand beside their mother. Mark sneaked in another quick scratch and a fleeting smile when one of the Border collies crowded up against his legs. But when he slipped his hand into hers and looked up at her, his gaze was anxious. Feeling as if she had failed him in every conceivable way, Kate stuck a plastic smile on her face and gave his hand a reassuring squeeze, wishing she could sit down right there and hold him. Lord, but she hurt for him.

Getting hold of Scotty's hand to keep him from getting into trouble, she tried to bridge the strained silence that had sprung up. "Is Burt still asleep?"

"Yeah. He usually sleeps for most of the morning. Ross will be right up."

Scotty glanced up at his mother, then looked at Tanner, his tone unsure and a little timid. "What are the dogs' names?"

Tanner indicated the two collies. "That one's Ben, and that one's Blue and," he said, pointing to the shepherd, who was checking out something in the long grass, "that's Mac."

Kate heard Scotty repeat the names under his breath, and she tightened her hold on his hand. Somehow she was going to put some joy back in their lives. Somehow.

The cook house was located at right angles to the attached bunkhouse, the structure situated on a naturally treed rise just east of the barn. The view was spectacular, marred only by a clothesline full of laundry flapping in the breeze, most of the items sheets and towels. That clothesline seemed out of context somehow, on a ranch with nothing but men on it.

Scotty gave her hand several tugs. "Can we stay outside, Mom?" he whispered, eyeing Mac, who had a big stick in his mouth. "We'll just sit on the doorstep, okay?"

Hesitating, she glanced down at Mark, who was watching her with hope in his eyes. It was the hope that did it. "Okay, but don't wander off." She gave her eldest son a warning look. "All right?"

He shrugged and grimaced sheepishly. "We'll be good. Honest."

Hoping she hadn't just made a mistake, she gave them one final warning glance, then followed Tanner into the porch that was attached to the cook house. A mouth-watering aroma of fresh bread greeted them as they stepped inside, and Kate experienced an unexpected flash of humor. So Cyrus couldn't cook worth spit, huh?

The main room was large. Off to one side was a large battered wooden table with at least a dozen chairs around it and a lazy Susan in the middle. At the far end of the room were a pool table, a couple of old sofas and some easy chairs, a large-screen TV and a shuffleboard.

"Cyrus?"

"You ain't getting any cinnamon buns, if that's what you're snooping around here for."

The lines around Tanner's eyes deepened. "Just get out here."

"This had better be good, Tanner. I'm a tad touchy this morning, and I ain't in no mood for twiddling my thumbs."

A wiry man with bow legs and a huge drooping white mustache came around the corner, a bowl tucked in the crook of his arm, a towel tucked in his belt. He was beating something in the bowl, and he was frowning fiercely at it.

A smile lurked around Tanner's mouth. "I brought someone down to meet you."

Cyrus's head came up, his expression brightening when he saw Kate. He stared at her for a second, then set the bowl down on the table and wiped his hands on the towel. He smoothed down his mustache. "Well I'll be jiggered. You must be Miz Quinn. Ain't you jest a sight for sore eyes. We was expecting some starchy old war-horse that was going to throw the fear of damnation into the lot of us. I can see that ain't going to be the case a-tall, a-tall." He gripped her hand and shook it, his brown eyes twinkling. "Welcome to the Circle S, ma'am." He pulled out a chair, motioning her into it. "Park yourself here, and I'll get you a cup of coffee and the best cinnamon buns you ever sunk your teeth into."

Feeling suddenly lighter, Kate did as she was told. He had to be at least sixty-five, with the quick, lean build of a man of action, and sharp, intense eyes. Stripping off his towel apron, Cyrus waved Tanner into a chair, as well. "You may as well park that ugly butt of yours, boss. No sense in standing there looking all hangdog." He returned with a handful of cutlery, three steaming cups of coffee, a pitcher of cream and a pan of cinnamon buns. He set them down in front of her, then reached for a chrome napkin dispenser and a bowl of sugar from the lazy Susan. "Help yourself. Afore Tanner gets his sticky mitts on 'em."

Kate shot an amused glance at Tanner. He'd doffed his hat and hung it on the ladder-back chair next to him, and he was watching the cook with barely disguised disgust. Managing to keep a straight face, she glanced at Cyrus, who was breaking apart the steaming buns with two forks, the melting icing making Kate's mouth water. Somewhat belatedly, she responded to his welcome. "It's good to be here."

"Damned good to have you. Ol' Burt's been almost more'n Tanner could handle." Plopping the buns on individual plates, he gave her a penetrating stare. "Two boys, right?"

"Yes."

"Well, where are they?"

Tanner answered. "They're outside with the dogs."

"Well, jest bring 'em here later for some of these here buns."

Licking the icing off her fingers, Kate swallowed her first mouthful of the roll. "They'll like that."

Tanner shook his head when Cyrus started to shove a bun toward him. "I want you to show Kate where everything is, and I'd like you to take her through the storeroom, as well."

"Will do." Cyrus rested his arms on the table, giving his employer a pointed stare. "I hope now that you got some help up at the house, you're going to lighten up some."

The silence could have been cut with a knife. Clasping her hands around her mug, Kate avoided looking at anyone. Out of the corner of her eye, she saw Tanner set his mug down. He didn't say a word; he didn't have to. Kate could feel the chill from two seats away.

Cyrus stared right back at him. "You can stare all you want. I ain't going to drop it. You've been holed up in this valley for twenty-eight years. Time to make some changes."

"Just show Mrs. Quinn around," Tanner snapped, shoving back his chair and standing up. Sweeping up his hat and settling it on his head, he gave his cook one final glare. "And make sure she knows the rules."

The slam of the outside door rattled the windows, leaving a strained silence behind.

Unsettled by the confrontation, Kate nervously wiped her fingers on a napkin, feeling as if she'd been privy to something she shouldn't have.

Cyrus heaved a heavy sigh, slowly shaking his head. "That boy's been up to his armpits in the swamp so long, he don't even know the alligators are all dead."

Kate folded her hands around her cup, not sure what to say, or if she should say anything at all. The silence finally got to her and she spoke, feeling compelled to defend him. "I imagine he has a lot of responsibilities with a ranch this size."

Cyrus's voice was gruff with emotion. "It ain't what *is* I'm worried about, Miz Quinn, it's what *ain't.*"

A shiver sliding down her spine, Kate stared at her cup. Cyrus's comment made a frightening, disconnected kind of sense to her. It wasn't what she'd done that terrified her; it was what she hadn't done that scared her to death. And that was why she was here; she needed space to collect her resources while taking that final step.

The old man's tone was gruff with kindness when he spoke again. "Don't let Tanner get you down, Miz Quinn. He's ten times harder on hisself than he is on any of us."

Disconnecting from her own disturbing thoughts, Kate looked at him, managing a polite smile. "I expect it will take us all a while to settle in."

Cyrus gave her a sly grin. "Oh, I 'spect you'll settle in right nice, Miz Quinn. You're going have Ol' Burt eating out of your hand in no time."

Kate shifted her gaze. It wasn't Ol' Burt she was worried about.

Chapter 3

Rain spattered against the window, the heavy skies filling the room with gloom. Kate cleaned carrots at the kitchen sink, listening to the sounds from Burt's room, monitoring the irritability levels in her sons' voices. It had been overcast and rainy for the past two days, and she was waiting for the boys to explode with boredom. The last time they'd had a chance to burn off any steam outside was on Wednesday, the day they'd gone down to the cook house to meet Cyrus. Granted, they'd run themselves and the dogs ragged. Cyrus had dug out an old wagon he used in the garden, and they had spent the rest of the afternoon building a fort and taking wild rides down the hill. They had burnt off so much energy and had such an overdose of fresh air that Scotty had fallen asleep at the supper table. But two full days of being cooped up inside was about their limit before they started tormenting each other. Today was the third.

She heard Burt say something and Mark answer, then heard them change the TV channel. Thank God for Saturday-morning cartoons and the big satellite dish beside the house. With a hundred and some channels, maybe they would keep the lid on things for a while longer, then she was going to throw them outside, no matter how wet they got. Tossing the carrots into the container, she turned on the tap and filled it with cold water, smiling to herself. She couldn't believe they had Burt Shaw in there watching "Sesame Street." But then, there were a few things she couldn't believe—like the fact that the two of them had smuggled their bubble blowers into his room and turned it into one big bubble factory. She wouldn't ever have found out about it if she hadn't heard both Mark and Scotty giggling and known, as sure as she lived and breathed, that they were up to no good. Burt, in that cranky tone of his, had told her to get of his room and mind her own business. The boys had loved it.

The back door slammed, and Tanner entered the kitchen carrying a large plastic bag, his long oiled canvas slicker beaded with rain, dark splotches marking the wide brim of his hat. She recalled Cyrus's comment about him being harder on himself than he was on anyone else; with those grim lines around his mouth, she didn't doubt it for a minute. He looked as if he had the weight of the world on his shoulders.

Setting the bag on the table, he swept off his hat and ran his hand through his hair, then put his hat back on, careful to avoid her gaze. "Here's that sheepskin you wanted for Burt."

Drying her hands on her jeans, Kate went over to the table and took the pad out of the bag. She thought it was unusually large until she opened it and realized there were two. "This is great. Where did you get them?"

"There's a place just outside of Calgary." For the first time since Wednesday, Kate caught a glimmer of amusement in Tanner's eyes. "He's not going to be too happy about this."

It was also the first time in two days that he'd met her gaze dead-on, and Kate experienced an unnerving flutter in her middle. Nervously fidgeting with the skins, she severed the contact. "Yes. Well..." Feeling very self-conscious, she smoothed her hand over the carded wool, then made an awkward gesture. "Thanks. It really will make him more comfortable." Sensing his gaze still on her, she turned to go, the flutter in her middle climbing up into her chest.

She stopped in the bedroom doorway, looked at the ceiling and heaved a weary sigh. Not again. This time they had made colorful paper chains and fans and hung them from the rigging over Burt's bed. And balloons. Balloons she remembered them saving from the school carnival. It looked like some sort of cheap bordello. Scott was lying on his stomach at the end of the bed, his head propped in his hands, and Mark was sitting beside Burt, the channel changer in one hand and the controls for the bed in the other. No doubt giving Scotty rides during commercials.

Burt gave her his best, bossy stare. "You can just turn yourself around and hightail it outta here. We ain't doing nothing, so there's no need to be looking at us like that."

Mark gave her his best angelic look. "Hi, Mom."

Scotty didn't even bother saying anything. He just gave her an absent wave.

Before Kate could get one word out, both boys got wide-eyed looks of alarm on their faces and immediately scrambled over the safety rails and off the bed. Burt glared at a spot over her shoulder. "And you can just cart your ugly hide out of here, Tanner McCall. You'd think this was Grand Central Station, the way people keeping coming and going in here."

His wide, fearful eyes fixed on Tanner, Scotty reached for Mark's hand, a flicker of defiance in the angle of his chin when he stammered, "Os-Oscar was having a birthday party on TV, and Burt said he never had one. So we decorated his bed."

When Tanner didn't respond, Kate did. "Fine. You'll have to move, please. I want to put this sheepskin under Burt so his back doesn't get sore."

Burt gripped his quilt, giving her a hostile look. "You ain't coming near me with that thing. The only good sheep is a dead one, and I'm not having no sheepskin in my bed."

Kate felt as if her patience had just run dry. Just once she would like things to be normal. Just once. She peeled the quilt out of Burt's hands. "This *is* a dead one, Burt. And, yes, you are having it in your bed."

Scotty shot Burt a worried look, then leaned over and whispered a warning. "You better not argue when she gets that look, Burt," he instructed urgently.

Mark tried to assure the old man. "It *is* a dead one, Burt. A dead one will be okay, won't it?"

His size accentuated by his hat and the oilskin duster, Tanner entered the room, his expression perfectly still. He looked like a gunslinger in that outfit. Pushing around the other side of the bed, he ended the discussion when he dropped the rail and picked Burt up, blankets and all. There was an odd tone to his voice when he said, "I wouldn't put up a fight if I were you, old man. I think the lady means business."

Burt glared at him but only made a disgusted sound when Kate spread the sheepskin on the bed, then fluffed up his pillows. Once she had the bed arranged, Tanner laid Burt back down, then stood with his hands on his hips as Kate tucked the bedding back under the mattress.

Knowing from experience that the less she said right now, the less she would have to regret later, Kate picked up three dirty glasses and some scraps of construction paper and marched out of the room, keenly aware that she had developed a splitting headache in the past five minutes. Both her sons and Burt deserved to be spanked.

Tossing the paper in the trash for the burning barrel, she put the glasses in the dishwasher and shut the door with more force than necessary. Why did everything have to turn into some kind of sideshow around here? Why?

"I take it you have a three-party insurrection happening here."

Kate jumped and clamped her hand over her breastbone. Lord, she hadn't heard him come into the kitchen, and she hadn't realized he was standing so close behind her. Inhaling carefully, she turned, a blush climbing up her cheeks when she saw the glint of amusement in his eyes. She had the uncomfortable feeling that his amusement was directed at her. "Yes, well . . ." What could she say? He'd seen the utter chaos with his own eyes. It was a wonder he didn't fire her on the spot.

He stood with his weight on one hip, his thumb hooked in the pocket of his jeans, the duster pushed back. And she could feel him watching her. Folding her arms tightly under her breasts, she made herself look up at him. His hat was pulled low over his eyes, the angle making him look distant and unapproachable. And solitary. Very, very solitary. His absolute stillness, his steady, level gaze, his unsmiling expression, did funny things to her insides—things that didn't make any sense—and she looked away, nerves making her heart race. She wondered what lay hidden beneath that inscrutable exterior.

There was a long, unsettling pause, then he spoke, his voice roughened. "I made an appointment with the principal of the elementary school in Bolton for Monday morning. I figured you'd want to get Mark enrolled right away."

Alarm shot through her, and Kate reacted, her gaze swiveling to his. Experiencing the first cold fingers of panic, she stared at him, trapped in her own omission. She should have foreseen this. She should have dealt with it as soon as she got off the damned bus. All she could do now was tell him a portion—a small portion—of the truth. Stuffing her hands in her pockets, she forced herself to meet his gaze. "Mark was so far ahead of the rest of his class that his teacher already passed him." Experiencing a rush of panic, she tightened her hands, her voice strained when she forced herself to go on. "There are only six weeks of school left, so I thought I'd give him a long break—and give him a chance to settle in here."

Tanner studied her, his eyes narrowed in a gauging, speculative look. He didn't say anything. Unnerved and anxious, Kate stared at him, afraid to take her next breath.

He dragged his thumb across his chin, his gaze cool and analytical, his eyes never leaving her. Finally he spoke, his tone a little too quiet, a little too edged. "Tell me something, Mrs. Quinn. Do you have legal custody of your boys?"

Feeling as if her knees were going to buckle, she leaned back against the counter and closed her eyes, her heart hammering heavily in her chest. She had never expected him to ask that. Never. But it was one question she didn't have to evade. This one she could answer truthfully. Feeling shaky inside, she opened her eyes and met his gaze. "Yes," she whispered, her voice breaking on emotion. "Yes, I do."

He stared at her for a moment, then reached down and took the bag with one hand. "*Was* he ahead of his class?"

"Yes."

He raised his eyes and looked at her, his face expressionless, the steadiness in his eyes making her think of a hunter's eyes, the angles of his face accentuated in the gloom. He was so still, so very still.

He held her gaze a moment longer, then picked up the receipt that had fallen out of the bag. Folding it in half, he stuck it in the breast pocket of his shirt. "Tell Burt I'll check in with him later. There are a few things I need to talk to him about."

Suddenly cold, Kate huddled in the warmth of her sweater. "Okay."

Tanner gave her one final glance and turned. Just then the back door opened and Cyrus called out, "Tanner? You in here?"

"Yeah."

"Hell's bells, it's rainin' cats and dogs out there." The cook came through into the kitchen, slapping his hat against his leg to knock the rain off. "The farrier's here. Wasn't sure what horses you wanted done and couldn't find Ross."

Tanner picked up a set of keys that had been lying on the counter and stuffed them into his jeans pocket, then turned up the collar on his coat. Another young man, his upper arm immobilized against his chest in a Velcro restrainer, followed Cyrus in, and Tanner shot Cyrus a questioning look.

The cook gave him a level stare. "I brought Buddy up here to set a spell with Ol' Burt. Figured I'd take Miz Quinn and them two boys down to see the new pups."

There was a long pause as Tanner stared back at him, then he spoke, his voice flat. "Then make sure they don't get in the way. We've got five horses that need to be shod, and Riley will be working in the barn."

Cyrus's chin came up, and his eyes narrowed. "Well, now," he retorted, his voice thick with sarcasm. "It's a good thing you told me that, Tanner. It's not like some old wrangler could figure that out for hisself."

Giving the cook a disgusted look, Tanner snapped a clasp on the front of his coat and headed for the door. Embarrassed by the byplay, Kate pretended she wasn't there, wishing heartily that it were true. It hurt that Tanner expected the boys to get in everyone's way, to be a big annoyance. She sighed. She had to be fair. There were times when they *were* annoying—very, very annoying—but she had already warned them that they

were never, never to go in the barn unless they were told to do
something or if she was with them.

"He jest gets a burr under his saddle now and again, Miz
Quinn. Them two tads could get hurt bad down there, especially if no one was watchin' out for 'em."

Kate looked up at Cyrus, wishing that he'd talked to her first
before setting off her boss. "I don't think this is a good
idea—"

"Horse puckies. Ain't going to put nobody out." He turned
to the young man. "You go on and settle yourself in there with
Burt. You can stretch out on that cot in the corner if yer arm's
paining you some." He looked at Kate. "Buddy here dislocated his shoulder a couple of days ago—old bronc decided to
peel him off the hard way." He strode across the kitchen.
"Hey, you boys. You wanna go see some pups?"

Kate winced when she heard someone fall off the bed, then
the two boys came boiling out of the room, wild excitement
lighting up their faces. "Puppies? Real puppies?"

Cyrus chuckled. "As real as they get."

Kate loved the rain, and she loved being outdoors. It didn't
matter if it was cold, or if the sky was so overcast that the
clouds shrouded the valley. She knew she wasn't going to be
able to get out that often, so she was determined to enjoy it
when she could. The boys' jackets were all-weather with
hoods, but she'd had nothing appropriate. Cyrus had found a
yellow slicker, which covered her from her neck to just about
down to her toes, and he'd jammed one of Burt's Stetsons on
her head to keep the rain off her hair.

The barn was down the hill from the house, sheltered from
the winds that Kate knew would howl in from the northwest in
the winter. The boys ran ahead, the three dogs trying to bounce
up on them, and Scotty's laughter carried clearly back to her.
Squinting against the rain that caught in her eyelashes, she
smiled and stuck her hands in the pockets of the slicker. In
spite of everything, this was going to be a good place for them.

The farrier was already at work in the barn, shoeing a big
bay gelding that was cross-tied in the alley between the long
rows of box stalls. The horse had a white blaze on its face and

bright, intelligent eyes, and Kate knew enough about these animals to know this one was a fine piece of horseflesh. As soon as the boys walked up to him, he dropped his head and nickered into Mark's outstretched hand. Mark thought he had died and gone to heaven.

Cyrus gave each of the boys a handful of crunchies, then showed them how to hold out their hands with the palms flat to feed the horse. Scott thought that was all right, but he was more interested in what the farrier was doing, and he squatted down beside him so he could see what the older man was up to. Kate knew the questions were going to start coming fast and furious, and she knew she was going to have to try to distract him, or he would drive everyone nuts. Before she had a chance to reprimand her son, Cyrus was explaining what the farrier was doing and why. *Then* the questions started. Why did the man have on a leather apron? Why did the man use that big file on the horse's hoof? Was it like Mom filing her nails? Did it hurt when the man nailed the shoes on? Why couldn't they just glue on the new shoe—and could he have the old one?

It wasn't just that Scott asked a ton of questions; he had to have everything qualified and verified—just so he had his facts straight. If he retained half of what he learned, he was going to be a walking encyclopedia by the time he was fourteen.

Mark was quieter. He didn't ask as much, but he stored up information like a sponge. Not only would he remember the step-by-step process, but he would remember the name of every tool, the number of nails the farrier used and anything else that he happened to notice—which was usually quite a bit. Kate thought about some of the things that had happened during the past year. Her stomach knotted. Sometimes Mark remembered far too much.

A tall lanky man in his early thirties, wearing a black hat, a black denim jacket and black shotgun chaps, came out of one of the box stalls, his spurs jangling against the cement alleyway. Cyrus called to him. "Ross. Come here for a minute."

The young man approached with the loose-hipped saunter of a man who'd spent hours in the saddle, his unshaven face unsmiling. "Ross, this here is Miz Quinn and her two boys—

she's the one Tanner hired to look after Burt. This here is Ross Wilson, our foreman."

Ross Wilson touched the brim of his hat, a flicker of something appearing in his eyes before his expression shut down. "Ma'am."

As Cyrus explained that he'd shanghaied Buddy to stay with Burt, Kate studied the younger man. He was younger than she had originally thought—maybe twenty-seven—but hardened beyond his years. He was, she inwardly recognized, a man you would want with you, rather than against you, if the chips were ever down. Scotty was watching him with absolute awe, as if one of his cartoon heroes had just sprung to life. Kate wasn't sure she liked the idea.

Their business concluded, Ross looked at her, touched the brim of his hat again, then headed out of the barn, something almost insolent in his swagger.

The puppies and their mother were in a box stall filled with fresh straw, with a wooden box in the corner that had an old quilt in it. Mark and Scott were on their knees in an instant. The mother, not one of the three dogs they'd seen before, was also a Border collie, and so were the puppies. The puppies, Kate could tell, were only days old, with their eyes barely open. And their bodies were so roly-poly, they could barely walk. They were adorable.

But before Scott could touch one, Mark caught his arm. "No, Scotty. Remember how Mom showed us with Brian Olsen's dog? Let the mom smell you first. She's got to get to know us. So she knows you're not going to hurt them."

Leaning back against the heavy plank wall, Kate watched them, a traitorous twist unfolding in her chest as Mark gently stroked the mother, his voice a soft singsong as he talked to her. Scott, abdicating to Mark's authority in this instance, carefully mimicked his big brother's slow, gentle strokes, but not exactly giving the mother dog his full, undying attention. He kept glancing at the puppies; he wanted to get his hands on one of them in the worst way.

Mark finally picked up one of the puppies and carefully showed it to the mother, his eyes lighting up when she licked his hand. "All right," he said softly, his tone underscored with awe. "You can pick one up now, Scott. But be real careful, okay?"

Cyrus, who had been watching the byplay, crouched down beside Mark and began stroking Bess's head with his weathered hand. "You handled that jest right, Mark," he said, his voice quiet. "Bess wouldn't have hurt you, but she wouldn't have liked it much if you'd manhandled her pups right off the bat. You done a good job."

Keeping his eyes averted, Mark gave an embarrassed little shrug, unaccustomed to praise from a male. He answered, his voice wobbling, "Thank you, sir."

Cyrus ruffled his hair, his own voice gruff when he responded. "I ain't no 'sir,' son. Cyrus works jest fine for me, if your mom don't mind."

Kate's chest felt painfully full. "It's fine with me," she answered, her voice uneven. Afraid she was about to cry, she looked away, struggling with the tightness pressing down in her chest. The feeling was instantly neutralized and her stomach dropped when she saw Tanner standing just outside the stall, his face set in that inscrutable expression, the unexpected starkness in his eyes making her heart contract. Pain. And a terrible, terrible aloneness. Abruptly looking away, she stared unseeingly at her sons, feeling as if she'd just stumbled on to something so private, so personal, that it was as if she had trespassed emotionally. The sensation unnerved her, and she experienced the weirdest sensation in the pit of her stomach. For some reason she recalled Cyrus's comment about Tanner hiding out in this valley for twenty-eight years. A life sentence. Shaken by that unexpected thought, Kate looked away, a stark realization hitting her. Twenty-eight years. He must have been little more than a boy. And she knew, without a doubt, that whatever had brought him here had left some very deep scars. Scars that went soul deep.

"—now like I said, if it's okay with your mom, I'd like you boys to help me look after Bess and these here pups. You'll have to make sure she's got food and water, and she'll need to be brushed once in a while."

Mark stared at him, hardly able to believe his ears. "You mean it?"

"Yep. I do. But," Cyrus added, raising a finger, a warning tone in his voice, "you boys ain't to go into any of the corrals unless someone is with you, and you can't go into any of the box stalls except this one. The hands sometimes bring their horses in, and some of them are unpredictable cusses. And you ain't to touch anything unless you check with either Ross or me." The older man gave the boys a stern look. "Now, I need your word on this. We can't have you getting hurt because you didn't pay no mind."

Their eyes wide, they both nodded, their responses coming out in ragged counterpoint. "We promise."

He stared at the two of them, then spoke, a hint of humor in his tone. "Good." Placing his hands on his knees, he got slowly to his feet. Without looking at the door, he spoke. "You got anything to add here, boss?"

The two boys looked up, alarm in their eyes; they'd clearly been unaware of Tanner's presence. Standing with his arms folded, Tanner looked down at them. "No. That pretty much covers it."

At the sound of his voice, the dog bounded up, her eyes keen with alertness as she came over to him. Smiling a wry half smile, he reached down and scratched her ear, his voice gruff. "It's okay, girl. You've got a few days of maternity leave coming to you before we put you back to work."

Huddled in Burt's yellow slicker, Kate watched him, feeling as if everything had just been thrown out of sync. She had told him two days earlier that she wanted this to be their home. He had, in his own taciturn way, just permitted her two small sons a place in the bigger scheme of things on the Circle S. Her chest suddenly tight, she stuck her hands in the pockets of her slicker and looked down, raking the loose straw into a pile with her foot. Kate knew he didn't want them there, but that bleak look in his eyes did awful things to her heart, and she shivered, hurting for him. And not even knowing why.

Chapter 4

"**M**om! Mom! You gotta come see! They're going to be bringing a whole bunch of cows through the pasture. And those big trucks—those cattle liners things are here and they're going to load 'em up. You gotta come see!"

Checking the oven setting, Kate shut the door and turned, heaving a sigh when she saw Mark. He and his brother had been out behind the cook house, shaking water off the trees, and, she suspected, sliding down the steep slope on pieces of plastic Cyrus had given them to waterproof their fort. His blond hair was soaked, with the moisture trickling down his face, and he was covered with mud and grass stains. He was so revved up on excitement that he could hardly stand still.

She met his gaze. "What are you talking about?"

"They're bringing the herd through. Cyrus says they can't take the trucks out to where they usually load 'em 'cuz it's too wet and they'll get stuck, so they're moving them up to the barn—so they can use that chute there. You gotta see it, Mom. It's going to be awesome."

Buddy, who was unloading supplies after a trip to town, set a box of groceries on the counter, wincing slightly as he jarred his shoulder. With only his upper arm strapped to his chest, he had the use of his arm from the elbow down, but Kate suspected carrying in boxes of groceries wasn't one of the prescribed exercises. She was about to scold him, but he gave her a sheepish grin. "My mama always said I was too stubborn for my own good." Shifting the sling, he cautiously rolled back his shoulder. "If you want to go with your boys to watch, I'll sit with Burt for a spell." He flashed her a broad grin. "Sometimes these range cows don't load worth s—ah, worth a dang, and it can get kinda interestin'. Last year one old whiteface tried to go through the chute and broke it all to hell . . . ah, excuse me, all to heck."

Kate wanted to go in the worst way, but she didn't feel right about leaving Buddy here to do her job. Except Burt was asleep, and she suspected the hired hand would be quite happy to sit up here with the TV remote control and endless sports channels.

"Come on, Mom. We can go over by the cook house and watch. There's an old picnic table there, and Cyrus said we could. He said for you to come."

It was the anxious, hopeful look in her son's eyes that made up her mind. "All right," she said, stripping off the towel she had tucked at her waist. She looked at Buddy. "If Burt wakes up, or if you have to leave, just phone down to the cook house, okay?"

"Will do, ma'am."

The ground was spongy, and the new leaves still glistened with beads of rain, but the thick, dense cloud cover had broken, allowing thin sunlight through. Her feet in a pair of Burt's rubber boots and wearing his slicker, Kate followed the boys down a trail through the trees along the brow of the hill. The tree bark was dark with rain, the tall grasses and low berry bushes shiny with moisture, and Kate inhaled deeply, the smell of rain and wet soil energizing her. The thick stands of spruce, aspen and poplar along the bluff were unusually quiet, the only sounds the swish of Kate's slicker against the long grass beside the trail and the soft, erratic tattoo of water dropping from the overhead branches. Huddled against the damp chill, Kate noticed a patch of wood violets among the undergrowth. She would have to remember where they were, so she could find them when they bloomed later in the summer. Again inhaling the fresh, clean fragrance of wet pine, damp soil and new growth, Kate ducked her head to avoid a low hanging branch, shivering when cold beads of water hit the back of her neck.

She had no misconceptions about this being the shortest route to the cook house. It wasn't. But it did skirt the barn and the corrals, and it offered a fantastic view of the mountains through the trees. It was so beautiful and wild and unspoiled, but then, most of the land on the Circle S was—right from the open rangeland to the wilderness of the foothills. God's land, Burt called it. Kate couldn't have agreed more. She loved it.

Cyrus was just coming out of the cook house carrying a large thermos when they reached the last jog in the trail. He was wearing a tattered slicker with a battered hat pulled low over his eyes, and he had his pants tucked into his boots. He set the thermos on the steps, pulled off his hat, spat on the ground, then grinned at them. "Well, howdy, Miz Quinn. Glad you could make it. This is always good for a show."

Tucking a stray curl back into the loose knot on top of her head, Kate grinned back at him. "So I hear. Buddy just came back with the supplies, so he offered to stay for a while."

The twinkle in Cyrus's eyes intensified. "Must be a baseball game on. I tell you, that boy's baseball crazy." He waved his hat at the weathered picnic table at the front of the cook house. "You jest plunk yourselves down here. Best seat in the house."

Kate ducked under a moisture-laden fir bough. "Will I be able to hear the phone from out here? I told Buddy to call down here if he needs me."

Cyrus motioned to Mark. "How about you skedaddle in and open the window for your mom and set the phone on the sill? Then we can hear it jest fine." He swiped most of the water off the plank seat with his hat, then waved her over. "Have a seat. I got a fresh pot of coffee brewing, so we'll nip into that as soon as it's done."

Stepping over the cross brace on the table, Kate sat down beside him, her spirits buoyed by the view. They were looking down the throat of a heavily treed pass to the mountains beyond, with the valley opening up to the rolling pastureland surrounding the ranch site. She took another deep, invigorating breath. God, but it smelled wonderful.

Cyrus shot her a sly grin. "Sounds like you've got yourself a fair slice of contentment there, Miz Quinn."

She gave him an amused look. "You could say that." Bracing her elbows on the table, she stared across the scene before her. "Actually," she said softly, "I love it. It's so beautiful around here."

Cyrus nodded in agreement. "Gets in your blood, it does. I've been in these here parts for fifty-eight years—my folks moved out when I was just a tad about Mark's age. Never been anywheres else, and don't have any urging to go anywheres else."

Kate could understand that completely. They fell into a companionable silence as Mark and Scott took turns swinging on the tire swing that Cyrus had rigged up in one of the massive cottonwoods. Kate shifted her gaze when she heard a diesel engine fire up, and with her chin propped in her hand, she watched one of the big cattle liners pull around, then back up to a chute by the big corral. She observed the maneuvering for a moment, then glanced at Cyrus. "Do you always sell cattle this time of year?"

He pulled down the brim of his hat and shrugged. "Depends. They always cull out the cows that don't drop calves—ain't no point in keeping them. But Tanner's culling 'em out now and shipping 'em off because beef prices are up a bit. He's shipping a few steers, as well—some of the ones we kept over the winter at the feedlot at the other place." He shook his head, giving a wry snort. "You jest watch. Next week the prices will be down a few cents a hundredweight jest like he figures, which don't seem like much when you think of a thousand-pound cow. But multiply it by a couple of hundred cows and Ol' Tanner will make a fair bit of change. Tickles me, it does, the way he outsmarts 'em."

Kate studied his profile, contemplating what he'd said. "You said something about a feed lot at the other place. What other place?"

Cyrus waved his hand in an easterly direction. "Out east about eight miles—four, as the crow flies. A fella had a big feedlot set up over there—computerized grain mills, big silos, the works—but he got hisself in trouble with the bank three or four years back, couldn't make a go of it with the cost of borrowed money and what it cost him for steers to fatten. Anyhow, Tanner figured since the Circle S had a ready supply of steers, he could make a clean profit, so he bought him out. He kept him on to run the place—first time Tom Benson had any real money in his pocket. Anyhow, Tanner turned it into a regular gold mine—drying, bagging and selling steer manure to greenhouses—got a regular manufacturin' operation going over there. And them city folk buy it by the truckload. Them steers is here because the road to the feedlot is all tore up. The county is fixing the grade, and it ain't nothing but a big soup hole with all this rain, so the boss had 'em moved over here day afore yesterday."

Tanner appeared around the front of the idling cattle liner, riding the big bay gelding Kate had seen in the barn. The horse pranced along, its neck arched and head tucked, its hide gleaming in the watery sunlight. His head bent, Tanner was shaking out the lariat on the far side of the horse, the reins looped loosely around the horn of the saddle. The animal tossed its head and danced sideways, and Kate heard Tanner speak to him. He rode with the loose-body ease of a man who'd spent a good portion of his life in the saddle, his black hat and his long oiled canvas drover's coat making him appear dark and dangerous. A funny feeling unfolded in her middle when she realized there was a rifle in the rifle scabbard. She would be willing to bet that Tanner McCall knew how to use it.

A gust of wind whipped through the branches overhead, sending a cold sprinkling of water down on Kate, and she shivered. But the shiver had little to do with the cold and everything to do with the man riding toward the cross-poled pasture gate. Dark and dangerous—and solitary. Always alone, always apart from his men, barricaded behind his cool aloofness. But she had seen the bleakness in his eyes, and that altered everything.

Her expression solemn, she watched him recoil the rope and settle it over the saddle horn. Picking up the reins, he nudged his mount over to the gate. Leaning down, he unhooked the chain, and the heavy gate swung open. Making it look much easier than it was, he closed the gate without dismounting; then, pulling the brim of his hat low over his eyes, he cued the gelding with a touch of his spurs. The muscles bunched in the animal's hindquarters as it responded to Tanner's signal, and in two strides it was in a ground-eating canter. She watched him ride off, so aware of the solitary rider that she experienced a peculiar heaviness in her chest.

"A good man, Tanner," Cyrus said quietly.

Surprised by his comment, she shot him a quick glance. He, too, was watching the horse and rider in the distance, his face solemn, but there was a look of sober recollection in his expression that made her pause. Feeling as if she'd just stumbled onto something private and personal, she looked away, suddenly heavy-hearted and not knowing why.

Heaving a sigh, Cyrus pushed himself up and stepped over the seat. "Think I'll wander down and see who's ready for coffee."

The first few head of cattle appeared through the trees twenty minutes later, with riders flanking the main body of the herd as it moved into open pasture. Everything went smoothly until they tried to funnel the lead cows into the open corral gate, then animals started to bolt. She heard a long whistle and a shout, and the three black and white collies streaked across the open field, all of them responding to Tanner's command to come. Two stayed on the near side with Tanner, and he sent the other one around the back of the herd to Ross. She'd never seen anything like it, watching those three dogs do what they had obviously been so well trained to do. With flawless execution and incredible speed, they worked the herd, following the commands from the two men as they systematically collected the herd and drove it forward into the penning area. The riders collected the odd stray, but for the most part it was the dogs who managed the final push of two hundred head of cattle. It was awesome to watch. And, for Kate, unexpectedly moving. Maybe it was the spirit of cooperation between man

and beast, or maybe it was the dogs' obvious love of the task—
or maybe it was the way all three dogs rollicked around Tanner's horse afterward, watching him with the bright-eyed en-
thusiasm of children, waiting for him to assign them another
task. They would, she suspected, follow him anywhere.

There were some shouts and a heavy clang as the metal ramp
of the cattle liner dropped into place on the loading chute.
Engrossed in everything that was happening, Kate shifted her
position so one foot was on the seat, then locked her arms
around her upraised knee and rested her chin on her hands.
They were going to load the upper deck first, and she was curious to see how they did it.

She heard the door of the cook house slam, then the sound
of voices through the open window, and she realized someone
had gone in for coffee. She considered getting a cup for herself, then changed her mind. She didn't want to miss out on
anything here, and besides, she hadn't met all the Circle S
hands, and she wasn't exactly comfortable with the idea of just
waltzing in there. Shifting her gaze, she checked on the boys.
They had moved down the hill and were standing off to one
side, well out of the way of anyone. Cyrus reappeared and
hoisted Scotty onto the top rail of the corral, putting his arm
around both boys' shoulders after Mark climbed up. She
smiled to herself. No doubt Scotty was asking questions a mile
a minute.

The voices inside moved closer to the open window, and
Kate heard the scrape of chairs as the men sat down at the table. Knowing they couldn't see her from the window, she remained still, not wanting to expose her presence. Engrossed in
what was happening down at the corral, she ignored the conversation until she heard Tanner's name mentioned.

An uneasy sensation settled in the pit of her stomach when
she realized it wasn't Circle S staff inside, but two of the drivers from the cattle liners.

"It's going to be mighty interesting to see how things shake
down here once old Burt kicks off. Folks have been speculating for years what the deal is—whether old Burt signed over
half, or if McCall is just a high-paid manager."

Another, deeper voice responded. "McCall ain't no high-paid manager, that's for damned sure. That half-breed is going to end up with the whole spread—see if he don't. Fred Carson says the Indian worked up north on the rigs a couple of winters, made big money and poured every red cent into cattle. McCall has a big stake in this spread, sure as hell. And Tom Benson said Tanner didn't even have to float a loan when he bought him out. Just sat down at the table and wrote out a Circle S check."

There was a derisive snort. "Well, it don't matter what the deal is. Even if he don't own half of it, Burt ain't going to leave it to nobody else, and McCall is going to be sitting on one hell of a pile of real estate. And that sure in hell is going to rub salt in a few people's saddle sores."

A sound penetrated Kate's consciousness, but she sat stock-still, almost afraid to move, praying she wouldn't be discovered. She let out her breath when the first voice continued. "Hell, who would have thought it? The breed ends up with the biggest spread in the country, while most of the folks around here pretend he don't even exist."

"There'll be talk, all right, that's for damned sure. My wife is friends with the cashier over at the drugstore, and she heard that McCall's got a young white woman stashed out here—supposed to be a nurse or something. The cashier knows one of the Circle S hands, or a drinking buddy of one of the hands—something like that."

"A white woman. Well, hell. Ain't that rich? Don't expect he's ever had one of those."

There was the sound of a chair scraping against the floor. "We'd better get back down there. It looks like they got Danny's rig just about loaded. And I ain't about to tick off Tanner McCall."

Paralyzed by a horrible, churning feeling, Kate stared blindly across the yard, stunned by what she'd overheard. It made her think of a pack of dogs she'd seen when she was a child, mean and vicious and snarling as they attacked a lone, injured animal—until the bleeding cougar had risen and challenged the pack. Then the balance of power had shifted, with the hunters becoming the hunted. But this was worse. Resentment, malice, spite—all were there in the tone of the conversation, but it was the sneering references to Tanner's mixed blood that upset her the most. It was the source of the resentment.

Suddenly cold and strangely shaky, she pulled the collar of her coat up around her neck. He knew, of course. That was why he was so solitary, so guarded. Feeling chilled to the bone, Kate stuffed her hands in her pockets, huddling bleakly in the shallow warmth of her slicker. No wonder he was so withdrawn. No wonder.

Another sound penetrated her consciousness, and she straightened, alarm clutching at her gut. It was the same sound she'd heard before—a very distinctive sound, only now it registered. It was the sound of shod hooves on gravel. Whirling toward the sound, she stiffened, her breath suspended on the kind of dread that made her heart race. The dread turned to horror when a horse and rider appeared on the trail leading down to the corral. It was Tanner, and he was carrying the large thermos she'd noticed sitting on the back step. Realization hit with upsetting clarity. He had ridden up behind the cook house to get it for Cyrus—straight up the hill from the gate. One look at his profile, and she knew with a sickening certainty that he, too, had overheard at least part of the conversation. Closing her eyes, she pressed her forehead against her upraised knee, the horrible sinking sensation making her feel sick inside. He didn't deserve this. There wasn't a human being alive who deserved this.

Realizing that if Tanner turned, he would know that she had overheard, as well, Kate got up, her knees unsteady beneath her. She would not add to his humiliation. Not if she could help it.

The kitchen was dark except for the light from the floor lamp standing in the corner beside a battered old easy chair. The worn maroon fabric was covered by a faded Mexican blanket, and the matching footstool, which was now shoved aside, held a stack of old cattle magazines and some farmers' almanacs. The chair, Kate had found out, was Burt's.

Folding laundry at the kitchen table, Kate rolled wool socks together, smiling to herself as she thought of Burt. The chair wasn't the only thing she'd learned about her eighty-year-old charge in the ten days she'd been there. He was stubborn, he was willful, he wanted things his own way and he liked everyone to think he was a crotchety old devil. But under all his bluster and fuss, he was nothing but a big marshmallow, and her kids had gotten around him in about two minutes flat. Unfortunately, they did practically anything he told them to, which had given her one or two near heart attacks. She had to watch all three of them like a hawk.

She supposed she should read the riot act to the boys, but Burt thrived on the sneaky little conspiracies the three of them cooked up. She knew how he hated the indignities of his inability to care for himself—the urine bottle, the bedpan, having to be fed. He could have made things so difficult for her, but he didn't. And since he endured those affronts to his dignity with a minimum of red-faced muttering, the least she could do was turn a blind eye to some of their shenanigans. Like the boys sneaking the pups in to show Burt—and everyone looking angelically innocent when she asked who'd piddled on the bed.

She heard the back door open, then quietly shut, and she closed her eyes, a flutter of nerves taking off in her middle. Waiting for the attack to ease, she glanced at the clock mounted on the valance over the kitchen sink. It was after ten o'clock. Tanner had gone down to the barn right after he'd put Burt to bed at eight. He'd said he had to check a mare that was due to foal, but Kate knew there was more to it than that. After overhearing the conversation two days ago, she had found herself dwelling on Tanner McCall more than she liked to admit. She had been so upset by that conversation that it had taken her the remainder of that afternoon and half the night to put her anger in perspective.

But it wasn't just the conversation that upset her. It was Tanner.

In the ten days she'd been there, he'd never come in before ten, and she had barely seen him since that first day, after he'd taken her to the cook house to meet Cyrus. Without fail he was gone in the morning before she got up, and he ate all his meals with the hired hands. The only time she saw him was when he came in to check on Burt, or if he came into the office to get something. At first she honestly hadn't thought much about it. When Burt had started fretting about it, wanting to know why Tanner was never around, she'd tried to reassure the old man, telling him that Tanner probably had a lot of work to catch up on. But that conversation between the two stockmen had forced her to reevaluate many things, one being Tanner's prolonged absences. And with a horrible, sinking sensation, she realized that Tanner McCall was very likely avoiding the house because of her. Sickened by the realization, she had not been able to get it out of her mind. She'd barely slept last night because of it, and she knew she wouldn't sleep again tonight unless she did something about it.

Her expression lined with worry, she started stacking the folded bath towels in a laundry basket, looking up when he entered the kitchen, her heart giving a painful little twist when she saw his face. His shoulders sagging with a bone-deep weariness, he looked unusually tired and preoccupied as he rolled back the cuffs of his shirt.

Kate stared at him, experiencing feelings she had no business feeling. He looked so solitary—so isolated and alone in his thoughts—and so damned exhausted. She would have given anything to have the right to comfort him, to draw his head against her breast and just hold him—to ease that awful aloneness she saw in his eyes.

Shaken by her thoughts and by the need they aroused, she set the rest of the towels in the basket, her hands nearly as cold as her insides. Raising her head to look at him, she spoke, her voice uneven. "Would you like something to eat? There's still some pie left from supper."

He jerked his head up, his gaze riveting on her, and Kate realized he hadn't seen her on the far side of the table. Gripping the wicker basket with both hands, she forced herself to hold his gaze. "I can make some fresh coffee, if you like."

He stared at her an instant longer, then looked down and finished rolling back his cuff. "It's after ten," he said, his voice gruff with censure. "You're putting in some pretty long hours. And they weren't part of the deal."

Struggling against the sudden thickness in her chest, Kate tried to camouflage the unevenness in her voice when she answered. "Cutting a piece of pie isn't exactly hard labor," she said, her tone gently challenging. "I think I can manage that before I drop from exhaustion."

He looked at her, a tiny glint in his eyes, one corner of his mouth lifted just a little. "Thanks, but I think I'll hit the sack." He held her gaze for an instant longer, then turned and started toward the living room. Experiencing a flurry of desperation, Kate clenched and unclenched her hands, her insides in knots. If she didn't say something, he was going to disappear on her. If she was going to talk to him, it had to be now, when there were no kids around and Burt was asleep.

Mustering her courage, she rubbed her hands against the seams of her jeans, her throat tight with dread. "Tanner?"

Pausing at the archway, he turned, his expression unreadable as he met her gaze. "Yes?"

She rubbed her palms again, then folded her arms tightly in front of her. "Could I talk to you for a minute?"

Bracing his shoulder against the wooden frame of the arch, he, too, folded his arms. "What's on your mind?"

She felt as if there were something hard pressing on her lungs. Lord, she did not want to do this. Swallowing the knot of nervousness, she took a fortifying breath, her voice only breaking a little when she asked, "Are you avoiding me?"

He stared at her for an instant, then dropped his gaze, carefully aligning a loose baseboard with the side of his boot. Finally he raised his head and looked at her, his expression impassive and sober. His voice was strained when he answered. "Yes."

Nervously fingering the material of her sleeve, she tried to get a breath past the thickness in her chest. She'd thought she'd been braced for that answer, but having him verify it hurt more than she liked to admit. She swallowed again, determined to get it all out in the open. "Have I done something wrong?"

Sliding one hand into the back pocket of his jeans, he once again toyed with the loose piece of baseboard. Just when she thought he wasn't going to answer, he spoke, his voice gruff. "You weren't quite what I expected. It wasn't until I saw you sitting in the restaurant that I realized I didn't have any idea how old you were—and I never really gave any thought to how old the boys were. My main concern was getting someone qualified to look after Burt. All the rest was irrelevant."

Feeling as if her legs were apt to give out, Kate leaned back against the wide window ledge, clutching her arms even tighter. "You're right. I didn't include how old I was in the application. By law, I don't have to."

Tanner looked up, a glimmer of humor in his eyes. "No, you don't. And I know that." He looked past her, clearly evaluating both her and the situation. Making a small dismissive gesture with his shoulder, he looked back at her, a wry half smile appearing. "Cyrus pretty much explained it. I guess we were all expecting someone older, someone who was..."

The knot of nerves eased just a little, and Kate managed a small smile as she supplied the description. "A little more starchy."

Tanner shot her an amused look, the half smile deepening into something warm and disarming, something sensual and oddly intimate—something that was enough to make her heart pound.

"Yeah," he agreed softly. "Someone a little more starchy."

Kate watched him, the wild flutter expanding, her breath suddenly jammed up in her chest. One smile—one full smile—and her legs wanted to cave in under her. One smile and she could feel every pulse point in her whole body. Leaning back against the windowsill, Kate rested her hands on the edge and gripped it tightly. Easing in a deep, shaky breath, she tried to stifle the nearly unbearable longing. She didn't dare even imagine what it would be like to be held by him. God, she couldn't remember wanting something as badly as she wanted to find out.

Unaware of what was happening with her, Tanner pushed himself away from the doorway and approached the table, his expression thoughtful as he fingered a blouse of hers that was folded on top of the towels. Finally he raised his head and looked at her, his expression taut. "I think it would be wise if I moved down to the bunkhouse while you're here."

His quiet statement was like a shot of ice water, and Kate stared at him, feeling oddly disconnected. Her voice came out sharper than she expected. "Why?"

He held her gaze for a moment, then began fondling the top button on the blouse. There was a trace of bitterness in his voice when he finally answered. "Bolton is a small town, and it has a lot of narrow-minded people in it. It's going to be all over town in a matter of days that I've got this young and very attractive woman living with me—and being what they are, the good people of Bolton are going to twist it all out of shape." He looked up at her, his gaze ruthlessly direct. "You're going to get hung with some pretty nasty labels—not the most offensive being Tanner McCall's white squaw."

Stunned by the explicit bluntness of his words, she stared at him, the first flicker of anger pumping through her. So it was true. She'd hoped that malicious bit of conversation was nothing more than two men gossiping. But that obviously wasn't the case. Fortified by a deep, energizing rage, she straightened, curling her hands into fists. "I don't really give a damn," she said, her tone quiet and precise, "what they say. And they can take their narrow-mindedness and stuff it." Her throat suddenly aching, she looked up at the ceiling, willing away the sudden sting of tears. Regaining control, she folded her arms again, meeting his gaze dead-on. "This is your home, Tanner. And if people are that small-minded, they're going to twist my being here into whatever they want, whether you're sleeping in the bunkhouse or not."

Exhaling heavily, he jammed both hands on his hips and stared at her. He finally shook his head, his voice flat. "You don't know these people, Kate."

Holding his gaze, she gave him an unsteady smile. "I don't want to."

There was a flicker of humor around his mouth; then his expression sobered, the bleakness in his eyes tearing at her heart. Intuitively knowing that there was more at stake than where he slept and ate, she gazed at him, silently imploring him. Sensing his resistance, she said it aloud. "Don't do this,

Tanner. Please. Burt doesn't understand what's going on, and I don't want you to leave because of me. Please, don't do this."

He held her gaze for a long, tense moment, then looked away, his face haggard with strain. Kate saw him swallow, and when he spoke, his voice was so gravelly that she could barely hear him. "I'm afraid you'll live to regret it if I don't."

What she was going to regret, she realized with a sudden wrench, was that her time here was going to be calculated in weeks, or, if she was lucky, maybe months. And when she left, she would regret leaving this man behind.

Hugging herself to ease the ache in her chest, she looked at him, her voice steady. "No," she said with quiet certainty. "I won't."

Tanner stared at her for a long time; then finally he straightened and spoke, his voice gruff. "I'll see you in the morning, then." He made it as far as the archway, then turned and indicated the laundry basket. "Does that go up?"

Affected by his thoughtful gesture, Kate had to swallow before she could answer. "Yes."

Holding it under one arm, he picked a book up off the counter, then cast her one final glance. "Go to bed."

Biting her lip against the increasing fullness in her throat, Kate nodded. "I will."

She finished tidying up the kitchen, checked on Burt one last time, made sure the night-light and the intercom were on and then she, too, went up to bed. But as tired as she was, she couldn't sleep. She had too many things racing around in her mind, and no matter how much she tried, she couldn't shut her brain off. She could see the digital readout on the clock radio on the dresser, and she watched the numbers change from 12:43 a.m. to 12:44. She shifted her gaze.

Lying on her side, her hand under her cheek, she watched the curtains billow and furl in the light night breeze, considering the fact that they were the only curtains in the whole house. She saw the fine hand of the Hutterite ladies in this—in the simple lace curtains, in the plain Shaker-styled, handcrafted furniture in her room, in the large handmade tufted floor mat by her bed. Tears trickled down the side of her nose, and she wiped them away. She could just envision it—Tanner

asking the ladies to fix up a room for the woman who was
coming to look after Burt, trying in the best way he knew how
to make her comfortable. It made her feel so desolate inside,
that aloneness she sensed in him, and the meanness that had
made him that way. She wondered why he had been targeted
the way he had, and what had happened to make him withdraw into such a solitary shell. She wondered why there was
such bleakness in his eyes when his guard was down. *Tanner
McCall's white squaw.*

That recollection triggered a churning in Kate's stomach,
and she abruptly sat up, pressing her forehead against her
knees. Twenty-eight years. He'd been living like this for
twenty-eight years. Locking her arms around her knees, she
stared into the darkness. He must have been little more than a
boy when he'd come to the Circle S Ranch, and she wondered
why he'd done it. She knew that Burt's grandfather had settled in the area when he was a young man, and she knew that
Burt had never married. And she also knew that the old man
loved Tanner like a son.

Resisting the unrelenting ache in her throat, she wiped her
face against the sheet, then rested her cheek on her knees and
watched the curtains move, thinking about what a paradox life
was. She felt more emotionally entangled with Tanner Mc-
Call after ten short days than she had with Roger Quinn after
ten long years. God, he made her feel things, made her want
things, made her ache inside, and she sensed such a terrible,
terrible loneliness in him. He made her think of an old song
about a man wanting to change his lonely life, about wanting
to know where love was. She could hear the melody, could hear
the poignant words in her head, and she closed her eyes, fresh
tears slipping from beneath her eyelashes. Two desperately
lonely people—and a huge, gaping chasm in between. God, he
made *her* feel so sad—and so alone.

Lifting her head, she wiped her face on the sleeve of her pajamas, her heart skipping a beat when she heard his door open.
Not moving a muscle, she listened, hearing the creak of the
third stair. Burt. She wondered if something was wrong with
Burt.

Scrambling off the bed, she rooted through the bedding for her housecoat, stuffing her arms into the sleeves as she opened her door. Soundlessly, she headed for the stairs, dread making her stomach knot. Please, God, please, please don't let there be anything wrong with Burt. Reaching for the banister, she stepped onto the first stair, her stomach falling away to nothing when she heard the distinctive beep of a computer booting up. Gripping the banister, she pressed her other hand over her eyes, emotion filling her chest and nearly strangling her. She didn't want him getting up because he couldn't sleep. She didn't want him downstairs by himself. She didn't want him doing balance sheets at one in the morning. She didn't. But there was a line she had no right to cross. And it had nothing to do with him being her boss.

Poised at the brink of doing something incredibly foolish, Kate stared down the dimly lighted stairs; then, collecting her resources, she turned and went back to her room. She had her own ghosts to fight. With her own life in such a mess, how could she even think about wanting to do battle with his?

Chapter 5

The sun was warm on Kate's back, the grass was finally turning green and the breeze carried the smell of spring. Just that morning, she'd found some daffodils blooming in a flower garden that had gone wild on the east side of the house, and the boys had brought her some crocuses yesterday. Burt fretted about the two blizzards that had hit southern Alberta that spring, and he fretted about it being such a cold, late season, worrying about the summer graze for the cattle. Kate realized that most of the fretting was because he was house-bound and that, for the first time in his life, he was unable to check the crop of new calves. She was hoping that now it had warmed up, she would be able to get him outside once in a while. Maybe then he wouldn't feel so removed from everything.

"Well, now, Miz Quinn. You could end up in Saskatchewan, with the wind and that sheet and all."

Kate finished pinning the wet sheet on the clothesline, then turned, the wind whipping her hair across her face. Holding it back, she squinted against the bright sunlight. "Good morning, Cyrus. Great day, isn't it?"

"It's a fine one, all right." He nimbly caught the trailing end of the last sheet as she lifted it out of the laundry basket, waiting for her to get it under control before he stepped away. The wind caught it, sending it flapping as she clipped it to the line; with the wind and the sun, the sheets would be dry in minutes, and smelling like heaven when she brought them in.

"You're looking a mite tired. Ol' Burt giving you a hard time?"

Kate's hand froze on the line; then she stuck on the final clothespin, her insides settling into a lump. Schooling her expression into a casualness she didn't feel, she turned. She forced a smile as she unhooked the bag of clothespins from the line and dropped it in the basket. "No, not at all. He doesn't give me any trouble at all." Remembering that her two kids and Burt Shaw were on their own in the house, she gave a little grin and amended her statement. "Well, hardly any trouble. My kids will do anything he tells them—and a few things he only suggests. All in all, it keeps things interesting."

Cyrus chuckled, shaking his head. "Ol' Burt's a hard man to keep down. Few years ago—he must've been, oh, seventy-four, anyway—anyhow, he got throwed from a horse and broke his leg. Bad break, too. He took the cast off hisself and was back on a horse in about ten days. Wrapped enough duct tape around it to choke a horse—said that was all it needed, tape and liniment."

Kate laughed and picked up the laundry basket. "I think I should have asked a few more questions before I took this job." Raking her hair back off her face, she looked at the cook. "There's a fresh pot of coffee on. Would you like to come in for a cup?"

"Sounds fine." He fell into step beside her, holding open the gate for her. "But I didn't jest come up here to scrounge a cup of coffee. Thought maybe you'd like to head to town for an hour or two. Figured I could get out the cribbage board—see if that old coot remembers how to cheat."

Kate stopped at the bottom of the steps and looked at him, considering his offer. It wasn't that she wanted to go to town; it was that she needed some things she wasn't about to put on any grocery list. "I'll have to check with Tanner first and make sure it's okay with him."

Cyrus looked directly into her eyes. "It was Tanner who suggested it. Said you're putting in some long hours, and he figured you could do with a break." Cyrus climbed the steps leading to the back porch, then held the door open for her. "We'll be moving out to the south cattle camp tomorrow. There's over a thousand head of cattle to move afore branding, and with corrals and holding pens to get fixed up, we're going to be running thin around here for the next week or so. Tanner's going to be ramrodding the cattle camp this year, so you're going to be pretty much on your own as far as Ol' Burt's concerned."

Tanner was going to be heading the cattle camp this year—the implication being that he didn't usually. Kate experienced a rush of guilt. It had been two nights ago that she'd confronted him. He hadn't moved down to the bunkhouse, but he was still eating his meals with the men, and now he was moving out to the cattle camp. She was beginning to wish she hadn't said anything.

Realizing that Cyrus was watching her, she managed a smile. "There are a few things I'd like to pick up. A trip to town sounds great."

"Fine, then. Let's jest go tell Ol' Burt he's gotta get his wits about him."

Setting the laundry basket on top of the washer as she passed, Kate entered the kitchen. She took one look, closed her eyes and slapped her hand over her face. She should have known better than to leave them alone for fifteen minutes.

Taking a deep breath and squaring her shoulders, she raised her head, thinking things no mother should ever think about her own children. Mark Andrew and Scott Allan had Burt—and his bed—halfway out of his room, with Scott pushing, Mark pulling and Burt waving instructions with his cane from the comfort of his bed.

Ignoring the chuckle she heard behind her, Kate took another deep breath and jammed her hands on her hips. "All right. What's going on here?"

Mark, looking hot and sweaty, straightened. "Burt needs to be by the kitchen windows. He says he can see the barn and corrals from there, and he can tell if everyone's doing what they're supposed to be doing.''

Scotty rubbed his nose on his sleeve and nodded. ''Yep. That's right, Mom. That's what he said.''

Burt folded his hands on his cane, looking as ferocious as possible, the foxy glint in his eyes ruining the image of a sick old man. She glared at him; he glared right back at her. ''Don't stick your nose up at me, woman. And don't you interfere with these here boys. They're doing what they're told, and that's more than I can say for some.''

Kate stared at him, her hands still on her hips. Burt continued to stare at her. She didn't dare let him get away with it. ''If you don't quit pulling stunts like this behind my back, I'm going to take the wheels off everything in this house.'' Her tone became more pointed. ''You could have simply *asked,* you know. You didn't have to turn it into some sort of cloak-and-dagger campaign.''

Burt gave her a huffy look. ''The lads were following orders.''

''The *lads* should know better.'' She looked at Mark, releasing her breath on an exasperated sigh. ''You'll have to move the table. You're going to shove it through the wall if you don't.''

Giving them all one final stern look, she headed for the living room and marched up the stairs. She went into the bathroom, shut the door and gave in to the nearly hysterical urge to laugh. God, the next time she was apt to find them on the road to the barn, pushing and pulling and Burt waving his cane. It took her three starts down the stairs before she had a grip on herself—if they ever found out that she'd been upstairs laughing, they would turn her life into a living hell.

By the time she entered the kitchen, they had the chairs and table moved, and Cyrus was helping them with Burt's big easy chair. He flashed her a twinkly look and smoothed down his mustache, his face poker straight. ''Where do you want this broken-down thing put, Miz Quinn? In Burt's room where the bed used to be?''

Not daring to look at him, she waved to a space along the wall between the kitchen and living room. "There will be fine," she said, her voice quavery.

The boys moved the footstool and lamp, casting worried looks at her. Kate clamped her teeth together. If she started laughing in front of them, she would never, *never,* be able to call her life her own again.

By the time they had Burt situated in front of the window and the electric motor of the bed plugged in, Kate was pretty much back in control. As she straightened his sheets under him and fixed his pillows so his head was supported, he watched her, his bright blue eyes twinkling with a sparkle that made her insides go all soft. "You're a good woman, Kate Quinn," he said, his voice gruff.

Kate's throat got tight, and for a minute she thought her eyes were going to fill up. God, but she loved this old man.

She finished tucking the blankets under the mattress, her voice catching a little when she was finally able to answer. "You're not so bad yourself, Burton Shaw."

In the end, the boys balked at going to town, wanting to stay with Cyrus and Burt. Kate had some reservations about leaving the two of them behind, but Cyrus insisted that he'd wrangled wilier colts than them and had always been able to outsmart 'em. Burt retorted that the only thing Cyrus had ever outsmarted was himself, which didn't count for much. Cyrus said Burt might as well shut his trap, 'cuz he wasn't going to get into a battle of wits with a man who was unarmed. Kate decided it was a match made in heaven.

The drive to Bolton was an eye-opener for Kate. Her only trip over the road had been on the night that Tanner had picked her up, and that journey had left her with an impression of hills and curves, but little else. The hills offered spectacular views, and the curves skirted picturesque little ravines, rocky outcroppings and stands of coniferous trees. To the east she could see the bleak and barren rolling hills of open rangeland, but here, caught between the barren hills to the east and the rugged, majestic Rockies to the west, was some of the most beautiful country she had seen in a long, long time.

Cyrus had warned her about Bolton. Located to the north along the secondary highway, the town was situated on a plateau of land above a fast-running river, the mountains creating a breathtaking backdrop. Kate knew that during the years of active oil exploration in the province, Bolton had boomed as an oil town. In a weed-infested lot, she spotted a relic from the past, a rusty derrick lying like a prehistoric skeleton in the hot sun.

Leaving the highway, she turned onto the main access road that took her into the center of town. Huge poplar trees lined the wide, paved streets, and the sidewalks in front of the businesses looked new. Small—a population of around a thousand, according to Cyrus, with not much to offer but a cold beer on Saturday night and a fair-to-middling Chinese restaurant—it was not quite the poky town she'd been led to believe. Besides the hotel and the Chinese restaurant, there were several small but thriving businesses—all the ones she'd expected to see in a small ranching town, and some she hadn't, such as the quaint little teahouse on the corner. Quiet and clean, the town gave Kate a feeling of durability and timelessness.

After having driven around to get her bearings, Kate parked the Bronco and headed down the main street, stopping in at the small drugstore to get the things she needed. The clerk was pleasant, and two of the other customers went out of their way to speak to her. A friendly little town, or so it seemed. She recalled the comment Tanner had made about the narrow-mindedness of the people of Bolton. After seeing the town and meeting some of its inhabitants, it seemed oddly out of whack. Why would anyone in a town this size care one way or another about what was going on at a ranch twenty miles away?

Deciding not to think about that night with Tanner, Kate took her parcel back to the truck, then decided to go for a little stroll to check out the shops. Absently fingering the dime in her pocket, she thought about her own situation. She felt a little more secure now that she'd seen the town. It was small enough not to be one of Roger's targets, and it was big enough that a stranger like herself didn't stick out. Maybe fate had treated her kindly this time around.

Spotting a small beauty salon squeezed between the post office and a small appliance repair shop, Kate waited for a pickup to pass, then crossed the street. Maybe she would be able to get an appointment to have her hair cut.

Half an hour later, with her hair trimmed to a manageable shoulder-length bob, Kate decided to check out the library she had spotted when she'd driven through town. Feeling more carefree than she had for a very long time, she rounded the corner, startling a huge raven from the gutter at the side of the road. The bird also startled her, and she stopped and watched it take flight, its wings snapping. It was the simple act of watching the bird gain altitude that altered her line of sight, and she saw it, her stomach giving a funny little skip. The Bruce T. McCall Sports Arena.

She stared at the huge lettering, trying to rationalize away the funny sensation in her abdomen. She recalled the comments from one of the drivers, about how it was going to rub salt in a few people's saddle sores when Tanner took over the Circle S.

The arena wasn't a new structure. Far from it. It was in excellent repair, but Kate guessed it to be at least thirty years old. Dragging her attention away from the huge lettering, she tried to dispel the sensation in her belly. She was making mountains out of molehills. McCall was a common enough name; there were probably a dozen of them listed in the phone book.

Determined not to look at the sign again, she gripped the strap of her shoulder bag and started walking. *Tanner McCall's white squaw.* Unsettled by the memory and driven by something that went beyond simple curiosity, she abruptly turned back, entering the video store she'd just passed.

Sticking a smile on her face, she approached the teenager behind the counter. "Could I borrow your phone book for a minute, please?"

The young girl smiled and reached under the counter. "Sure can."

Feeling a little foolish, Kate flipped it open, hoping for something that would dispel the uneasy sensation in the pit of her stomach. One McCall—B.T., with two numbers. Closing the book, she slid it back across the counter. Inhaling unsteadily, she forced another smile. "The sports complex across the street—the Bruce T. McCall Arena—who's it named after?"

The girl gave Kate a shy and slightly embarrassed smile. "I don't know all that much about him—he's pretty old now but he owns a ranch around here, and a big auction mart somewhere. He donated all kinds of stuff to the town." She gave Kate another embarrassed smile, making a self-conscious gesture with her hand. "Mrs. Kerby at the library knows all about him. She's kind of the town historian."

Kate thanked her and left, feeling suddenly light-headed. She didn't like snoops, but she didn't like the gnawing feeling in her stomach, either. There were just too many pieces that seemed to be connected.

Mrs. Kerby was a pleasant-faced woman of about sixty— one of those perpetually kind, sweet, affected people who tend to gush. When Kate explained that she was new to the Bolton area and wanted to know who Bruce T. McCall was, Mrs. Kerby pressed her hand to her breast and raised her gaze heavenward. "Oh, my. You *must* be new, my dear. *Everyone* around here knows who Bruce McCall is. He's just the most generous man. Made a large—*large,* mind you—donation to the arena years ago. We would never have managed it without his financial support, and he's made very, very generous donations to our library and the senior citizens' lodge. The family settled here in the late 1800s, with a huge land grant from the crown. The McCall name was a *very* big name back then. Very influential, very prominent—still is, actually. The original McCall ranch—the Bar M—was absolutely monstrous and has been written up in several prominent historical accounts. Amazing, amazing people, the McCalls—have always been politically connected and still have tremendous influence."

The light-headed sensation turned into something akin to motion sickness, and Kate felt herself go pale. Suddenly the room was very, very hot. Wiping her clammy hands on her jeans, she drew a shaky breath; then, schooling her face into an appropriate expression, she made herself say the words. "It sounds like a fascinating family." Her heart beating like a wild thing in her chest, she made herself relax her clenched fists, then asked the question that was foremost in her mind. "I don't suppose you could tell me what the *T* stands for."

Mrs. Kerby gave her an affronted look. "Well, of course. It's Tanner. Bruce Tanner McCall."

Kate was never sure afterward how she got out of the library and back to the truck. Once inside, though, she sagged in the seat and closed her eyes, her legs shaking so badly that she wasn't sure she could even drive. Bruce Tanner McCall. A man of influence, a man of prominence. A man who was somehow a player in a drama she didn't even pretend to understand. And what about Tanner? He had been only a boy when he'd come to the Circle S—just a boy. What was the history behind the sneering, demeaning comments she'd overheard, and what had happened to give the whole town license to slander him? *Tanner McCall's white squaw.* God, it was all beginning to make sickening sense.

A rap on the passenger window brought her back from all the questions racing through her mind, and she turned, a flurry of alarm taking off in her chest. It took a moment for the face at the window to register, and she managed a weak smile when she recognized Rita. Reaching across the cab, she unlatched the door, hoping she didn't look as shaken as she felt.

The older woman swung the door open, a friendly smile on her face. "I thought I recognized the vehicle. So how's it going?"

Kate managed to return the smile. "Just fine. I didn't expect to see you here."

Rita indicated the hotel with a jerk of her head. "I manage the coffee shop at the hotel, so I try to spend a few hours a week here to keep things on track and the books up-to-date." She made another gesture with her head. "Come on. I'll treat you to coffee and a fresh piece of pie."

Kate remembered Rita's kindness the night she arrived, the depth of humanity in the other woman's eyes. She also remembered her saying that she and Tanner McCall went back a long way. Her chest suddenly tight, Kate had an image of Tanner standing by the laundry basket, his expression unreadable as he fingered her folded blouse, and for an instant she wasn't sure she was going to be able to respond. Struggling against the impeding tightness, she tried to smile. "I'd like that."

With Rita preceding her, Kate entered the café, the breeze catching her hair as she stepped inside, the door sighing shut behind her. Rita waved her into the corner booth, telling her that she would be right back, then disappeared into the back. Kate slid into the booth, still experiencing the aftermath of shock. Bruce T. McCall. Rubbing her arms against a sudden chill, she wondered what had put that bleak empty look in Tanner's eyes.

Disturbed by her thoughts, Kate anchored her sunglasses on her head, then tipped her head back to ease the knot of tension in her neck. Resting her arms on the table, she stared out down the street, feeling almost as barren as the country that stretched endlessly out to the east.

Rita returned, carrying two servings of still-steaming peach pie and some cutlery. She placed the pie and cutlery on the table, then took a seat across from her. "Perfect timing. A fresh batch of coffee's perking, and the pie's fresh out of the oven."

Kate drew the pie closer, then reached for a napkin. "It smells terrific."

Rita settled back into the booth, her gaze intent as she looked up at Kate. "So how is it going? I missed Tanner when he brought the sleeping bag back, and I was wondering how you were managing with Burt."

Kate responded with a wry grin. "Burt on his own I can manage. It's him and my two boys who are driving me crazy." She went on to elaborate about them moving Burt into the kitchen.

Rita let loose a hearty laugh, her face scrunched up as she shook her head. "Sounds like you're going to have your hands full, all right. And old Burt will play it for all it's worth." She paused as the waitress set two cups of coffee on the table, acknowledging the girl with a smile and a glance. She pushed the container of cream over to Kate, her tone mild when she asked, "And how's it going with Tanner?"

Caught off guard, Kate looked down at her coffee, her movements deliberate as she poured cream, her tone artificial when she answered. "Fine. Just fine."

There was a brief pause; then Rita spoke again. "You got something on your mind, or am I just imagining things here?"

Kate looked up, her expression immobilized by surprise. She stared at Rita for a moment, then looked back down and stirred her coffee. She didn't say anything for a moment, then she finally met Rita's gaze and answered, her voice uneven. "Who is Bruce T. McCall?"

Her broad face giving nothing away, Rita stared at her, clearly weighing Kate's question and the intent behind it. When she spoke, her voice had a slight edge to it. "Why do you want to know?"

Kate's vision suddenly blurred, and she looked away, her emotions raw and unpredictable, the tightness in her chest swelling to nearly unbearable proportions. It wasn't the tone of Rita's voice that had done it; what got to her was the sudden mental image of Tanner standing in the kitchen, telling her why he should move down to the bunkhouse. Trying repeatedly to will away the knot in her throat, Kate gazed out across the street, wishing she could get that image out of her mind. It nearly killed her, seeing that aloneness in him.

Rita's voice had lost its edge and was tinged with something closely related to amusement when she said, "So that's the way the wind blows."

Quickly wiping away the tears, Kate pulled another paper napkin out of the holder and blew her nose, still trying to get rid of the damned lump. Avoiding Rita's gaze, she picked up the mug and took a sip of coffee, not sure if she was going to be able to swallow or not.

Rita leaned forward and rested her arms on the table, toying with the spoon beside her saucer. "Tanner's got a pile of hurt in him," she said quietly. "And I don't want to add to that."

Kate looked at her, her gaze steady. "Neither do I."

Rita studied her for a moment, then began folding the napkin by her cup, her expression sober and inward. "Bruce McCall is Tanner's father," she said, her tone gruff. "He was never married to Tanner's mother, but they lived together for years. She came from one of the reservations in the States, and apparently old Bruce brought her home after he'd been down there on a cattle-buying trip, or so the story goes. They lived on the McCall ranch, and eventually they had Tanner. He made sure Tanner was legally registered as a McCall. Some say he did it to rile his old man, some say he did it for Tanner's mother. Anyhow, no one knew much about her, except she was a real beauty and apparently thought Bruce could walk on water.''

Determined not to let Rita see how the news that Bruce T. McCall was Tanner's father affected her, Kate forced herself to take a bite of pie. She wasn't sure how she managed to get it down, but she did. There was only a slight quaver in her voice when she nudged the other woman to continue. ''What happened? How come Tanner ended up as part owner of the Circle S?''

Rita sighed, her expression indicating her lack of knowledge. ''No one knows for sure what happened between Tanner's mother and Bruce. All anyone knows for sure is that when Tanner was around six, Bruce came home from a trip to Texas with a very rich wife.'' A wry smile appeared, and Rita's tone was underscored with amused sarcasm. ''Our very own Miss Ellie.'' Her expression sobering, she shook her head, her attention again focused on the napkin. ''Tanner's mother got on her horse and rode out to McKinnon Falls. They found her body two days later. Actually, it was Burt Shaw who found her.''

Kate set her cup down, coffee sloshing into the saucer, the warmth draining from her in a sickening rush. For an instant she thought she was going to be sick. Weakly resting her elbows on the table, she closed her eyes and rested her forehead against her clenched fists. Six years old. He had been left all alone when he was just six years old. About Scotty's age.

Rita shifted, leaning back in her seat and stretching her legs out in front of her, her tone somber when she continued. ''Ellie thought the little half-breed at the Bar M was pretty cute, at least until she found out the half-breed was Bruce's kid. All hell broke loose, and that was when Bruce built that big house here in Bolton. Miss Ellie wouldn't go near the Bar M after that. Rumor has it that Bruce didn't draw a sober

breath for over a year. Then Miss Ellie had Chase, and I guess
things straightened out."

Trying to waylay the growing tightness in her throat, Kate
waited a moment, then lifted her head and looked at the
woman across from her. "What happened to Tanner? Who
took care of him?"

Rita gave her a wry smile. "You mean once Ellie found out
who he was and gave old Bruce the ultimatum?" she said, that
same sardonic undercurrent in her voice. "Well, since Bruce
wasn't about to risk losing Miss Ellie's considerable bankroll,
he stuck Tanner in a foster home. A couple that lived on a run-
down farm east of town. They were dead-set religious—went
to church three or four times a week. I guess Bruce figured if
they were good Christian people, Tanner would do okay, but
it turned out they were a pair of religious fanatics, into devil
possession and punishment. They used to whip him, trying to
beat the devil out and obedience in, saying they were the in-
struments of God, and God had brought him to them to be
shaped."

Heartsick and hurting for the boy—for the small, confused, defenseless boy—whose whole world had been turned
upside down, Kate clamped her teeth together, her vision
blurring. So small. And so alone. With no one to hold him or
comfort him. God, she couldn't even bear to think about it.
Abruptly wiping away the tears with the side of her hand, she
had to wait for the awful contraction to pass before she could
speak. "Nobody did anything? They just left him there?"

Rita gave her a mirthless half smile. "I don't think anyone
really knew. He was away from school more than he was there,
and his foster parents didn't have anything to do with anyone
in the community. It wasn't until he was about eleven or
twelve—his first year of junior high—that Mrs. Whittaker got
suspicious when he came to school with burns on the palms of
both his hands. She finally got it out of him what was going
on, and she raised Cain. Cyrus was working for Bruce by
then—he was foreman at the ranch—and he and his wife
marched out to the farm and collected Tanner, lock, stock and
barrel, then took him home to the Bar M with them. Ellie
threw a fit when she found out he was back on McCall land,

but rumor has it that Millie threatened her if she did anything about it. Those next couple of years were probably the best in Tanner's entire life. At least until Millie died.''

Hurting right down to her soul, Kate rested her head against the high back of the booth and stared off into space, a thousand questions churning through her mind, the information she was receiving not nearly enough to fill in all the spaces. She hadn't known Cyrus had ever been married, but Rita's account explained Tanner's association with the cook. It also explained the softening she saw in Tanner's expression whenever he was around the older man.

Wiping her face with the side of her hand, she let her breath go, then met Rita's gaze. "How come he ended up on the Circle S?"

Rita shrugged. "No one knows what happened there. At least, not all of it. When Tanner was about fourteen, he got tangled up with a girl. He was a hell of an athlete—excelled at everything he tried. She was a year or so older and was pretty taken with him—the star athlete, the dangerous reputation, the half-breed—but her old man raised holy hell. From all accounts, Bruce thought the whole thing was a big macho joke—figured it was all right, his fourteen-year-old kid getting it on with a cheerleader. Bruce had a real reputation as a womanizer, so I guess that all fit. But something happened after that. All of a sudden Cyrus was gone from the Bar M to the Circle S, and so was Tanner. Old Burt never had had much use for the McCalls, least of all Bruce, but he figured Tanner's mother was all right, so it caused quite a ruckus around here when Bruce found out where Tanner had gone."

Rita shrugged, meeting Kate's gaze with a wry smile. "And Ellie threw a regular fit. She wanted Tanner gone, not sitting just outside of town on the Circle S, rubbing her nose in the fact that by all accounts Tanner had legal rights to the McCall money. To my knowledge, Tanner hasn't seen his old man for years. There was a big falling-out between Bruce and Chase—that's Bruce's oldest son by Ellie. He'd be seven or eight years younger than Tanner. Anyhow, Chase was a real hell-raiser and made it clear he didn't have any use for his old man. Rubbed both Ellie's and Bruce's nose in it when he took off when he was about eighteen and hired on at the Circle S. He was there for a year or so, then he hit the rodeo circuit. It's rumored around that Tanner bankrolled Chase when he started rough-stock contracting to the pro rodeo circuit in the States. Bruce's other son is one of those who doesn't have a whole hell of a lot of backbone—nice enough person, but took everything old Bruce dished out. And I don't know what happened to Eden. That's the daughter. She hasn't been around for years.

"Of course, the Bar M isn't what it used to be—the original ranch ended up being split three ways when Bruce's father died. Divided it between Bruce and his two sisters—that was just after Tanner disappeared. That really shook Ellie up—she always thought Bruce would get it all, since the ranch had always been passed on to the oldest son."

Feeling as if every ounce of energy had been drained out of her, Kate reached for another napkin and blew her nose, her hands icy. Stuffing the tissue in her pocket, she wrapped her hands around the warm coffee mug. There was a long silence, each woman deep in her own thoughts. Then Kate looked up at the older woman. "Rita?"

"Hmm?"

"Tell me about you and Tanner."

Rita looked at her, her gaze sober as she gave a small shrug. "Not much to tell." Then she gave Kate an amused look and added, "At least, not in the romance sense. But we've been friends for a lot of years." She looked down and began fiddling with the napkin again, her expression strained. "I was placed in a foster home when I was nine. Mine was better than Tanner's, but you still grow up knowing you don't really belong. That feeling carries over into everything, and things weren't great for either Tanner or me in elementary school."

Her smile twisted with the unpleasantness of remembering, her voice growing even huskier when she continued. "Tanner and I were pretty much outcasts. Nobody was going to fight our battles for us or much cared what happened to us. We stuck pretty much together—comfort in numbers, I guess. It was worse for him, though. He was so withdrawn and quiet, and he missed so much school that he was always pretty far behind. And I don't know if it was because no one wanted to cross Ellie, or if it was because he was part Indian or what, but there were a couple of teachers who used to really pick on him. Of course, the more they belittled him, the more closed up he got. It wasn't until Cyrus took him that things picked up for Tanner."

Rita made a gesture with her hand. "And Mrs. Whittaker made a big difference. She figured out right away that he wasn't stupid like his other teachers claimed—he'd just missed so much school. He'd been brought up thinking he wasn't worth nothing, and he was so ashamed of being dumb. I guess he figured they'd really humiliate him if they found out he couldn't read, so he never let on. She was the one who never let on, though—just started working with him, after school and at noon hour, then got him playing sports. Millie used to work with him at home, too."

Rita's expression altered, her face growing solemn and introspective. She folded the napkin into a precise square, her thoughts clearly focused on the unpleasant past. It was a long time before she spoke, her voice heavy from the weight of remembering. "His foster parents did a good job of that, of drumming shame and humiliation into him. And there was one teacher, Mr. Rutherford, who got some sort of sick pleasure from picking on kids, especially Tanner. He taught grades four and five, and he used to make fun of Tanner every chance he got. Found out years later that he was in Ellie's bridge club. It was so bad, he started going through Tanner's lunch in front of the class and showing everyone what Tanner was given to eat. Which usually wasn't much—maybe a cold baked potato."

Knowing she was approaching emotional overload and knowing she couldn't handle many more of the graphic details without coming completely apart, Kate swallowed and rubbed her forehead, trying to dispel the headache that was developing. God, it was so awful, so horrible—and so unbearably sad.

Rita glanced up as a customer entered the café, then began toying with the napkin again. Her face softening with a reminiscent expression, she shook her head and gave a chuckle.

"He showed 'em, though. A few years back, Tanner and Burt bought an old run-down farm that was adjacent to the Circle S, half a section that was nothing but a big gravel pile—couldn't grow much of anything on it. Different ones in town did a lot of snickering about it, making snide comments about him buying a pile of rocks. Just after that, there was a big push for road upgrades in this end of the province, and the contractors were desperate for gravel. Tanner knocked off the top of a hill, brought in a crusher and made a small fortune off that damned farm—in fact, that gravel pit is still making him money. The place they're living on now wasn't part of the original Circle S—they bought that just before they started mining gravel, so they paid that off right quick. After the gravel pit episode, people were laughing out of the other sides of their mouths, I can tell you. Especially when the Circle S hands rolled into town that fall in a whole new fleet of vehicles. The same thing with the Benson place—there were quite a few who thought he was a fool for buying an operation that had already gone belly-up, but he turned that into a gold mine, dehydrating and bagging steer manure, if you can believe it."

"So," Kate said, her voice breaking a little, "things haven't changed that much as far as the community is concerned."

Rita looked up at her, her gaze somber and steady. She considered Kate's question for a minute, then gave a small, dismissive shrug. "There's still some of that old attitude around, no doubt about it. Bruce and Ellie still like to swing their weight around, and there are still a few people in town who play their game. But there's a lot of decent folk around here. They see Tanner for what he is, and Tom Benson can't say enough good things about him. But Tanner isn't going to make an effort to build any bridges, that's for damned sure. You don't ever forget what it was like to be a half-starved, half-breed kid who was stripped of everything, who wasn't allowed one ounce of dignity or human kindness. He didn't have anybody—not one person who cared a damn about him. I just think what it must have been like for him when I first knew him—just a little guy, and so quiet and solemn. It was just after Christmas, and everyone else was rattling on about what they got, and he just sat there looking at the floor and not saying anything. You never forget things like that—the humiliation, knowing that you're not worth anything and feeling ashamed about it. He's never going to forget what it felt like to be that kid who got nothing. And you can be sure he's going to make damned sure he never leaves himself open for it to happen again.''

Unable to see for the fresh blur of tears, Kate rubbed an imperfection on the side of the mug, the cramp in her throat so painful she couldn't even swallow. She had wanted answers, and she had gotten them. But they hadn't eased the pain around her heart. Knowing only made it worse.

But it wasn't until she was on the road leading out of town that her concentration fractured and she found herself remembering the look in Tanner's eyes that first morning, when he had stood looking out at the valley. The memory of that terrible bleakness set off another rush of emotion, one that finally swamped her. Lord, it had hurt then, but it hurt even more now, knowing just how isolated his life had been. No one should have to live like that.

But he had. And knowing that changed everything.

Chapter 6

Unable to sleep, Kate turned onto her side and stared into the darkness of her bedroom, listening to the light tattoo of rain on the roof. She couldn't stop thinking about what Rita had told her. She couldn't imagine what it must have been like for Tanner. So little, so helpless, and almost overnight his whole world torn apart. After his mother had died, he had been abandoned by his father, and then taken from the only home he'd ever known and sent to live with strangers who treated him like an animal. She wondered how many times he had cried himself to sleep. Knowing she didn't dare continue that line of thought or she would end up in pieces again, she shoved back the covers and got up, the awful pressure in her chest weighing heavily on her heart.

Raking her hair back, she went to the window and pushed back the curtain, staring out at the yard. The yard light created a faint luminescence, backlighting the steadily falling rain with a silver aura. The rain beat on the ground and drizzled down the window, the chill seeping into the room with an insidious dampness. Kate stared out, watching the rain perforate the mirrored surface of the puddle beneath the light pole, her thoughts straying and somehow fractured. She didn't know why, but the rain comforted her, as if it enclosed her in some sort of safe isolation.

Sighing heavily, she was about to drop the curtain and turn when she caught a glimmer of lights through the trees along the main road. Drawing the curtain completely back, she watched, her insides giving a funny little lift when the lights turned into the Circle S lane. God, she hoped it was Tanner. He hadn't shown up for supper, and Burt had fretted so much about his absence that she had finally called down to the cook house. But Cyrus hadn't known where he was.

She knew that his absence had contributed to her own sleeplessness—that she'd been lying there wondering where he was, worrying that something had happened, waiting for him to come home. Tightening her grip on the curtain, she watched and waited as the vehicle turned toward the house, afraid that it might be one of the hands bringing Tanner's truck home. The vehicle parked on the gravel pad, the lights went off and a moment later Tanner climbed out.

Experiencing a weakening rush, Kate rested her forehead against the window and closed her eyes, her relief unexpectedly intense. She was so damned glad to have him home.

Hearing the back door open, she drew an uneven breath and straightened, letting the curtain fall. Rubbing the sudden chill from her arms, she turned, nerves unfolding in her midriff. She had made a decision on her drive home from Rita's. She had evaded the truth about why she hadn't put Mark in school, and she didn't want Tanner thinking she was hiding something from him. She owed him that much. At least.

She reached for the sweat suit lying on the end of the bed, her anxiety setting off a flurry inside her. It was going to be hard to face him. Not only would she be dredging up her own past, she would be coming face-to-face with his for the very first time since she'd found out the truth.

Slipping from her room, she headed toward the stairs, the nervous flutter getting more frantic with every step. She didn't dare analyze why she felt compelled to do this; she just knew she had to, or she would never be able to look him in the eye again. Reaching the living room, she closed her eyes and took a deep breath; then, clenching her hands to still their trembling, she turned toward the kitchen. He was at the sink washing his hands. Or at least she thought he was washing his hands, until she saw the first-aid kit sitting on the counter. It was then that she noticed the drops of blood on the kitchen floor. Alarm shot through her. "Tanner? What happened?"

He ripped off some paper towels from the dispenser by the sink, then turned, pressing the wadded-up toweling to the heel of his hand. Leaning back against the cupboard, he gave her a wry look. "Not much. We had one old cow rush a fence, and one of the top rails came loose. There was a spike in it, and it scraped my hand. That's all."

She could tell by the drawn look around his mouth that it wasn't all. She crossed the kitchen. "Let me see it."

"It's just a—"

"Let me see it," she demanded, gripping his wrist. Pushing his other hand out of the way, she lifted the toweling to reveal his palm. There was a nasty gash across the base of his thumb that clearly needed stitches. But it wasn't the ragged cut that made her stomach roll; it was the purple puncture wound in the middle of his palm. Bracing herself, she carefully turned his hand over, her stomach dropping again when she saw the identical wound on the back of his hand. The spike had gone clean through, then had cut through the fleshy pad beneath his thumb when it had been torn out. It was a mess.

Knowing how much it must hurt, she carefully turned his hand back over, a wide track of blood running down his wrist. Picking up one of the packs that held a sterile dressing, she ripped it open with her teeth. Gently supporting his hand, she pressed the gauze dressing firmly against the wound. Her voice wasn't quite steady when she spoke. "This needs stitches, Tanner."

There was a brief pause, then he finally answered, his voice gruff. "I know. I've got some veterinary supplies here with sutures—I'll do it myself."

Startled, she looked up at him, horrified by his matter-of-fact tone. "You can't do it yourself. You need to get it checked, to make sure there isn't any muscle damage."

He held her gaze for a minute, then looked away, the muscles in his face suddenly taut. "It's not as bad as it looks, and the cut isn't that deep. I'm not driving all the way to Pincher Creek to get half a dozen stitches.''

It was on the tip of her tongue to suggest going to the small hospital in Bolton, but she caught herself. He would drive all the way to Calgary before he would ever go to the hospital in Bolton. Distressed by the thought of him doing it himself, and more distressed by the idea of him having done it by himself in the past, Kate studied his profile for a moment longer, then looked back down, carefully peeling back the compression pad. The gash was a mess, and it was deep, but not deep enough to warrant more than surface suturing. It was the puncture wound in his palm that made her shudder. She had a mental picture of him throwing up his hand to protect his face as the wood snapped against the force of the charging cow. Drawing a steadying breath, she pressed the pad back down. ''Are your tetanus shots up-to-date?''

''Yes.''

He tried to withdraw his hand, but she maintained a grasp on his wrist. ''I want to clean this with some antiseptic first,'' she said, digging through the well-stocked first-aid kit. ''And I'd feel a whole lot happier about this if you were on antibiotics.''

''There's penicillin in the fridge. We had a horse with an abscess.''

Alarmed by his comment, she looked up at him. He met her gaze, the corner of his mouth lifting a little. ''I've done this before, Kate. I can manage by myself. You may as well go back to bed.''

Kate looked down, feeling just a little too vulnerable. He wasn't going to manage on his own, and she certainly wasn't going back to bed. Not with his blood smeared across her hand. ''Just keep some pressure on the cut,'' she said, her voice uneven.

She found the antiseptic swabs and the throwaway plastic forceps that went with them, her hands not quite steady as she broke open the seal. She knew why her hands weren't quite steady; the thought of poking around in that wound to clean it made her stomach shrink into a hard little knot.

"You don't have to do this," he said gruffly, taking the forceps out of her hand.

Experiencing a growing pressure in her throat, she shook her head.

"Look at me," he commanded, his voice quiet.

Blinking rapidly to will away the burning in her eyes, she waited for the moment to pass; then she looked up at him. There was a solemn intensity in his expression, something that made her heart accelerate, and she saw the muscles along his jaw tense. He stared at her, his gaze darkening, and the muscles in his throat contracted as he reached up. For one heart-stopping instant she thought he was going to touch her, but then he clenched his hand and let it drop.

He glanced down; then, after a brief pause, he looked back at her. The corner of his mouth lifted in a semblance of a smile, but his voice was uneven when he spoke. "I don't expect you to clean this up, and I don't expect you to play Florence Nightingale. And I'd rather you didn't go poking around in there with those swabs." A hint of amusement appeared in his eyes, and his expression relaxed a little. "In fact, you'd make me real happy if you just threw them in the garbage and got the bottle of antiseptic out of the cupboard by the fridge."

Feeling as if she'd had a close brush with something sweet and dangerous, Kate held his gaze for a moment, then managed a small smile as she tossed the swabs in the garbage. She found the bottle of antiseptic—a plastic squeeze bottle with a nozzle—and returned to the sink. Setting the bottle down, she rolled up his cuff, then very carefully peeled the bloodied pad off the gash. Before she had a chance to act, Tanner reached in front of her and grasped the dispenser, thoroughly irrigating the wound and the puncture, the sudsy liquid turning red as it sluiced through the cut.

"That should do it," he said, setting the bottle down. Her shoulder brushing against his arm, Kate tore open another sterile pack and blotted the wound, then pressed a fresh dry pad against it to staunch the renewed bleeding. She was keenly aware of how close he was, of the warmth of his arm against hers, and she closed her eyes, the heat from his body making her go weak. Swallowing against the sudden frenzy in her chest, she supported his hand as she tore off some paper towels, carefully skirting the sterile pad as she wiped the rest of his hand. He went very still, and she heard his breathing stop when she dried between his fingers, and Kate closed her eyes again, the wild flutter in her chest robbing her of common sense. It was all she could do to keep from cradling that damaged hand against her breast.

His closeness overwhelmed her senses, and she swallowed hard, trying to struggle against the longing that surged through her, making her heart race even faster. She wondered what it would be like to be held by him, to feel the weight of his arms around her. And she wondered what it would be like to lie with him, to feel the full, hard length of his body against hers. God, it would be heaven to feel his warmth, to experience the comfort of his embrace. To be touched by him.

His hand jerked when she touched his palm, and he spoke, his voice roughened by strain. "The sutures are in that green container in the cupboard, if you want to get them. We may as well get this over with."

Kate drew a deep stabilizing breath, reaching down deep for control.

She wasn't sure how she got through the next half hour, so aware of him as a man, and so aware of the growing heaviness low in her body, she could barely function. But somehow she did. Between the two of them, they closed the torn flesh with seven stitches, then she covered them and the puncture with an antiseptic cream and dressed his hand, knowing he would never keep it clean if she didn't. After tucking the final wrap into place, she put the gauze and scissors back in the kit, feeling so shaky and emotionally exposed that she was afraid to look at him.

"Thanks."

Her voice was unsteady when she answered. "You're welcome." Her insides in a turmoil, Kate rose and began tidying up. Reaching across the table, she picked up the cap for the antiseptic cream and screwed it back on the tube, so sensitized to him that she was conscious of every movement, every breath. Tanner rolled down his sleeve, traces of dried blood on the back of his knuckles, and Kate had to clench her hand to keep from wiping them away. She wanted to touch him so badly, to cradle his head against her belly and stroke his hair. It was a big aching emptiness inside her, this need to hold him. She wanted to fill up her arms with him; it was as if holding him would fill up the emptiness inside her and replenish her soul.

Tanner rose, closing the lid on the first-aid kit, then put it away in the cupboard by the fridge. Kate leaned back against the counter and tightly folded her arms, the emptiness inside compounding as she watched him, far too aware of the tight lines of pain around his mouth. He turned and found her watching him, his expression suddenly unreadable as he braced his good hand against the side of the cupboard. "Something on your mind?"

Her chest clogged with a host of feelings, she gazed across the room at him, loneliness rising up in her with a desolating force. She could love him. So easily, she could love him. Wrenched by that thought, she hugged herself, the ache in her throat so tight that she could barely speak. "I wanted to tell you why I didn't put Mark in school," she said unevenly. "I didn't want you to think I was lying to you."

He bent his head and stared down at the floor, his profile rigid, the muscles along his jaw tense. Finally he lifted his head and looked at her. "Why didn't you put him in school?"

A chill slithered down Kate's spine, and she swallowed, her voice uneven when she spoke. "I left my husband a little over a year ago. We agreed on a divorce, but right after he signed the preliminary papers, things started to get nasty. Roger took the kids once, but he brought them back when I said I'd reconsider. It got so bad that I finally moved, but he tracked us down and started pressuring me, threatening to take the kids again if I went through with it. I moved again, only this time I didn't tell anyone where I was going. He showed up at Mark's school about two months later and tried to take him. The school called the police, and I found out he'd tracked us down through a combination of airline tickets, school records and medical records."

Having blurted out the worst of it, Kate looked up at the ceiling and took a shaky breath, the knot in her stomach unwinding just a little. She waited to regain her composure, then she looked at Tanner, certain she didn't have a speck of color left in her face. "Your ad in the paper was heaven-sent. A decent job, a place to live for me and the boys and nearly total isolation. He's never going to find me here, as long as I don't give him a paper trail to follow." Her knees feeling suddenly unsteady, she redistributed her weight and rested her hands on the counter, bracing herself against it. Her voice was nearly as shaky as her legs when she continued. "That's why I didn't put Mark in school. I didn't want to leave a paper trail."

His hand still braced on the side of the cupboard, Tanner stared at her, a muscle in his jaw flexing. He didn't say anything for a moment, then he spoke, his voice flat. "Was there abuse involved?"

Drained of all warmth and unable to hold his gaze, Kate looked away and shook her head. "Not physically. Manipulation and emotional battering, and a whole campaign to terrorize me, but nothing physical. What he did was ten times worse."

There was a long, strained pause, then Tanner straightened, his voice cold and quiet when he spoke. "He won't get to you here. You can be damned sure of that." He gave her one final, chilling glance, then yanked his jacket off the back of the chair.

He turned toward the archway, and Kate stared after him, feeling more alone than she could ever remember. Curling her fingers around the edge of the counter, she braced herself for the worst. "Do you want us to leave?"

He paused, his jacket scrunched in his good hand, his shoulders stiff with tension. After a moment he turned, his expression solemn as he ran his thumb across the tape on his bandaged hand. Finally he shook his head. "No," he said, his voice husky with strain. "I don't want you to leave."

Letting her breath go in a rush, Kate closed her eyes, a thousand feelings speeding through her. And every one of them was tied to Tanner McCall. Waiting for the awful fullness in her chest to ease, she swallowed and opened her eyes. The archway was empty. She hugged herself, the ache spreading. God, she hadn't known she could want anything as much as she wanted to have him hold her.

The clouds were turning indigo and crimson when Kate finally rolled onto her back, the bedding crumpled and twisted from a long, sleepless night. She looked toward the window, the sky turbulent with heavy clouds, the first rays of dawn burnishing their undersides with a vibrancy of color. Her eyes gritty and her head throbbing, she shoved away the covers and got up, shivering slightly as she went to the window and pushed back the curtain.

Lord, it was a sight, this big, endless sky, the indigo and crimson shades now slashed with fingers of orange, the bottom edges of the dark clouds kissed with gold. The trees along the ridge stood in a ragged silhouette, the rain from the night before leaving the air clean and fragrant.

She stood at the window for a long while, watching the colors fade and change; then she rubbed her arms and turned back to the bed, reaching for her housecoat. It was too early to use the bathroom up here. She would wake the boys for sure, and she needed the absolute stillness, the solitude, of a silent house.

After she'd showered and dressed downstairs, she went in to check on Burt and found him lying on his back, one bony hand curled around the top of the quilt. His mouth was open, and he was snoring slightly, a thin trail of spittle at the corner of his mouth. Gently wiping his chin, she tucked the covers around his shoulders, then quietly closed his bedroom door, not wanting to wake him.

She had just put the coffee on and had everything assembled to make baking-powder biscuits when she heard the shower in Tanner's room. Going still, she stared down at her hands, then picked up the pastry cutter and began working the shortening into the flour mix, her insides knotting. She wondered if he would be leaving for the cattle camp first thing, or if they would all pull out later in the day. And she wondered how long he would be gone. She dumped the dough out on the counter and began working it. She didn't even want to think about what it would be like with him not there.

She had the biscuits in the oven and ham and cheese diced for an omelet by the time he came downstairs. He paused at the door, surprise registering on his face, then he dropped to the floor the canvas duffel he was carrying. "Good morning."

Kate noticed that the dressing was gone, replaced by a wide adhesive bandage. She pasted on a smile. "Good morning. I was going to make myself an omelet. Would you like one?"

He hesitated, then began rolling back his cuffs, his expression set. "An omelet sounds fine."

Kate set about preparing his breakfast, her pulse leaping into overdrive when he came over to the counter and got himself a cup of coffee. He was so close that she could smell the soap on his skin, and she closed her eyes, the surge of awareness nearly overwhelming her. Lord, but he was big. And male.

Forcing herself to disconnect from the feelings warring inside her, Kate looked away and took a deep, steadying breath. She wasn't sure whether she could get through this without coming undone altogether.

She busied herself at the counter while Tanner ate his breakfast, the silence between them thick with undercurrents. Knowing she couldn't avoid the situation without making him wonder, she took her own breakfast to the table, certain she wasn't going to be able to swallow a bite. But she was halfway through her omelet when Tanner pushed his plate aside and rested his arms on the table, his expression somber.

Finally he looked at her, his gaze shuttered. "If you need to get hold of me, use the cellular phone number. We might have some dead spots in coverage depending on where we are, but you'll get me eventually. Buddy is staying behind, and Ross and a couple of others will be riding in and out from here, so you won't be completely on your own."

Kate nodded, something in his face making her pulse race. Tanner watched her for a moment longer, then dropped his gaze and lifted his mug, the silence suddenly strained. Her insides churning with uncertainty, Kate looked down at her plate.

Tanner set his cup down. "I've left some cash in the top drawer of the desk, in case you need anything, and I left a message on Doc Casey's answering machine, so he knows what's going on.'' There was a pause, then he looked at her, a grim expression compressing his mouth into a hard line. ''And I'm going to talk to the hands about the situation with your boys. I don't want any carelessness about strangers showing up.''

Her stomach reacting, Kate abruptly set her fork down, her expression frozen as she stared at him. Of all the things she might have expected from him, this was not one of them. Realizing he was watching her with a steady, unreadable look, she gave herself a mental shake and looked away, her pulse suddenly uneven. She didn't know how to respond. Or what to say. She hadn't meant to drag him into her mess. Feeling as if she'd misused him in some way, she looked up at him, sickened by the fact that he had misconstrued her intent. ''I'm not worried about the boys, Tanner,'' she whispered unevenly. ''That's not why I told you.''

Tanner stared at her, the expression in his eyes darkening, the muscles in his jaw tight. Finally he spoke, his voice strained. ''I know.''

Her heart suddenly hammering, Kate gazed back at him, the clamor in her chest making it hard for her to think. He did know. Maybe more than she wanted him to. Unsettled by that thought, she dragged her gaze away from his, needing to be absolutely honest with him. ''I feel perfectly safe here,'' she said huskily. ''And I don't want the men having to be responsible for us.''

''They *are* responsible for you. As of today.''

Kate looked up at him, caught off guard by the glimmer of humor in his eyes. She didn't know how to respond. The glimmer deepened, and suddenly the knots in her stomach relaxed. She gave him a warped smile, her tone dry when she responded. ''No doubt they'll be thrilled.''

It happened again, that disarming, sensual, intimate smile that did unbelievable things to his eyes and even more unbelievable things to her insides. The smile held, the creases around his eyes deepening, the glint in his eyes turning her heart to jelly. ''No doubt,'' he allowed.

Smiling back at him, she fell victim to the sparkle of amusement, to the glimmer of intimacy that she saw in his eyes. Oh, yes. She could very easily care for this man. So very easily. Burt wasn't going to be the only one who was going to feel his absence the next few days.

Flustered by that random thought, she dragged her gaze from his, her pulse erratic. She had to stop doing that—letting her mind wander—or she was going to end up in very big trouble.

She heard his chair scrape back, and she looked up, experiencing a sinking feeling. He pushed his chair back against the table, then lifted his mug and finished off his coffee, his shirt stretching across his shoulders. He set the cup back down, then picked up some papers lying by his plate. "You be sure and take a cellular phone if you're out on your own. I don't want you stuck out in the middle of nowhere if you have car problems."

Experiencing an unexpected awkwardness, Kate rose, shoving her hands in her pockets. "I will."

He stared at her for a moment; then, sticking the papers in the breast pocket of his shirt, he turned and picked up his duffel bag. Anxiously fingering a safety pin in her pocket, she followed him to the utility room, an awful hollow feeling settling around her heart. She didn't want him to go. And it made it even harder, knowing why he was leaving. She felt as if she were driving him out of his own home.

He paused in the utility room and lifted his hat off a hook, then settled it on his head. Adjusting the brim, he turned to face her. "Buddy's going to the city today, and he'll be picking up a portable intercom, so you have some way of monitoring Burt."

She met his gaze, her own solemn. He looked so tired and serious, so somber. She thought about the joyless existence he'd had, of never having anyone to love or comfort him, of always being separate and alone. It broke her heart just thinking about it.

He held her gaze for a moment, then he looked away, his profile tense. "If you need anything, let me know," he said, his voice gruff. "I'll check in when I can." He finally raised his head and looked at her, his expression desolate, something in his eyes making her heart contract.

Lacing her hands together to keep from touching the tension lines around his mouth, she swallowed hard and nodded. His expression cast in harsh lines, he collected his slicker, and with it clasped in one hand, along with his duffel bag, he pushed open the screen door. Shifting everything to his good hand, he glanced at her, his gaze dark and unreadable, then he turned and stepped outside. Catching the screen door so it wouldn't slam shut behind him, she watched him go down the back steps, her heart climbing higher in her chest. Lord, she didn't want him to leave. But what made it even worse was that she had a feeling that *he* didn't want to leave, either.

It was not a good start to what turned out to be a bright, sunny morning. Trying not to think about how empty the house felt, Kate launched herself on a make-work program, determined not to let that emptiness turn into something more. By the time she got Burt bathed and settled, and the boys fed and shipped outside, she had managed to cram everything back into perspective—at least she thought she had, until she walked into the living room.

She rarely spent any time in there. It was somehow Tanner's reserve, and she always felt as if she were trespassing when she went in. But as she entered the room, her gaze was drawn to the rows and rows of books lining two walls. Setting the vacuum down, she stared at them, remembering what Rita had told her about how the kids had made fun of Tanner in school. When she thought about the kind of childhood he'd had—the abuse, the neglect, the emotional poverty, the sick, twisted existence he'd been forced to endure—it was a miracle he'd even survived. She thought about what the mortification must have been like, going into junior high and being unable to read. God, each and every day must have been an agony of dread. And now he had amassed literally hundreds of books.

Drawn by some internal need, Kate started idling her way along the bookshelves, noticing for the first time the titles and content of the volumes. There was everything—books on astronomy, geology, world religions, two whole shelves on history and biographies, books on archaeology and anthropology, two sets of encyclopedias, one very recent and one several years old, rows and rows of *National Geographic* and three shelves of classics. But the most significant were the literally dozens of volumes on American Indian tribes and cultures, with a good portion of those focusing on the Plains Indians. Kate touched the worn bindings, her expression sobering. A man in search of his roots.

Straightening, she let her gaze sweep down the full length of shelving, a funny feeling settling in the pit of her stomach. This encompassed a lifetime of self-education—and a lifetime of shame. The result of a childhood of humiliation and loneliness. Disquieted by that realization, she moved slowly along, cataloging the vast collection of knowledge before her. She came to the sound system and paused, then crouched down and opened the set of doors beneath it, a funny sensation unfolding in her when she saw the collection of albums. She stared at them, the hollow flutter moving to her stomach. In all the time she'd been there, she had never once heard the stereo on, not even at night, after she'd gone to bed and he was working late.

She opened the next set of doors and found custom-built pull-out trays specifically designed for CDs. Dozens and dozens of CDs. Kate stared at them, her insides tightening into a painful knot. She hadn't realized just how guarded he was until now. How very little he gave away. He left no part of himself unprotected, even his love of music. And because of her presence, he'd denied himself this pleasure rather than open himself up for any kind of speculation.

Roughly closing the unit, she stood up, a chilling anger building in her. If she ever got her hands on Bruce McCall and his social-climbing wife, she would strangle them both.

Going to stand before the windows of the sun room, she stared out, a terrible emptiness settling inside her. That feeling was compounded when she recognized the rig heading toward the main road. It was Tanner's truck, hauling a six-horse trailer. She watched, trying to will away the ache that was growing around her heart. She knew he was leaving because of her. Because of what people would say. He had a lifetime of experience to draw from. His aloneness, his wariness, created such a vast hurt in her that she could barely stand it. He so desperately needed someone to show him what love was. Hit by a rush of emotion, Kate locked her jaw against the awful constriction in her throat. She had never realized until this instant, as she watched him leave, how much she wanted that someone to be her.

Chapter 7

It was the fourth night of steady rain since Tanner had left. Unable to sleep, Kate stood in the darkened kitchen, watching the rain batter the growing pool of water beneath the power pole, the illumination from the yard light blurred and indistinct. It was late, and the only sounds were the wind-driven rain lashing against the windows and the scraping of the lilac branches along the west side of the house.

Drawing her robe around her, Kate stuck her hands in her pockets and stared out, loneliness pulling at her. It was a bad night for feeling lonely. For some reason the rain seemed to intensify the feeling of isolation, of being separated from those who mattered.

Folding her arms, she rested her shoulder against the window frame, the emptiness expanding in her. She knew why she couldn't sleep. She was waiting for Tanner to call. He had checked in regularly for the first two days, just brief calls to make sure everything was okay, but he hadn't called today. And the longer she waited for the phone to ring, the more alone she felt, so aware of his absence that she was left with this huge hollowness in the middle of her chest. She wondered where he was and if he was cold and wet. She knew—

logically, she knew—that the cellular coverage in this area was spotty; he'd told her so more than once. But on a night like tonight, logic didn't cut it. She just wanted to know he was somewhere dry and warm.

A sharp jangle behind her broke the silence, and she turned and picked up the phone before it had a chance to ring twice. "Hello."

There was a hiss of static, and the gruff, male voice seemed to come from a long way off. "I'm sorry it's so late, but we've been moving cattle, and I've been out of range up until now."

She could hear both the frustration and the weariness in his voice, and she wished he wasn't so far away. "Don't worry about it. I was up anyway." Tightening her hold on the receiver, she closed her eyes against the sudden ache, her voice very husky when she spoke. "It sounds like you've had a long day."

She heard him heave a frustrated sigh. "And it isn't over yet." There was a static-riddled pause, then he spoke again, his tone gravelly. "It's getting pretty ugly out here. We're breaking camp and moving the herd to a more sheltered location. If all goes well, Cyrus and a couple of the other hands should be home sometime tomorrow." There was another pause, then he spoke again, his voice clearer, as if he'd shifted the phone closer to his mouth. "How are things there?"

Wishing she could ease the weariness in his voice, Kate shifted the receiver, trying very hard to keep her tone light. "Wet. I think you could float a canoe in the north pasture."

There was a hint of amusement in his voice when he answered. "I don't doubt it. " He hesitated, then spoke again, his tone gruffer than before. "You'd better warn the boys to stay away from the creek, Kate. With the spring runoff and all this rain, it's going to be pretty wild."

Kate stared off into the darkness of the kitchen, loneliness making her voice catch. "I will."

She heard him exhale heavily, and the weariness was back in his voice. "I'll try to check in tomorrow, but I can't promise anything. We're going to be heading into the back country."

Sensing the desolation in him, Kate drew a shaky breath. Needing to reach out to him in some small way, she tightened her grip on the phone, the thickness in her throat growing. "Take care, Tanner," she said, her voice uneven. "And stay safe."

There was a long, static-filled pause, then Tanner answered, his voice gruff. "Call if you need anything. Okay?"

"I will."

Kate listened until she heard the disconnection; then she closed her eyes and clutched the receiver to her chest. Five minutes on the phone with him weren't enough. Not nearly enough. Feeling more alone than ever, she reluctantly replaced the receiver, the empty feeling expanding. He sounded so tired and so alone.

"Katie? That you?"

Raking her hair back from her face, she straightened, then turned toward Burt's bedroom. "Yes, Burt. It is."

The night-light by his bed cast his room in a soft amber glow, and the sound of the rain rattling against the windowpanes was heightened by the wind. He shifted his head to met her gaze, his voice slurred with sleep. "Was that Tanner?"

Lowering the rail, she pulled the covers up, then sat on the edge of the bed. "Yes, it was."

"Where is he?"

Realizing that the old man's hands were cold, she warmed them with her own as she relayed her conversation with Tanner. Burt watched her, his eyes sharp. When she'd told him all there was to tell, he tightened his bony fingers around hers. "Did he say when he'd be home?"

She gave him a small smile. "No, he didn't."

He stared up at her, watching her with an intentness that belied his illness. Finally he spoke, his voice gruff. "That boy's like family, you know."

Already on shaky ground emotionally, Kate had to swallow before she could answer. "I know he is," she responded unevenly.

His grip tightened with surprising strength, and he continued on as if he hadn't heard her, his voice cracking. "I would have married his mama if she would have had me. Nearly broke my spirit when she died. Seems right that he ended up here." His hand shaking, he clumsily wiped the corner of his eye, his finger stiff and gnarled. "He's had a powerful lot of disappointment in his life, Tanner has. Powerful lot. I don't want to see him get any more."

Her throat tight, Kate gently smoothed down the thin wisps of hair along his temple, nearly overcome with feelings for this old man. The awful constriction finally eased, and she brushed her thumb across his sunken cheek as she forced an unsteady smile. "Neither do I," she whispered shakily.

He gazed up at her; then, giving her hand a spastic squeeze, he closed his eyes, a thin trail of moisture tracking down his temple. "You've got soft hands, Kate Quinn. Soft hands."

Feeling more emotionally raw, more lonely, than she could ever remember feeling, Kate continued to stroke the old man's temple until his grip slackened. Assured that he was asleep, she carefully pulled the blankets over his cold hands, then tucked them around his shoulders. Fighting against the persistent lump in her throat, she leaned over and kissed him on the cheek, so many feelings jammed up in her that she could barely identify them all. Lord, but she loved this man.

"Ma'am?"

Rapping the ladle against the rim of the pot, Kate set the utensil on the saucer by the burner, then turned from the stove, the rainy-day gloom infiltrating the room. Wiping her hands on the towel over her shoulder, she glanced at Buddy, who was standing in the doorway, beads of moisture clinging to his hair. His face was unnaturally white. She frowned. "What's wrong?"

He gave an apologetic shrug, wincing as he shifted his shoulder. He cautiously repositioned his strapped arm, his face turning even whiter. "I don't think I'm going to be able to make that trip to Pincher Creek, ma'am," he said, his voice uneven. "That black mare got ornery when I tried to bring her into the barn, and she jarred my shoulder some."

Crossing the room, Kate tossed the tea towel on the table. "Does if feel like you've dislocated it again?"

Buddy tried to smile. "No, ma'am. I don't think so. It just hurts like hell—like the dickens, ma'am."

Kate eased his slicker off and hung it on a hook inside the utility room, then very gently checked the area around his shoulder. The joint felt properly seated, and the strapping was tight. Recognizing the lines of pain around his mouth, she indicated a kitchen chair. "Sit down and let's get some ice on it. I saw some painkillers in the first-aid kit."

Supporting his arm, the hired hand wiped his feet on the mat, and Kate saw him sway slightly. Without giving him a chance to argue, she propelled him into the kitchen and plunked him down in a chair. "Sit. And don't argue."

Buddy managed a weak smile. "Yes, ma'am."

By the time Kate had his shoulder packed in ice, his color was somewhat better, but it was obvious that he was damned sore. Kate hadn't been too keen about him driving all the way to Pincher Creek with only one arm in the first place. Granted, once he hit the pavement it would have been smooth sailing, but there were seven miles of gravel road before getting to pavement, and those seven miles were something else altogether; they were bound to be a mess. Now his going was clearly out of the question. Under the circumstances, it wouldn't have mattered one way or the other, but Burt had taken the last pill of one prescription that morning, and since it was for his high blood pressure, she did not want him going without. Which meant a trip to Pincher Creek. And in spite of what Buddy thought, she was more than capable of driving on muddy country roads.

Buddy looked absolutely appalled when Kate suggested it. Amused by his reaction, she didn't give him a chance to give her that code-of-the-west, little-woman routine. She gave him a dry, chastising look. "Don't go all male on me here, Buddy," she said, her tone slightly scolding. "My father and grandfather were both fishing guides up north, and I've driven places in four-wheel drives that would make your head spin. So don't worry. I can make it from here to Pincher without putting the truck in the ditch."

Buddy fidgeted. "I don't know, ma'am. This side road is going to be heavygoing. And if you run into trouble, Tanner'll have my hide."

Avoiding his gaze, she bound his shoulder in gauze to keep the ice packs in place, thinking that what he considered heavygoing and what she did were two different things.

Tucking in the loose end of the binding, she looked down at him, reassuring him with a smile. "I have to get the prescription filled," she pointed out. "And I'll need you to stay with Burt."

He gave her a worried look. "I don't mind at all staying with Burt, ma'am, but I do mind you heading off by yourself. It's damned—um, real miserable out there."

Kate gave him a reassuring pat, her tone businesslike. "Believe me, I'll manage."

It had been days since Kate had been off the ranch property. It had been raining almost nonstop, but she had no idea just how much rain had fallen until she drove across the little bridge spanning the creek that wound its way through the Circle S pasture. The creek that Tanner had warned her about. It was deep and muddy and churning, the turbulent water breaching the steep banks and ominously spreading out through the willows into low-lying areas. There was water everywhere.

In fact, the entire countryside was sodden, with ditches full and pastures flooded, with every ravine and gully a catch basin for the steady, eroding runoff. About three miles from the ranch there was another stream that cut through a sharp coulee, its meandering course now obscured by the overflow. The water was level with one shoulder of the road, the four-foot culvert either blocked or unable to handle the runoff. There were also other places along the road where the water was backed up, and one spot where the road itself was nearly submerged, the deep ruts full of water, the thick grass along the shoulders marking the edge of the ditch.

Grateful that the boys had refused to come with her, Kate dumped any idea of spending an hour browsing in the shopping mall. If any more vehicles passed this way, this portion of road would be so chewed up that it would be impassible. And the last thing she wanted was to get stranded several miles from home.

The rain had eased up a little by the time she reached the outskirts of town, but the streets and back alleys were flooded—rushing storm sewers, hubcap-deep puddles at intersections, the sidewalks awash with muddy water thrown up by passing cars.

After getting the prescription refilled, she picked up some things she'd promised the boys—two new games, some comic books and some chocolate bars, then headed back to where she had parked the Bronco. The street was dismal and cloaked in gray, the brick-and-sandstone structures dark from days of rain, the lights from the shops visible in the unnatural dusk. Rain rattled against the cars parked along the curb as the steady drizzle suddenly turned into a drumming downpour.

Rain bounced like pellets off the pavement, and traffic crept down the street, brake lights flashing as drivers slowed to accommodate the blinding rain. Turning her face from the slanting wetness, Kate pulled her hood closer and huddled in Burt's good canvas slicker, her purse and parcel hugged against her chest. Avoiding two pedestrians, she stepped to the corner, squinting into the downpour as she waited for a break in the traffic to cross the street. A truck passed from her left, and she stepped off the curb, catching a glimpse of a red car that was angled to pull out of a parking spot on the opposite side of the street. A red car that looked frighteningly familiar.

The rush of alarm was so intense that for an instant she thought her heart would stop altogether. Clutching her parcel tighter, she stared at the vehicle, her heart suddenly jammed against her ribs, hammering frantically as fear churned through her. God, it couldn't be! There was no way that Roger could have tracked her here—no way. She had been so careful.

Realizing that once the oncoming van passed, the car would have a clear lane to leave, Kate reacted. Darting around the back of the van, she sprinted across the street, panic compressing her lungs and a frantic prayer circulating in her mind. She had to find out. She had to know. God help her, she had to get close enough to see the back license plate. Dodging a group of Hutterites coming out of a store, she flew down the sidewalk, careless of the puddles collecting on the cement, disregarding the muddy water splashing up her legs. If the car got away before she got close enough, she would never know if he was closing in. And then her life would turn into another nightmare.

Just as she darted around a car coming out of an alley, the van stopped, allowing the car to pull away from the curb, the large vehicle blocking her line of sight. Fear rising in her, she lengthened her stride to an all-out sprint, her breathing coming in labored gasps as she raced past the van, frantic to see the plate on the departing car. Praying that the driver couldn't see her in his rearview mirror, she twisted past an older woman with an umbrella; her dash brought to an abrupt halt by a large dog bounding between the parked cars. Grabbing a light standard to catch her balance, Kate jerked around, a sickening rush clutching at her when the red car turned the corner and she knew she'd just lost whatever chance she had. Her chest heaving and her lungs on fire, she propped her forearm against the light standard and covered her face with her hand, the sharp rush of panic giving way to crushing despair. God, she'd been so close. So close. One red car, one damned red car, and she was right back to where she'd started. Looking over her shoulder at every turn.

She didn't know how long she stood there. Long enough, though, for her breathing to level out and her mind to clear. Swallowing against the sudden tightness in her throat, Kate dropped her hand, feeling as if her insides had turned to lead. Grasping the bag in one hand, she turned, her legs trembling, dread rising up like a sickness. She couldn't think about it. She had to shut off her mind and not think about it. He would never find her at the Circle S. And the boys were safe. Safe.

Mindless of the rain, she started walking back toward the truck, her heart still slamming in her chest, the need to panic nearly overwhelming her common sense. He couldn't get to them. There was no trail to follow. God, let there be no trail to follow.

Rounding the corner, she stepped into the full force of the wind-driven rain, the cold drops pelting against her face and running down her neck. The wind made her shiver, and suddenly, in her mind, she saw him as she'd seen him the last time they had come face-to-face. The panic broke free, and she started to run. She had to get home. She had to get to the boys.

The trip home was a jumble of rain and panic and short periods of trying to convince herself that she was overreacting. It wasn't until she slowed for the turn onto the gravel road that she realized she had no recollection of leaving Pincher Creek, of passing Rita's service station, of making the turn onto the secondary paved road. Nothing. She remembered nothing. Except driving as fast as she dared and checking repeatedly in the rearview mirror to see if she was being followed.

A bad case of the shakes hit her as she turned onto the gravel road, and she braked, closing her eyes tightly as she rested her head against her hands. God, she had been so scared. So damned scared. Determined not to let fear overwhelm her, she made herself concentrate on taking deep, steadying breaths, making her muscles relax. She had to calm down or she would end up in the ditch for sure. Taking one final stabilizing breath, she raised her head, deliberately loosening her grip on the wheel. Focusing strictly on the mechanics of what she was doing, she set the transmission for four-wheel drive, then took her foot off the brake. Seven miles. She had seven miles to go. That was all. Then she could have a cup of tea and a hot bath. And find some excuse to hold her boys. Kate clenched her jaw and tightened her grip on the wheel, trying to will away the sudden sting of tears. Seven miles. Just seven miles.

The road was a mess, churned up from her trip out and worsened in the interim by the steady rain. By the time she reached the first bad mud hole, Kate was so intent on her driving that everything else had been eliminated from her mind. She stopped on the slight rise just before it, chewing thoughtfully on her bottom lip as she considered the stretch of road. The deep, gouged-out ruts were now completely filled with water, and only the deep ridges of the ruts and the grass along the edges protruded above the water. She could tell by the lay of the land that the ditches on either side were not that deep, but they weren't really the problem. The road itself was the problem. It had been soft before, but it was going to be worse now. She had ample clearance as far as the vehicle was concerned, and ample horsepower, but she had thirty feet of gumbo to plow through before she got to solid ground on the other side. Not her idea of a sure thing.

Exhaling heavily, she tightened the tension on her seat belt, then put the vehicle in gear. She was going to need a damned good run at it or she would get mired up to the axles about halfway through.

It was one wild ride. It wasn't until the vehicle started to lose momentum that things got really dicey. Kate's heart lurched in alarm as the truck slewed wildly, the rear end sliding perilously close to the invisible shoulder. It took all the skill she had to navigate back to the center, the cab rocking wildly as the wide tires settled back into the deep ruts. With the engine howling and wheels churning, she fought the drag as the vehicle slid sideways, knowing that if she lost momentum, the game would definitely be over. Inch by inch, she plowed through the mud hole, fighting both the weight of the road and the truck, mud flying from the clawing wheels. It seemed like forever, but finally the front wheels grabbed solid graveled ground, and with a final, lurching fishtail, she broke free. Letting go a shaky breath, Kate eased her grip on the steering wheel.

But then the absolute recklessness of what she'd done hit her, and her throat closed up with another painful cramp, only this time her vision blurred with tears. She wasn't even rational. If she'd caught the crumbling shoulder with the roadbed so soft, she likely would have rolled the truck—and into a ditch of water to boot. Reaching the crest of the hill, she pulled to the side of the road and stopped, covering her face with her hands. God, she was coming apart piece by piece. Home. She just had to get home and make sure the boys were okay.

Drying her eyes with the back of her hand, she swallowed against the unrelenting knot, remembering that she had promised she would call Buddy when she turned onto the gravel road. Reaching for the cellular, she tipped it to look at the readout. A jolt of near-panic coursed through her when the readout flashed the red no-service warning. But then the red light turned green, and Kate inhaled unevenly, her legs suddenly trembling. Lord, she had to get a grip or she would never make it home. Fortifying herself with another deep breath, she shifted the phone to her other hand and punched in the number, then hit Send, closing her eyes as she waited for the call to go through.

Buddy answered, and Kate shifted the phone closer to her mouth. Striving to keep any traces of panic out of her voice, she told him where she was, and that she would be home soon. Keeping her voice level, she also told him that the road wasn't in very good shape, and that it might take her a while. She listened to his caution; then, swallowing hard, she tightened her grip on the phone and asked how the boys were doing.

"They're doing just fine, ma'am. They went down to feed the dogs, and now they've got Burt playing Chinese checkers."

Knowing fear was making her irrational, but unable to stop herself, she said, her voice uneven, "You'd better keep them in the house, Buddy. I don't want them going anywhere near the creek. It's too dangerous."

"Will do. I'll tell Burt you called. He's been fretting about when you'd be getting home."

Kate looked out the window, struggling to will away another rush of tears. "Tell him I'm on my way. Okay?"

"Will do."

She had trouble seeing the End switch, and her hands weren't quite steady when she placed the phone back in its holder. Their security hadn't been breached. They were all safe and sound, and she was only minutes away. Just minutes away.

Raking her hair back from her face, she closed her eyes and released a shaky sigh; then, collecting herself, she put the truck in gear, automatically checking the rearview mirror before she pulled onto the road. There was nothing behind her but the falling rain and a long stretch of empty road.

Suddenly so drained that she could barely function, Kate fixed her attention on the road, the shrouding gray drizzle and the *whip-whap* of the windshield wipers making her feel oddly disconnected, as if her mind were separated from the rest of her body. She wanted nothing more than to close up in a tight ball and try to convince herself that the red car meant nothing, that paranoia had sucked her into a frightening flashback.

But despite her self-lecture, the awful ache would not go away, and no amount of blinking would clear her vision. She would have given anything if she had someone to lean on for a while—someone who could stand between her and the terrifying reality of what was waiting for her out there. Just for a while.

If she had felt drained before, she felt absolutely beaten when she crested the rise of land rimming the ravine and saw what lay between her and the ranch. The water had risen dramatically and now completely obliterated the road, but what alarmed her was that it had turned into a rushing torrent. Pulling off to the side, Kate put the vehicle in Park and stared at the churning, muddy water, stunned by what had transpired in a matter of two hours. It was as if a dam had broken somewhere upstream.

Reliving the awful feeling that had churned through her when she'd spotted the red car, and now unable to get to her boys, Kate braced her elbow on the window ledge and covered her eyes with her hand, finally giving in to the intolerable pressure in her chest. It was the panic that had unraveled her—and the awful tension that had dogged her every mile on the long drive home. And it was also the accumulated strain of months of worry and moments of heart-stopping fear. For months she had shoved the constant anxiety to the back of her mind, refusing to give in to it. But now, stranded and alone, huddled in the cab of Tanner's truck, she let it take her under, as if, after months of stockpiling the fear and the panic and the frightening uncertainty, her own internal dam had broken.

It seemed like an eternity before she cried herself out, her harsh sobs dwindling to the occasional ragged one. Pressing the heels of her hands against her throbbing, swollen eyes, she forced herself to dredge up some control, then she reached for her purse and located a packet of tissues. She blew her nose, then closed her eyes and tipped her head back, waiting for her emotions to settle. God, she didn't know she could feel so inadequate, so exhausted, so emotionally depleted.

Releasing a heavy sigh, she wearily lifted her head, knowing that although a damned good cry might take the edge off, it didn't fix anything. Especially the washout blocking her.

She went still when she spotted the truck parked on the other side of the gully, a truck that hadn't been there moments before. A movement at the side of the road caught her attention and she shifted her gaze, her heart lurching when she recognized the figure in the dark canvas drover's coat and black Stetson coming up the hill toward her, his shoulders hunched against the driving rain. She stared at him, her mind numb; then her throat cramped up again and her vision blurred. Tanner. He was home—and he was here. Afraid she would break down again if she didn't do something, she quickly wiped her eyes and reached for the door handle, the wind and rain buffeting her as she stepped out.

Slamming the door, she hunched against the driving rain and started toward him, slipping haphazardly in the mud, praying he wouldn't notice the mess she was in. If he showed any concern at all, she wasn't sure if she could keep it together or not.

Feeling as if she were hanging on by a mere thread, she stopped and tried to fortify her reserve, waiting for him.

Reaching her, his head tipped against the slanting rain, he turned so that she was sheltered by his large frame. He glared at her from beneath the brim of his hat, his face fixed in harsh lines. "Damn it, Kate. You should have called me to get the prescription. Buddy was damned worried about you."

She looked up at him, her hair plastered to her head, the water running down her face and dripping off her eyelashes and nose, the feeling of fear and helplessness surging back. She knew that if she opened her mouth to answer, she was going to cry. Dragging Burt's canvas slicker tighter around her, she tried to swallow, the growing pressure making it impossible.

His gaze narrowed, and the angle of his jaw hardened. "What's wrong? What happened?"

Her panic, her fear, her relief at having him there, came dangerously close to the surface, and Kate clutched her coat tighter and answered, her voice breaking badly, "I thought I saw the boys' father in Pincher. I thought—" Closing her eyes against the sudden welling of tears, she clenched her jaw, feeling as if she were about to shatter.

She heard him swear; then he gripped her chin and brought her head up, forcing her to look at him. Rain angled in under the brim of his hat and sluiced down his face, but he didn't seem to notice. "Kate, listen to me," he commanded gruffly. "We can't talk about it now. That culvert could go at any time, and if it does, there's no other way around. If we don't get across now, we won't be getting across at all."

Startled into stillness, transfixed by his touch, Kate stared up at him, the urgency of his words registering. She closed her eyes, and a violent shiver coursed through her, then she forced herself to pull it together.

Concentrating on what he'd told her, she met his gaze, indicating with a small movement of her head that she understood. Tanner stared at her, his eyes dark, then he gave her head a gentle little shake. "Okay?" he asked, his voice soft and husky.

She managed a weak smile and nodded again. "Okay."

He wiped away the water caught in her eyelashes, with his thumbs, then let her go, his voice gruff and tinged with humor when he said, "Do you think you can make it across without losing both your shoes?"

She tried to smile. "I think so."

Fighting against the new wave of feelings jamming up in her chest, Kate looked away, fresh tears filling her eyes. His slicker rustled, and he caught her under the chin, forcing her face up. His expression was intent, his gaze meeting hers with unwavering steadiness. "He won't get to you here, Kate," he said, his tone firm. "But if he does, he's going to have one hell of a battle on his hands."

Comforted by his assurance and warmed to the soul by the feel of his hand on her face, she gazed up at him, wanting with all her heart to curl up in his arms. Unsure if she could answer him, she held his gaze, her mouth trembling as she nodded again.

His expression altering, he tucked a wet strand of hair behind her ear, then slid his hand across her shoulders and turned up the collar of her coat. "You're starting to shiver," he said, his voice rough. "And that water's rising, Kate. We've got to get you home."

But Kate knew her shivering had nothing to do with being cold.

The rain beating down around them, they returned to the idling vehicle, the raindrops sounding like hail against the metal. Tanner opened the door and reached in to turn off the lights and the ignition, then removed the keys. He reached under his slicker and stuffed them in the back pocket of his jeans, then handed her her purse. He indicated the parcel she had retrieved from the floor behind the driver's seat. "Does that have to go?"

Shivering in earnest, Kate avoided his gaze, knowing he would never understand why, after experiencing the kind of terror she had, it was so important that she keep her promise to her sons. Unable to look at him, she answered, her voice unsteady, "It's for the boys."

The wind cut between them, making her shiver more. He took the plastic bag from her. "I'll carry it," he said, his tone quiet. Blinking rapidly, she swallowed hard, trying to collect herself as he pressed the automatic door lock and slammed the door. Shifting the bag to the other hand, he touched her arm. "Come on," he said. "You look like you're just about done in."

Unable to answer, Kate stumbled alongside him, something nearly unbearable unfolding in her chest as he steadied her, then took her hand, his warm, strong grip anchoring her.

By the time they got to the bottom of the hill, Kate was soaked and cold, but feeling a whole lot better than she had twenty minutes earlier. Tanner stopped a few feet back from the washout, and Kate looked at the muddy water, then glanced up at him. For the first time in hours, she experienced a flicker of humor. She gave him a wry smile. "It isn't heated, is it?"

The creases around his eyes crinkled, and a glint appeared. "Think of it as a once-in-a-lifetime experience."

She gave the swirling water a dubious look, then heaved a sigh. "I guess standing here isn't going to get it done, is it?"

"No," he said, his tone oddly husky. "It isn't." He let go of her hand, then took her purse from her and looped the strap over her head. Adjusting the strap so it fell diagonally across her body, he tucked it under her arm, then pushed the purse on to her back. He stopped her when he saw her about to kick off one shoe. "Leave your shoes on. It's pretty roughgoing in there." Satisfied with the security of her handbag, he looked at her, rain trickling off the brim of his hat, his expression intent. "It's probably going to be past your knees in the middle, and the current is swift, so be careful." He caught her hand and drew it under his slicker, positioning it at the small of his back. "Get a good hold on my belt, and watch your step, okay?" Pushing aside her coat, he grasped the back of her jeans, and she felt his fingers tighten around her waistband. He gave her a crooked smile. "Do me a favor and hang on. I'd rather not have to go fishing for you in this."

Kate wasn't too keen on the idea herself. Slipping her fingers under his belt, she took a deep, fortifying breath. "Lead on, Macduff."

It was cold, painfully cold. The footing was rocky and perilous, the current swift and treacherous. Kate was certain she would never have been able to stay on her feet if Tanner hadn't acted as a breakwater, and if he hadn't been there holding her up. And she would have been in very big trouble when, three quarters of the way across, she took a step and there was nothing there. Before she even realized what had happened, he had hauled her up hard against him and half carried, half dragged her onto solid ground.

It wasn't until she was standing at the driver's door of the truck that she realized she was wet to the waist and had lost one shoe. Opening the door, Tanner tossed the plastic bag onto the floor by the passenger seat, then dragged the purse strap over her head and tossed the purse on top of the bag. His face cast in grim lines, he rapidly peeled the slicker off her and threw it in the box of the truck, then pushed her inside. He waited until she'd slid past the steering wheel, then pointed to the compartment behind the seat. "There's a jacket back there," he said, his tone brusque. "You'd better get it on."

He stripped off his own slicker and threw it in the back, as well. Taking off his hat, he slid behind the wheel and closed the door, dropping his hat behind the seat. Kate closed her eyes and clamped her hands between her thighs, shivering and too cold to move. Tanner started the engine, and as a blast of warm air filled the cab, she felt him turn. Something warm and fleecy settled around her shoulders, and Kate opened her eyes, numbly watching his face as he tucked the fleece-lined jacket snugly around her. He was so close, and he smelled so warm, and suddenly Kate felt very fragile and very shaky inside, and she closed her eyes, clenching her jaw against her own emotions.

It had been a long time—a very long time—since someone had taken care of her. It nearly put her in sensory overload when he dragged her wet hair free of the jacket and pulled the collar up around her neck, his touch sending a trail of shivers down her back. Tension blossomed in her, and she pressed her thighs more tightly together, holding her hands immobile. She wanted to touch him so much, so very much.

"Slide over," he commanded roughly.

Avoiding looking at him, she numbly did as she was told, then sat huddled in the warmth of his coat, wet and cold and so bereft she could hardly bear it.

Tanner leaned across her and opened the glove compartment, taking out a pair of dry socks. "Here. Put these on."

Unable to respond, Kate gripped the flaps of the coat and pulled it tighter around her, and Tanner glanced at her, his face only inches from hers. He stared at her for a moment, the muscles in his jaw hardening, then he sat up and swore, hitting the steering wheel with the side of his hand.

Confused and shaken, Kate stared at him, her stomach dropping away to nothing. Not sure what was going on, she softly whispered his name. "Tanner?"

He turned and looked at her, his expression bitter, his voice harsh with self-contempt. "I came within an inch of losing you out there, Kate. An inch."

Something gave way around her heart, and she shivered. Feeling almost too raw to speak, she reached out and wiped the moisture off his face. "No you didn't," she countered unevenly. "If you hadn't been here, I would have tried to come across by myself. *Then* you would have lost me." She felt his jaw harden beneath her touch, and without any warning, her eyes filled up. A feeling of desolation washed through her, and she dropped her hand and laced her fingers tightly together in her lap, fighting to contain the tears. She shouldn't have touched him. She never should have done that.

Tanner shifted, then he cupped her jaw, lifting her face. "Don't, Katie," he whispered gruffly. "Please, don't."

She looked up at him, her eyes awash with tears, and Tanner brushed his knuckles across her cheek, then brushed her dripping hair behind her ear. His expression etched with strain, he let a wet strand curl around his finger, then swallowed hard and looked at her, his eyes dark and tormented. Then, releasing a long, shaky sigh, he shifted and pulled her across his legs, gathering her up in a tight, enveloping embrace.

Kate sagged against him, unable to hold in all the raw and turbulent feelings that surged through her. She'd thought she was all cried out. But the miracle of being held by him, of having someone to share her fear with, of finally experiencing the feel of his arms around her, was just too much to handle, and she huddled in his arms, pressing her wet face into the curve of his neck. On a day when her ongoing fear had once again resurrected itself, it was just too much.

Arranging the coat around her and drawing her deeper into his warmth, he cradled her head even closer, his breath warm against the side of her face. He didn't say anything; he didn't have to. He was holding her, and that was all that mattered.

Neither of them spoke; neither of them made any move to draw away. It was almost as though each was drawing warmth and comfort from the other.

But that private, comforting cocoon was invaded moments later when the cellular phone buzzed. Holding her head against him, he retrieved it, pressed a button and held it to his ear. "Tanner."

He listened for a moment, then turned and looked out the window, his voice gruff. "No. I've got her. We'll be home in five minutes."

Sensing his instant withdrawal, Kate disentangled herself and moved over onto the seat, desolation once again sweeping through her. The walls were back up, and she was outside them. She started to shiver, a different kind of cold settling in.

Chapter 8

The water gurgled out of the old tub as Kate folded the towels and hung them up on the antiquated brass bar, the late-night silence of the house weighing down upon her. She straightened the items on the vanity and put the cap on her body lotion, then dropped her hairbrush in the drawer. She felt as if every nerve in her body were stretched to the limit, the knot in her stomach sitting like a rock. She had gone to bed hours ago, shortly after she had settled Burt for the night, and she had even managed to fall asleep.

But something had brought her sharply awake, her heart pounding, the tentacles of fear leaving her cold and shaking. But it wasn't that unknown fear that had driven her from her bed; it was the anxiety of not knowing how to handle the situation with Tanner. He had been gruffly considerate ever since he'd brought her back, giving her time to collect herself before she had to deal with either Burt or the boys. He had, she realized with a pang, made sure she had her feet under her before he withdrew.

But that wasn't what made her chest tighten and her throat ache. It was recalling how, once they'd gotten back to the house, he had pulled back into himself, and although he had been very careful with her, he had avoided any eye contact, not even so much as a casual glance. It was as though he wanted to disassociate himself from everything that had happened in the truck. But then she had caught him watching her when she was getting Burt ready for bed, and the bleak look in his eyes had done terrible things to her already raw emotions. She'd sensed that she had somehow been responsible for that look, and that had upset her. It still upset her now.

She zipped up the front of her lightweight housecoat, then picked up her watch and sweat suit and left the bathroom, switching off the light after her. Attuned to the stillness in the house, she crossed to her room, starkly aware of the dark doorway at the end of the hall. Panic might have wakened her, but it was Tanner's absence and her own sense of guilt that were keeping her awake.

Pushing open her door, she entered the darkened room and put her things on the chair, then went to the window, her mood bleak. His truck was there, but there were no lights on in either the cook house or the barn. Realizing that her window vigil was only making things worse, and knowing that there was no way she could stay in bed until he came in, she rubbed her arms and turned. She needed something to do, something to take her mind off the sickening feeling that kept churning inside her. Something to take her mind off the dark, haunting eyes of Tanner McCall.

Avoiding the creak at the top of the stairs, she started down, her insides dropping away to nothing when she heard the sound of castors on hardwood—a sound coming from directly below her. Pausing on the third step, she gripped the banister, her heart suddenly clamoring. He was here. He must have come in when she was running the tub. Feeling shaky with relief, she took a deep, painful breath, trying to will away the frantic flutter that had climbed into her throat. Now what? What did she do now? Did she confront him? Did she leave it be?

She remembered how he had hung on to her when the torrent had swept her feet out from under her—how he had drawn her into his lap and wrapped her up in the dry warmth of his coat. And that moment in the truck when everything was on the surface—the comfort, the warmth, the loneliness.

But she had wanted that comfort, that warmth; she wanted everything with him. God, but it was frightening how much she wanted that, and it was even more frightening knowing that if she wanted it, she was going to have to reach out for it. She didn't know what she would do if he didn't reach back.

Trying to quell the uncertain flutter in her heart, she took a deep, steadying breath, her heart climbing higher and higher; then, marshaling every ounce of courage she possessed, she started down the stairs.

Tanner was sitting at the desk, his profile hard and unyielding in the circle of illumination from the banker's lamp, a computer printout spread before him. Uncertainty gripping her, she paused on the second from the last step, her insides balling up into a hard lump. There was no acknowledgment from him, and her doubts swarmed in on her. God, she was so scared.

Gripping the newel post, she spoke, her voice strained. "I was afraid you'd gone back to the cattle camp."

He swiveled his gaze to look at her, his surprise registering on his face. Realizing that he hadn't heard her and oddly bolstered by that, she came down the last two steps and clasped her hands in front of her, her legs suddenly unsteady.

Tanner stared at her for a moment, then looked down and began making lines in the margin of the printout, his expression unreadable. "I had some things to do in the barn."

She wished he would put the pencil down. She wished he would look at her. She wished she didn't feel so damned uncertain. He seemed so aloof, so detached. So unapproachable.

She rubbed her fingers across the corner of the desk, then collected her courage. "I wanted you to know how glad I was to see you today," she said, her voice unsteady. "And it had nothing to do with the scare I had in Pincher Creek."

His profile taut with strain, Tanner continued to sketch shapes in the margins, the large plaster bandage on his hand standing out against the darkness of his skin, something almost defensive in the set of his shoulders. Her pulse frantic in her throat, Kate hugged herself, waiting for him to say something. When the silence stretched on, realization finally filtered through; there wasn't going to be a response. Rejection in words would have been bad enough, but rejection by silence was even worse, and she turned, feeling like a fool. God, how could she have been so stupid?

But before she had time to reach the first stair, a strong, callused hand gripped her wrist. She tried to pull free, but he held her fast, his voice gruff and unsteady when he whispered, "Don't, Katie. Don't."

A single sob broke from her, and he pulled her around, gathering her up in an embrace so strong, so tight, that Kate felt almost lost in it. His hand rough against her face, he tucked her head against him, then molded her tightly against him, as if trying to warm her. Kate shivered, so many sensations breaking loose inside her that she could barely handle them all. But what finally unhinged her was the way he tucked back her hair, then pressed his face against hers. It was the tenderest of touches and did unbearable things to her heart, and Kate abruptly turned her face into the curve of his neck, sliding her arms around him.

"Ah, Katie," he whispered hoarsely against her hair. "What am I going to do with you?" He smoothed back her hair with his thumb, then brushed his mouth against her temple. And that one single, gentle caress devastated her, and she caught him by the back of his neck and turned her face against his. There was an instant, just an instant, when he went absolutely still; then he inhaled sharply and lifted her face, covering her mouth in a hot, starving kiss.

It was like being touched by a high-voltage wire, and Kate made a low sound, succumbing to the urgency clamoring in her, her mouth going slack beneath his, desperate for the taste of him. His fingers tangling in her hair, Tanner shifted his hold and dragged her up against him. A frenzied weakness pumped through her when she felt him against her thigh. Another low sound was driven from her, and Tanner spread his hand wide against the back of her head, increasing the pressure of his mouth as the kiss turned wet and urgent, as though some grinding need had broken loose. Feeling as if she were drowning in the fever he created in her, Kate clung to him, yielding up everything—*everything*—the searching, hungry heat of his mouth electrifying her, the feel of his hand against her face destroying her. God, she was drowning, drowning, drowning....

A violent shudder coursed through him, and Tanner tore his mouth away, his breathing harsh and labored in the silent room. His arm around her hips, he dragged her higher, crushing her against him, and Kate sobbed out his name when she felt the hard, thick ridge of flesh against her. Frantic to feel him pressed intimately against her, she wrapped her legs around him and pulled herself flush against his hardness. Tanner shuddered, his arms convulsing around her. Roughly grasping the back of her head, he angled her face and took her mouth in another wild, plundering kiss, and Kate surrendered everything to his hot, searching mouth. As if driven by an out-of-control need, he rocked his hips against her, and Kate clutched his shoulders, the feel of him rubbing against her blinding her with desire. Sobbing incoherently against his devouring mouth, she lifted herself against him, counterstroking along the length of him, trying to relieve his need—and hers.

He jerked against her, his fingers snagging in her hair as he roughly tore his mouth away and jammed her head against his neck. His breathing harsh and labored, he folded her even tighter in his embrace, locking one arm around her hips. He dragged in a deep, ragged breath of air, then slid his hand up the back of her neck as he tucked his face against hers. "Come upstairs with me," he whispered hoarsely, brushing her jaw with an unsteady kiss.

Not knowing if she could bear to let go of him, she clung to him even harder, her voice breaking when she answered. "Oh, yes."

Shifting the angle of her head, he kissed her on the mouth, his chest expanding raggedly when he dragged his mouth away. He stroked her back, then nestled her head against him and spoke, his voice gruff and unsteady and thick with desire. "Get the light as we go by." Then, adjusting his hold, he cradled her close and started toward the stairs.

Feeling as if she were on the verge of splintering, she hit the light switch when Tanner paused. Darkness enveloped the stairwell, hiding them, keeping their intimacy from view, and Tanner pressed a rough kiss against her temple, then started up the stairs. Overloaded with sensation, Kate tightened her arms around him and closed her eyes, her breath catching as she opened her mouth against the soft skin of his neck, desperate for the taste of him. A tremor coursed through him, and he stopped, grasping her by the back of the neck and forcing her head into the angle of his shoulder. He didn't move for a moment, his breathing ragged, then he started climbing again, his body trembling against hers.

At the top of the stairs they turned and entered his room. Once inside, he shouldered the door shut behind him. The instant it clicked shut, he caught her head and covered her mouth in a kiss that made her sob, made her move against the hardness of him, made her crazy with wanting. Cupping her buttocks, he twisted his pelvis against her, then slid his hand up her naked back, dragging her housecoat higher as he slid his hand between them, cupping the fullness of her breast. Making a low, incoherent sound deep in his throat, he fingered the hardened nipple, then plundered her mouth with his tongue, and Kate clutched at him, a jolt of sensation driving her deeper and deeper into the heat of urgency. Stroking his tongue with hers, she moved against him, desperate for the feel of him, silently begging for more.

His hand holding her face, Tanner widened his mouth against hers, and Kate shuddered as he carried her across the room, the movement of his thighs and hips making her ride hard against him. Crushing her against him with one arm, he carried her down onto the bed, and Kate cried out against his mouth as his full weight settled between her thighs.

Lifting her hips to accommodate him, he began thrusting against her, his mouth hungry and wild, and Kate clutched at him with her legs, frantic for the tormenting, assuaging rhythm, frantic for the feel of his hardness against her, frantic for the feel of him deep inside her. She couldn't stand the swelling, throbbing heaviness in her. She couldn't stand the barrier of clothes that separated them. She couldn't stand the torment of being denied the final consummation. Dragging her mouth away, she drew up her knees and arched beneath him. "Please, Tanner," she sobbed desperately. "Please."

A violent tremor coursed through him, and he abruptly turned his face into her hair, his whole body rigid with a shattering tension. He made a rough sound and dragged one arm from beneath her. Roughly pressing her face against his neck, he eased his weight to one side and cupped her heat, his fingers sliding into her as he began stroking her. Realization about what he intended penetrated the frenzied fog in her mind, and she grabbed his hand away, crying out from the agony of separation. "Please, Tanner," she pleaded desperately. "Please."

Dragging his hand free from her hold, he caught her along the jaw and pressed her head tight against him, then answered, his voice so ragged, so tormented, so strained that she could barely hear him for the thundering in her ears. "I can't, Katie. I can't. I have nothing here to protect you."

Destitute, desperate and needing him so much she couldn't bear it, she fumbled for the buckle on his belt. Right then nothing mattered—nothing but having him inside her. Nothing but the final, explosive, rendering, pulsing culmination. Clawing at the fabric of his jeans, she arched against him, sobbing with desperation and need. "Oh, please. Please."

With an agonized groan, he clutched her head, turning her face toward a fierce, wild, hot kiss, then he shifted, and she went a little crazy when she felt him reach down to free himself. When she felt the long hard thickness of him against her, she ground her mouth against his and lifted her hips to meet his thrust, impaling herself on rigid flesh. Buried deep inside her, he rocked against her, and Kate lost all contact with reality as the sensations inside her started to gather and gather, pulling into one hot, pulsating center. He moved again and again, and the sensations converged, and she cried out and arched stiffly against him, the explosion rocketing her off into a splintering release. But before the first contraction finished shuddering through her, he clutched at her, a low tormented groan ripped from him as he jerked free of her, his own release spurting wetly, hotly against her thigh. Fierce spasms continued to convulse through her body, and she clung to him, sobbing, incoherent and shredded with pleasure.

Fighting for breath, she cradled his head against the curve of her neck, a fierce, almost frantic protectiveness welling up in her. God, but she loved him. So much. So very much. And at that instant, she was sure the only thing that was holding her together was the savage strength of his arms.

It took a long time for her to come down, for the storm of emotion to ease, but when she could at last collect her senses, she hugged him and stroked his hair, profoundly moved by the care he had taken with her, knowing the pleasure he had forfeited to give her what protection he could. Closing her eyes against the sting of tears and an unbearable constriction in her throat, she continued to stroke his head, needing to give comfort, so full of feeling for him that she could barely stand it. God, but she loved him—beyond all reason, she loved him.

Tanner stirred in her arms, and she lifted her head and found his mouth, kissing him with infinite gentleness and care. Brushing the hair back from her temple with his thumb, he released an uneven sigh and kissed her back, his mouth warm and moist and gently, gently searching.

He exhaled raggedly, then tucked her face against the curve of his shoulder. Kate rubbed the back of his neck, wishing he was naked against her. Tanner tightened his hold on her, his chest expanding as he took a deep, unsteady breath. Fingering the soft silk of his hair, she kissed his temple, a nearly unbearable tenderness filling her chest. "You didn't have to do that," she whispered unevenly against his cheek. "It would have been okay."

Bracing his weight on one arm, he lifted his head, his touch leaving her breathless as he kissed the corner of her mouth. "I couldn't take that kind of chance," he said, his tone husky and intimate. "Not with you."

Fighting against the tears clogging her throat, she parted her lips and kissed him, the caress gentle and searching. Inhaling unevenly, Tanner slid his arms around her in a warm, enveloping embrace, deepening the kiss as she smoothed her hand up the center of his back.

It was as though he couldn't get enough of that soft, caressing intimacy, and it was a long time later when he reluctantly eased away. Brushing her hair back with his knuckles, he lifted her chin and gave her another light kiss, then released his breath in an unsteady sigh. "Come to bed with me, Katie," he whispered gruffly.

Sensing how exposed he was feeling right then, and knowing how much he was risking with that one single request, she wrapped her arms around his neck and kissed him. She didn't know why, but the huskiness in his request made her want to cry. Fighting against the surge of emotion, and praying she wasn't making a mistake as far as the boys were concerned, she whispered her answer against his mouth. "Yes, I'll stay."

Sliding his hand up the back of her head, he deepened the kiss, molding her against him with the weight of his body. Finally he eased away and gave her one final kiss, then rolled free. His profile outlined by the faint illumination coming from the yard light outside, she watched him shed his clothes, longing to caress the muscled length of his back. Leaving on his briefs, he turned back to her, lifting her into a sitting position as he stripped her short housecoat off over her head. Cupping her jaw, he kissed her, then whispered unevenly against her mouth, "I need to hold you like this." Overwhelmed by emotion, Kate turned into his embrace, and Tanner drew her down with him as he stretched out, his kiss intensifying when her naked breasts grazed his chest. Slipping his hand up her hip and across her back, he separated his legs and settled her between his thighs, and Kate's breath caught at the feel of his nearly naked body molded fully against hers. Raking her hair back, Tanner drew back from the kiss, then firmly nestled her head again in the curve of his shoulder. "Go to sleep, Kate," he whispered gruffly.

Kate closed her eyes, loving the feel of his arms around her, loving him, feeling safe and secure for the first time in a very long time.

The room was still dark, but early-morning sounds were filtering in when Kate awoke and rolled onto her back, a sweet lethargy pulling at her. Then recollection took shape, and she came wide-awake. Her heart suddenly hammering with alarm, she twisted her head, discovering that the space beside her was empty, the blinds drawn and the clock on the dresser confirming her fear. Late. God, it was after eight. She *never* slept in, and now the boys would be up. Horrified that they might find her in Tanner's bed, she threw back the covers, her insides giving a funny little lurch when she realized she was naked. Closing her eyes, she drew up her knees and pulled the sheet around her, memories swarming in and making her go weak inside. She locked her arms around her legs and rested her forehead on her upraised knees, the flurry in her chest leaving her light-headed. Lord, but it had been unbelievable. But what made her pulse labor was recalling how she had wakened in the middle of the night and found Tanner curled around her back, his arm securing her against him, holding her in the shelter of his body.

. Finally the flurry eased, and Kate awkwardly got out of bed, feeling as if one stray thought could bring her to her knees. She didn't dare think about last night. And she didn't dare think about facing Tanner.

By the time she had a quick sponge bath and was dressed, she felt a little more collected, but her nerve faltered when she reached the bottom of the stairs and heard a deep male voice coming from the kitchen. Closing her eyes, she hauled in a shaky breath, trying to override the renewed frenzy in her chest. This was not going to be easy.

Bracing herself for that first confrontation, she squared her shoulders and entered the kitchen, a bright smile plastered on her face. "Good morning."

Mark was nowhere in sight, but Scotty was hunched over a bowl of cereal, playing with a plastic toy that had obviously come out of the cereal box. He finished powering the bright green dinosaur through some spilled sugar, so intent on his sound effects that he pretty much ignored her. "Hi, Mom."

Knee-weakeningly aware of the large male form leaning against the counter, she rubbed her hands against her thighs, then looked at him, a funny catch in her voice when she acknowledged him. "Good morning."

His arms folded across his chest, a coffee mug in one hand, he watched her, his eyes dark and intent, his expression unsmiling. A fluttery weakness pumped through her, and it was all she could do to keep from tipping her head back and closing her eyes, letting those sensations wash over her with an arousing fullness, letting herself get lost in them. Letting herself want him, want him.

He stared at her across the room, the muscles in his jaw tightening; then he turned and dumped his coffee down the drain, setting the empty cup in the sink. He turned to face her, his expression taut as he motioned toward the utility room. "Could I talk to you for a minute?"

Rattled by the feelings swamping her, she followed him into the utility room, so aware of him and what they had shared the night before that she felt physically disconnected. As soon as she entered, he shut the door and rested his weight against it. Feeling raw and exposed, she looked up at him, feeling as if every nerve in her body were stretched to the limit. Avoiding her gaze, he brushed her cheek with his thumb, then carefully looped a strand of hair behind her ear. His touch set off a new wave of weakness, and she closed her eyes, struggling against the throbbing thickness that made her heart pound and her lungs refuse to function. Overwhelmed by sensation, she turned her face into his hand, and Tanner inhaled sharply and cupped the back of her neck. Murmuring her name, he drew her into his arms and covered her mouth in a kiss that set off a frenzy of sensation inside her. A sudden, frantic, mutual need seemed to travel from one to the other, and she clung to him, opening her mouth beneath his. Gripping her by the back of the head, he widened his stance, pulling her between his thighs and hard against his groin, and a low sound was dragged from deep inside her when she felt him hard and fully aroused against her.

Want escalated into an incoherent need, a need to feel him pressed against her, and she locked her arms around his neck, desperately pulling herself higher, tighter, against him. Widening his stance even more, Tanner shifted his hold on her back and dragged her up, resealing his hot, hungry mouth against hers in a kiss that seemed to ravage her very soul. A kiss that was fueled by loneliness, by need, by a fever of want.

It went on and on until Kate was nearly senseless, and the only thing that kept her grounded was the fierce pressure of his arms. As if realizing that she was beyond recovery, Tanner twisted her against one thigh and shifted his hold. Tightening his arm around her torso, he slid his hand under the waistband of her slacks and beneath the elastic of her panties, absorbing her cry as he touched her where she so desperately needed to be touched. Kate clutched at him, her body going rigid, and he jammed her face against his neck as she involuntarily arched against the stroking pressure of his fingers. An explosion detonated inside her, and a chain of convulsions ripped through her as she came apart in his arms. Cupping her hard, Tanner hugged her against him, his arm supporting her back, his hand splayed wide in her hair.

Unable to speak, Kate sobbed his name against his neck, and dragging his hand free of her clothing, he wrapped her up in a powerful, enveloping embrace. Cuddling her tightly against him, he tucked his head against hers and began stroking her back. Kate tried to shift her position to absorb more of her own weight, but he tightened his hold on her, his voice strained when he whispered against her temple. "Don't. Just let me hold you."

Too emotionally raw to make a response, Kate tightened her arms around him, tears matting her eyelashes. *Please, God,* she prayed fervently, *please, please let this work out.*

Inhaling unevenly, Tanner leaned his full weight against the door, drawing her deeper into his embrace, his touch meant to comfort as he massaged the base of her spine. Pressing his head closer, Kate turned her face against the curve of his neck, a wave of guilt washing through her. He had given her so much but had taken nothing for himself. Closing her eyes in shame, she hugged him against her. "I'm sorry," she whispered unevenly.

He smoothed his hand up her back, resting his jaw against her temple. There was a hint of amusement in his voice when he answered, "I'm not."

She lifted her head and looked up at him, not sure about his amusement. He gave her that slow, sensual smile that turned her insides to honey, an unmistakable twinkle in his hazel eyes. "This beats the hell out of what I had in mind."

She loved his smile, and she loved his amusement, but she felt ashamed that their encounter had been so one-sided. Her throat tight, she softly caressed his cheek, unable to hold his gaze. "I wish it could have been different," she whispered, a catch in her voice. She looked up at him, her expression solemn. "This has all been so one-sided, Tanner."

He stared at her for a moment, then became intent on her mouth as he ran his thumb along her lower lip. "Don't worry about it," he said, his tone gruff. "We'll get it together sooner or later."

Taking his face between her hands, she stretched up and kissed him softly on the mouth, her breath catching as he pulled her hips closer and took control of the kiss. It was long and lingering and oh, so sweet, and by the time he let her go, Kate felt as if her legs were going to give out under her. Releasing his breath in a long, shaky sigh, he wrapped his arms around her and rested his cheek on the top of her head. They remained like that for several moments, simply taking comfort and pleasure from each other. Then a sound from outside broke the spell.

Straightening, Tanner looped his arms around her hips, pressing a kiss against her temple. "I've got to go, Katie," he said, his tone rough with regret. "We're going to have to blow an old beaver dam downstream to drain the water that's backed up on the road, and Ross is waiting for me."

Loath to let him go, Katie closed her eyes and caressed the back of his neck, the silk of his hair tickling the back of her hand. Finally she spoke, a funny wobble in her voice. "Will you be coming back here tonight?"

He drew his hand across the curve of her hip, pressing her closer. "Yeah," he answered, his voice low and husky. "I'll be back for supper." His expression somber, he lifted her chin and gave her one final kiss. Then, without looking at her again, he turned and swept up his hat and settled it low on his head. A minute later the screen door slammed shut behind him. Miss-

ing his warmth, Kate huddled against the chill, watching him
cross the gravel drive to Ross's truck; then she turned and
reentered the kitchen.

Scotty, his head propped on his hand, was making bomb-
blasting sounds over his cereal, and she was just in time to see
him launch the bright green dinosaur with bull's-eye accu-
racy. Milk splattered onto the tabletop. She heaved a sigh and
looked in supplication at the ceiling. It was obviously time to
come back down to earth.

"You do that again, Scott Allan, and your dinosaur is going to be history."

He fished it out of his cereal and sucked it dry, then swiveled his head to look at her, his eyes narrowing. "Mr. McCall
said you had a bad day yesterday so we should let you sleep in
this morning."

She thought about the red car, then made herself disconnect from the flicker of fear. She picked up a tea towel that was
draped over the back of a chair and folded it. "It was sorta a
three-kite day, all right."

Scotty knew exactly what a three-kite day meant. It was in
reference to the day last spring when he and Mark had totaled
three kites and he got his mouth washed out for saying *that*
word. He grinned at her. "Did you say a swear?"

She gave him a pointed look. "I brought you treats, remember?"

His grin broadened into pure mischief. "You said a swear,
didn't you?"

"You," she said, changing the subject, "can quit with the
bombing runs and clean up your mess. And go make your
bed."

He heaved a world-weary sigh and rolled his eyes. "Do I
have to?"

"Yes, you have to."

He heaved another dramatic sigh and slid off his chair. Kate
hung the towel on the handle of the fridge, then started toward Burt's room. She heard another bomb blast just as she
entered the room.

Burt gave her a fierce look the moment she entered. "Well,
where have you been? Tanner was going to feed me some of

that slop he calls porridge, but I said I wouldn't eat that if he stuck a cattle prod in my ribs."

Kate restrained a grin, folded her arms and stared at him. "Well, well. And who made you king for the day?"

Burt stuck out his chin and glared at her, unable to hide the glint in his eyes. "I've always been king, and don't you forget it."

Kate nearly laughed. God, but she did love this cantankerous old man.

Mark came out of the bathroom, doing up the snap on his jeans, a rolled-up comic book tucked under his arm. He gave his mother a censuring look. "Burt's getting hungry, you know."

Staring at her young son, Kate responded, her tone dry, "The crown prince, I presume?"

Mark looked at her as if she'd lost her mind, and Burt snorted. The old man patted the space beside him on the bed. "Don't give her any mind, boy. She's got a bean up her nose this morning. Now, you climb up here and finish reading me that story about BlastoMan."

Kate rolled her eyes heavenward and turned. A bean up her nose, an eighty-year old comic connoisseur and exploding dinosaurs in the kitchen. Maybe she had lost her mind.

By ten o'clock the clouds had started to break up, the sun was trying to break through, and the boys started pestering her to go out. Knowing that Buddy was in the barn, she finally gave in and let them go down to feed Bess and play with the puppies. She bathed Burt and shaved him, then got him settled for his nap. Tanner had told him about the washout, and Kate got a big lecture about deep water and taking chances, and she assured him that she wouldn't even cross the Circle S creek for the remainder of the summer.

Once Burt was asleep, Kate went upstairs to vacuum, a funny flutter taking off in her chest when she came abreast of Tanner's door. Setting down the vacuum, she took a breath and pushed it open.

She had never been in it before last night; after his issue over her doing light housekeeping duties, she'd thought it was best if she didn't push that limit. But now it was different. He had taken her there.

It had been dark the night before, and the blinds had been pulled when she'd gotten up, so she'd been left with only shadowy impressions. Crossing to the two windows set in an alcove, she released the blinds, then turned, a fluttery sensation settling in her belly when she saw the jumbled bedding. It made her heart race just thinking about what had happened in that bed.

Knowing she was going to be in big trouble if she let her thoughts ramble, Kate studied the room. Big and sparsely furnished, with low walls and a gabled ceiling, it was painted the same white as the rest of the upstairs, but here the floors were hardwood, and the wood moldings and baseboards had been stripped and refinished. The mattress was king-size, set in a heavy wooden frame with a hand-carved headboard. There was a matching highboy, a very old steamer trunk with brass bindings and a huge oval handmade braided rug on the floor beside the bed. What surprised her was the large, un-framed canvas on the one full-size wall in the room, the one along the hallway. It was a landscape, bleak and beautiful, of the barren rolling hills, with a horse and rider off to one side. The colors were all earth tones, the colors of autumn, but the scene depicted the first snowfall, with the rider and horse be-ing buffeted by swirling snow and a cold wind. The rider was clearly Tanner, and the painting was stunning—and from the technique and the use of color, Kate was sure it had been painted by a woman.

Experiencing a sharp, unpleasant twist, she moved closer to see the signature. The signature was clear, and Kate straight-ened, startled by her discovery. Eden McCall. The half sister Rita had mentioned. The half sister who had gifted her fa-ther's bastard with a stunning piece of work, and the half brother who clearly valued the gift. Kate studied the painting for a long time, then entered the bathroom to collect the tow-els.

It had obviously once been a small bathroom, but the dark brown ceramic tiles, the refitted window, the Jacuzzi tub and the large opaque-glass shower indicated a fairly recent renovation. It was very modern, very uncluttered and, somehow, very Tanner. Aware of his presence around her, she picked up the towels and went back into the bedroom, determined to keep her mind on what she was doing. Dumping the towels on the rug, she went to the bed and stripped off the plain navy comforter and navy top sheet.

She froze, a galvanizing heat pumping through her when she saw the stain on the bottom sheet. Clutching the top one against her chest, she closed her eyes, remembering how it had gotten there and why. She waited until her pulse settled, then resolutely finished stripping the bed. Gathering everything up, she went out into the hall and pushed the bedding down the laundry chute. She would vacuum and dust his room; she would make his bed with fresh linen and clean his bathroom, and she would try not to think about last night. Nor tonight. She would be a mess in seconds if she did.

By afternoon the sky had nearly cleared, and for the first time in days there was real warmth in the sun. Cyrus showed up right after Burt woke up from his afternoon nap, a cribbage board in one hand, a big bouquet of tulips in the other. He handed Kate the tulips, then swept off his battered Stetson and hung it on a hook. "I figured you might enjoy these, Miz Quinn. There's an old patch down by the bunkhouse that don't usually amount to a hill o' beans, but for some ornery reason, they decided to do something with themselves this year. Probably because it's been an ornery spring. They're kinda bright and cheery, ain't they?"

Kate wiped her hands on her butcher's apron, then looked at the flowers. She could tell by the depth of color and size of their blossoms that they didn't come from some neglected patch but from a well-tended garden. Cyrus covering his tracks again. She breathed in the fragrance, then met his gaze and smiled. "Thank you so much, Cyrus," she said huskily. "They're lovely."

He gave her an offhand shrug. "Now, I rightly don't know what you can find to stick 'em in. Old Burt and Tanner ain't exactly the type to have fresh flowers delivered regular."

Kate grinned at him, fully appreciating his frank humor. "I'll find something. And if I can't, I can always stick them in Burt's water jug."

Cyrus grinned back at her. "That'd put a kink in his tail, that's for sure. But it'd give him something to rant and rave about, instead of laying there just chipping away at things."

In the back corner of a top cupboard, Kate found an old two-quart stoneware crock that had to be eighty years old. The metal parts of the wooden handles were rusted, but the lid was still intact, and she suspected it had been used to store butter. She cleaned it up and placed the flowers in it, then put them in the center of the table. It couldn't have been more perfect for a ranch kitchen. Cyrus came for a coffee refill as she was standing back admiring it.

"That looks right pretty there, Miz Quinn. Sorta fits right in. Jest like you do."

Startled by his comment, Kate shot him a quick look, but his expression was as innocent as a baby's. Too innocent, as a matter of fact. But in spite of that, or maybe because of it, his comment touched her. "Thank you for bringing them, Cyrus. It was really sweet of you."

He gave her a sheepish grin. "Well, now, ma'am, I'm right tickled that they please you. There's a hardiness in tulips I rightly admire. They get on with growin', no matter if there's a spring blizzard or poor soil, or even if they've been neglected. They just got this powerful need to grow and blossom. Figured tulips were your kind of flower somehow."

Stunned by his perceptiveness, Kate stared at him, a funny flutter unfolding in her chest. Without looking at her, he replaced the coffeepot, then returned to Burt's room, leaving behind a strange silence. Kate stood unmoving, a nearly unbearable cramp taking hold of her throat. Trying to short-circuit the ache, she polished away a dusting of pollen on the table with the corner of her apron, wishing this was more than a place to hide, wishing that her life wasn't such a mess. Wishing that Tanner was there.

Kate managed to keep herself busy for the rest of the afternoon, and it wasn't until she started getting supper ready that she began having a major problem keeping her mind from wandering. Every time she thought about Tanner coming in for supper, she got weak and flushed and her insides tied themselves in a million knots. She was beginning to wonder how she was going to be able to manage it when he did come home; just thinking about it was almost more than she could handle.

Needing a distraction, she fixed a cranberry and ginger ale drink for Burt and poured a fresh cup of coffee for Cyrus, then took the beverages in to them. Scotty was out cold on the cot under the window, and Mark was sitting cross-legged beside Burt, holding his cards for him. It gave her a funny feeling, knowing how the two boys naturally gravitated to the crusty old man, and how he egged on their shenanigans. It had become a conspiracy of kindred souls, an allegiance that bridged the generations.

Cyrus looked up, an obvious twinkle in his eye. "Well, now, Miz Quinn. That's what I call perfect timing. I've pretty well humiliated myself here, so being handed an excuse to fold my hand and lean back is mighty welcome. And that coffee smells fine."

Kate smiled as she handed the coffee across the bed to him. "Somehow I don't think you ever really needed an excuse for anything, Cyrus."

Burt snorted. "Need an excuse? He *is* an excuse. Never saw such a sorry excuse for a card player in all my life. Couldn't give a dead man a decent game."

Cyrus unwrapped a flavored toothpick and stuck it in his mouth, then rocked back in his chair. "Now, Burt," he said, the twinkle in his eyes intensifying. "That ain't hardly fair. After all, I couldn't very well whip you when you're so sickly and all."

Burt gave him a fierce glare, and Kate could almost see the wheels spinning in his head. His eyes glinting with mischief, Cyrus eyed him over the rim of his cup, then wiped his mustache and set the mug on his knee, turning his gaze to her. "There are some mighty fine smells coming from that kitchen, Miz Quinn. I set a pot of stew to simmer afore I came up, but after a spell, a man gets to appreciate someone else's cooking."

Kate thought about his blatant maneuver to let her know that he had a meal already prepared for the men. She thought about how much she didn't want an audience when Tanner came home. And then she thought about the beautiful bouquet of tulips that he had forfeited out of his garden. She also noted the sudden brightness in Burt's eyes. Helping Burt with his drink, she relented. "If that's the case, why don't you stay and have supper with us?"

Tipping his head in acceptance, Cyrus grinned at her. "Well, now, thank you, ma'am. I was hoping you'd ask."

Burt snorted, his testy expression almost camouflaging the sly glint in his eye. "Hoping? You've been laying snares all afternoon. You'd stoop to herding sheep to get out of eating your own cooking."

Cyrus turned his attention to his old friend, an undercurrent of humor in his voice when he responded. "Well, now, I reckon that's true. Especially when there's such a pretty lady doing the cooking. Makes the digestion all that much easier."

Wanting to laugh, Kate gave Cyrus a scolding look. "Someday you're going to get indigestion from all that charm, Cyrus. Especially if you keep laying it on so thick."

Her retort tickled Burt to no end, and he cackled and winked at Kate, his eyes sharp with delight. "You'll do, Kate Quinn. You'll do."

Kate gazed down at him, then very carefully wiped his chin. Her voice wasn't quite steady when she answered, "So will you, Burt Shaw. So will you."

Kate had the table set and Cyrus was wheeling Burt out of his room in the wheelchair when Tanner finally showed up. He'd entered the kitchen, mud caked on his jeans, his black hair flattened from the crown of his hat, and Kate could tell by the lines of fatigue and the set of his jaw that he'd had a bad day.

He had some papers in his hand, and his expression wasn't exactly one of delight when he looked from Burt to Cyrus to the carefully laid table, then back at her. His face was expressionless. "Don't wait for me," he said, his tone curt. "I'm going to have a shower first."

Kate stared at him for an instant, her stomach nose-diving, then she dragged her gaze away and began placing some hot pads on the table. She tried to keep her voice steady when she answered. "It's not quite ready, so you've got a few minutes."

Burt asked about the road, and Tanner gave him an equally curt answer, then Kate heard him climb the stairs. She tried not to let his reaction bother her, tried not to acknowledge the sinking feeling in her abdomen. He was tired and irritated, that was all. But the awful knots in her stomach told her there was more to it than that.

Chapter 9

Supper wasn't quite the strain Kate had thought it would be. When Tanner came back downstairs, she was so busy getting food on the table that she didn't have time to think about his reaction, so she was able to handle it. Almost. Every time he spoke, her insides would go into a twist and she would feel as if her stomach had no bottom.

It helped that the boys were all wound up over the novelty of having Burt and Cyrus at the table, and then there was a brief shoving match over who got to sit beside their best friend Burt. Before Kate had a chance to intervene, Cyrus made the comment that he would be right honored if one of them would sit by him. The boys both figured Cyrus was right up there next to God, and there was another loud debate over that. When they finally got to the table, Cyrus had Mark by him, and Scotty was beside Burt, making quiet bombing runs with his dinosaur. Kate set the mashed potatoes down, confiscated the dinosaur, gave Scott a warning look, then took the seat on the other side of Burt. The men immediately launched into a discussion about the flooding, and Burt, distracted from the indignity of being fed, ate far more than he usually did. Kate decided she would have to do this more often—get him out with the rest of them at mealtimes.

Somehow or another, Scotty managed to worm his way onto Burt's lap as soon as everyone finished eating. When Kate returned to the table after clearing away some of the dishes and caught him there, she gave her son a stern stare and lifted her finger at him. He gave a sigh of resignation, but before he had a chance to move, Burt clumsily anchored his arm around him and gave her a bad-tempered look. "Just mind your own business," he growled. "The boy ain't doing no harm."

Kate nearly laughed. Instead she gave him a long, quelling look and raised her finger at him. Burt raised his in return.

Restraining her amusement, she looked up, her gaze connecting with Tanner's. He was sitting with his elbows on the table, his hands clasped in front of him, absently rubbing his bottom lip with his thumb. His serious expression gave nothing away, but there was something in his eyes that made her pulse jump into overdrive. The hint of amusement instantly faded, replaced by a glint that was more heated, far more potent, far more intent. Far more male. And Kate remembered that instant when he'd entered her, when she'd experienced the full thrust of him, and she tightened her grip on the two serving bowls she held, her breath jamming up in her chest.

Tanner's hand stilled, and his eyes narrowed, and Kate could feel the heat of his gaze from across the table. Lord, but she wished they were somewhere dark and private, somewhere where...

"Well now, Miz Quinn, that was a right fine meal, and I thank you mightily. I do appreciate the company and the conversation. The boys in the bunkhouse ain't exactly scintillatin' at the supper table—lean more to simple digestion than discussion."

Tanner looked away, the muscles in his jaw clenching, annoyance flaring in his eyes. He shot Cyrus a disgusted look, then shoved his chair away from the table and stood up, his mouth compressing into a hard line as he went into the living room.

Upset by Tanner's reaction, Kate watched him, experiencing a rush of guilt. God, why hadn't she just kept supper simple? Realizing that Cyrus was watching her with sharp interest, she dredged up a smile, trying to act as if nothing was wrong. "It was nice having you, Cyrus."

"My pleasure, ma'am. My pleasure." Noticing that Burt was beginning to sag, Cyrus pushed his chair back. "Come on, old man. I think you need to flatten out them old bones for a spell." He glanced at Mark. "How about you trot on ahead and straighten that sheepskin, son?"

Knowing the bed needed straightening, and feeling at a loss anyway, Kate set the serving dishes on the counter and continued on into Burt's room. By the time Cyrus got there with Burt and the boys, she had the bottom sheet stretched tight, his pillows fluffed and the bedding folded down. Leaving Cyrus to it, she picked up the insulated water container and returned to the kitchen.

Through the archway to the living room, she could see Tanner standing by his desk, a sheaf of papers in his hand. His expression fixed and unreadable, he flipped through the sheets, then paused, a frown appearing. Kate stared at him for a moment, then turned back to the sink and began rinsing off plates. Damn it, she should have used her head. She should never have asked Cyrus to stay to supper, and she should have fed Burt in bed the way she always did. She should have accommodated Tanner's need for privacy, but instead, she'd caved in to a big dose of cowboy charm and a bouquet of tulips. She should have—

A muscled arm reached in front of her; her heart lurched and she went still, giving her pulse a second to settle.

His shoulder brushing against her, Tanner placed his empty coffee mug in the sink, then slowly wiped the droplets of water off her nails. "You have nice hands," he said gruffly.

Experiencing a heady rush from his caressing touch, Kate closed her eyes, her pulse going wild. Unable to answer him for the crazy flutter in her stomach, she turned her hand, sliding her wet palm against his. She heard him inhale deeply, then he lifted her hand and kissed her fingertips, and Kate turned her face into his shoulder, her strength sapped by the sensations that surged through her. Shaken by the intensity of her reaction, she laced her fingers through his, needing time to get herself together. He had overwhelmed her; with one single kiss, he had simply overwhelmed her.

Tanner slipped his other hand under her hair and began massaging the back of her neck, his touch meant to comfort. "Burt's calling me, Kate," he said softly, his voice thick. "And I don't want him sending one of the boys out here to get me."

Kate nodded, feeling as if she'd disintegrated into a million pieces. He gave the back of her neck a reassuring squeeze, then turned and left, and she leaned on the counter and closed her eyes, waiting for her insides to settle.

By the time she got the kitchen cleaned up and Burt's laundry done, she'd more or less pulled herself together, but she felt strangely rootless. When she put the boys to bed at nine, tiredness began to seep in. After turning off all the lights in the living room except Tanner's desk lamp, she curled up on the leather sofa and watched a special on Alaska, the sound on the TV turned down.

The next thing she was aware of were voices in the kitchen, and she came sharply awake, immediately checking the digital clock on the TV. It was after ten o'clock. And Cyrus was leaving.

Scrambling from under the Navaho blanket covering her, she sat up, trying to rid herself of the last vestiges of sleep. Pulling down her T-shirt, she started toward the kitchen to say goodbye, but she heard the outside door close before she got there. Tanner was just entering the kitchen when she walked in, and he paused to turn out the light in the utility room. He looked at her, a tiny flicker of amusement lurking around his mouth. "I thought you were out for the count."

She remembered the blanket and realized he had covered her. That realization did funny things to her heart. Clasping her hands together, she managed a small smile, experiencing a twist of sudden nervousness. "Is Burt settled for the night?"

Tanner nodded, his eyes narrowing slightly. He braced one hand on the wall and the other on his hip, his gaze intent as he studied her. His eyes were dark and steady, and the flutter of nerves climbed to her throat. It had been so much easier last night, when things had just happened. She didn't know how to proceed from here, how to handle the awkward silence and her own uncertainty—or his stillness. She twisted her fingers together, trying to think of something to say. Finally he straightened and came toward her, his expression intent and unsmiling.

The instant he moved, Kate's senses went crazy, and she closed her eyes and drew a shaky breath, trying to curb the feelings inside her. Opening her eyes, she looked at him, almost afraid to move for fear of doing something to break the spell. His expression compressed into hard lines, he stared at her, his eyes giving nothing away. Then he held out his hand, and Kate let out a tremulous sigh and took it, her grip urgent and tense, almost desperate. He held her gaze for an instant, his hair shining blue-black in the overhead light, his high cheekbones accentuating the lines of strain around his mouth. He looked dark and foreboding and unapproachable, but the look in his eyes made her heart pound and her knees go weak, and she swallowed hard. There was a flare of emotion in his eyes, and he tightened his grip on her hand and slowly, so slowly, stroked the palm with his thumb. It was too much. That one slow, sensual touch put her in such sensory overload that the brightness from the light made her skin feel too tight. Lacing his fingers through hers, Tanner shut off the light and drew her toward the stairs.

Kate was trembling so hard that she wasn't sure how she made her legs function. The only thing that kept her together was the tight grip Tanner had on her hand. Once inside his room, he shut the door behind him. She heard the lock turn, then he pulled her into his arms. Locking her arms around his torso, she closed her eyes and sagged against him, the feel of him setting off a new fever of sensation. Tucking her face against the curve of his neck, he drew her firmly against him and smoothed back her hair, his touch not quite steady when he kissed the curve of her neck. "You're shaking like a leaf," he whispered roughly.

Tightening her arms around him, Kate pressed her face deeper against his neck, feeling as if she were on the verge of shattering. Her voice catching on raw emotion, she struggled to get out the words. "Don't leave me tonight, Tanner. Not like last night. I couldn't stand it if you did that again."

He went still, then released an unsteady sigh and slid his hand under her hair and up the back of her neck, spanning the base of her head. "I don't think I could stand it, either," he answered, his voice thick with strain. His chest expanding, he turned her head and covered her mouth with hot, wet kisses. She made a low sound and opened to him, the thrust of his tongue sending a hot, weakening need through her.

Moaning against his mouth, desperate for the feel of him, she pulled his shirt free, then tore open the snaps, a paralysis of wanting compressing her lungs as she ran her hands over his smooth, muscled chest. Desperate to breech his reserve, she drew her thumbnails across his hard, male nipples, and he shuddered and crushed her against him, trapping her hands.

Kate was lost. Lost to the hunger. Lost to the sensations pumping through her. Lost to the urgency of his questing hands. And it wasn't until they were naked on the bed, their bodies straining together, his mouth hot and demanding on hers, that a sliver of reality surfaced. Tearing her mouth away from his, she clung to him, frantic for his assurance. "Please don't leave. Promise you won't."

His breathing harsh and labored, his body rigid with tension, he twisted her head back and trailed hot, openmouthed kisses down the arch of her neck. "I won't." He groaned and rocked his hips against her. "Ah—Katie. I couldn't."

He reared away from her, and Kate choked out his name, terrified that he was going to stop. Kneeling between her thighs, he reached for something on the bedside table, and when she heard the rustle of foil, awareness filtered in. Crying and about to shatter into a million pieces, she touched his engorged flesh, fumbling with haste as she helped to sheathe him. A violent tremor shuddered through him at her touch, and the instant the protection was in place, he came down on top of her and gathered her up in a crushing embrace, a low groan breaking from him as she guided him into her. She could feel how hard he was, how hard he was struggling to hold back, but she didn't want his restraint. She needed him hard and deep and out of control. Feeling her whole body collect and tighten, she arched her head back and rose up against him, choking out his name. He shuddered again, then clutched her against him and drove into her again and again and again, finally sending her over the edge of a high, splintering precipice. He thrust into her once more, grinding against her, then stiffened, an agonized groan wrenched from him as he climaxed deep inside her.

A nighttime stillness had settled outside, and a breeze rustled through the leaves on the old poplar tree just beyond Tanner's window, filling the room with a soft, whispering sound. Unwilling to let him leave her, Kate draped her legs over the backs of his and smoothed her hands up, slowly mapping the contours of his back. Too spent to move, not wanting to speak, she savored the heady sensation of contentment, loving the feel of his smooth skin beneath her touch. She found a ridge of scar tissue on his shoulder and lightly traced it. Dredging up energy from somewhere, she spoke, her voice husky. "What's this?"

Stirring heavily, Tanner reached back and caught her wrist, pulling her arm down. He placed a kiss on her palm. "Nothing."

His mouth was moist and warm and slightly swollen, and she drew her thumb across his bottom lip, thinking about the care he'd taken with her. "Tanner?"

"Hmm?"

She raised her head and kissed his jaw. "I thought you said you didn't have anything here," she whispered.

He didn't answer right away. Finally he shifted; as if it took every ounce of strength he had, he dragged his arms free. Bracing his weight on his forearms, he cupped her face, adjusting the angle of her head as he kissed her. Releasing a long sigh, he dried her bottom lip with his thumb. There was a hint of humor in his voice when he finally answered. "I made a point of going to Pincher Creek today."

She knew the road was impassable. Closing her eyes as he placed a string of kisses down her neck, she tightened her legs on top of his. "How?"

She felt him smile, then he lifted his head and looked down at her, the faint glow from the yard light catching in his eyes.

"I rode over to the cattle camp. We left one of the trucks there."

Slipping her arms under his, she smiled, using both hands to massage the small of his back. "That was very resourceful of you, McCall."

He brushed back the hair at her temple, then lowered his head and kissed her. "I thought so."

Neither of them spoke for several moments, content with gentle stroking and even gentler kisses. Finally Tanner released a reluctant sigh, easing his upper body away from her. Kate smoothed her hands up the contours of his biceps, her voice husky as she whispered, "Don't go."

Bracketing her face with his hands, he leaned down and kissed the bridge of her nose. "I have to." Covering her mouth in a drugging kiss, he withdrew from her, taking her with him as he rolled onto his back. Making room for her knee between his, he nestled her head on his shoulder, his touch caressing as he stroked the outline of her ear. After a comfortable silence, he tucked in his chin and brushed a kiss against her forehead. "Kate?"

Drowsy with contentment, she sleepily watched the shadows of the leaves on the wall, comfortable in the cradle of his arm. "What?"

He hesitated, then spoke, his voice quiet. "I stopped by the RCMP detachment when I was in Pincher Creek today. One of the officers hunts out here every fall, so I had him do some checking around. No one has been there looking for you, and there's no record of a Roger Quinn having checked into any of the motels or hotels."

Kate lay absolutely still for a split second, then she rose up on one arm, bracing her hand on his chest as she looked down at him. "You didn't have to do that, Tanner," she scolded softly.

Avoiding her gaze, he carefully tucked her hair behind her ear. He finally spoke, his tone gruff. "I'm not going to let him terrorize you, Kate."

Cupping his jaw, she stroked the curve of his cheekbone with her thumb. She didn't know what to say. With the exception of her grandfather giving her money, it had been a long,

long time since anyone had done anything for her. A very long time.

He clearly didn't want her to say anything. His fingers snagging in her hair, Tanner pulled her head down, distracting her with a long, sensual kiss. "I don't want to talk about it now," he whispered against her mouth. "Not tonight. I just didn't want you to worry."

Catching her by the hips, he drew her fully on top of him, then settled her between his thighs, running his hands along her rib cage until he reached her breasts. His touch sent spirals of sensation through her, and Kate closed her eyes, yielding to his mouth. No, not tonight. Especially not tonight.

Kate didn't make it up before the boys the following morning, either. But she had awakened before dawn and slipped silently from Tanner's bed, then returned to her own. It had been so hard to leave him. Especially after it had been such a night of discovery for her. She'd discovered an astounding physical intimacy with him that had empowered her, and he had uncovered a sensuality in her that she hadn't even known she possessed. And he had made her feel things she hadn't thought possible.

But after she had gone back to her own bed, she had lain there, unable to sleep for the fluttering of anxiety churning around in her abdomen. This was a fantasy come true, but at some point she was going to be forced to deal with her life. She couldn't keep Mark and Scotty out of school forever. But this time with Tanner was a gift, and she wanted to hold on to that gift for as long as she could. She was realistic enough to know that there were countless hazards along the way, and any one of them could destroy something so fragile and new. That realization filled her with such cold, hard dread that it sat like a rock in the pit of her stomach.

And there was Tanner himself. He carried deep, damaging scars from the past, and he would never let anyone get close enough to inflict that kind of damage again. The only thing that was for certain was the here and now. She had made up her mind that she was going to celebrate the gift she had been given for as long as it was hers to hold. She would make the most of what she had today and worry about tomorrow tomorrow.

She could hear the boys at the table as she came down the stairs, and she turned toward the kitchen, hoping that Tanner would still be there. He just was coming out of Burt's room when she entered. When he looked up and saw her, his eyes lightened. "Good morning."

The husky intimacy in his tone set off a wild flutter inside her, and she laced her fingers together, wishing the boys weren't there. "Good morning."

Mark looked up. "Hi, Mom. How come you put your T-shirt on inside out?"

Kate looked down, feeling like a fool. Damn it, how had she managed that? Restraining a sigh, she gave him a level look. "It's made that way."

He grinned and made a face. "Yeah, right."

Scotty, thinking no one was watching, covertly lifted his bowl. Kate knew exactly what he was up to. "Don't even think it, Scott Allan. If you're going to drink out of your dish, you can can go live with Bess in the barn."

Mark grinned at his brother. "Wow. Then you wouldn't have to make your bed, Scotty, and you'd never have to clean up."

Scott tried to kick him under the table, and Kate interceded. "That's enough, Mark. And, Scott, you keep your feet to yourself."

Conscious of Tanner leaning against the counter watching her, even more conscious of all the places where he had touched her last night, she crossed the room, aware of the rapid pulse in her neck. She didn't know why, but she felt all shaky inside. Just before she reached him, Tanner lifted a mug off the rack and poured her a cup of coffee.

He handed it to her, retaining a hold on it when she tried to take it from him. She looked up at him, the intimate gleam in his eyes making her heart speed up. "I think," he said, just loud enough for her to hear, "that Bess already has her hands full."

Kate wanted to hug him so much that she could hardly stand it, her senses overdosing on the scent of him, on his closeness.

"Providing, of course," she said solemnly, "that she had hands."

He flashed her an amused look, the creases around his eyes crinkling, the intimate glimmer setting off sensations in her midriff that made her pulse skip and falter. He held her gaze, that almost-smile in his eyes, then lightly touched the small gold stud she wore in her ear. The movement exposed the adhesive bandage on his hand, and she turned her head ever so slightly, brushing her mouth against it.

The phone rang, and he clenched his jaw and angled his head in annoyance. Releasing a heavy sigh, he turned and set his mug on the counter, then answered it. The conversation was brief and curt, and he replaced the receiver with more force than necessary. He turned back to her, his expression tight and shuttered. "We'll be moving some cattle today, but we should be back by late afternoon. Cyrus will know where we are if you need anything."

Feeling almost bereft from his withdrawal, Kate followed him into the utility room, leaning against the door frame as he stuffed a pair of gloves in his back pocket, then pulled on his boots. He lifted his hat off the hook and settled it on his head, and Kate could tell he was still irritated by the interruption.

Unable to let him go with all those old defenses erected, she crossed to him and straightened his collar, then smoothed it down over his collarbone. She glanced up at him, giving him a teasing smile. "I guess this means you aren't going to kiss me goodbye like you did yesterday morning."

He stared at her, then a glimmer of amusement appeared in his eyes, and he gave her a lopsided smile. "I don't think my jeans could handle the strain two mornings in a row."

His response both surprised and delighted her, and Kate reached up and kissed him soundly. After having spent two very intimate and sexual nights with him, she had discovered another aspect of Tanner's reserve—another aspect that made her ache for the harsh, bleak childhood he'd had. He had been so deprived of any kind of physical association that now he had this deep need to touch and be touched—it was as if, after that first complete and explosive consummation, he was starved for that kind of intimacy from her. But he was very,

very reserved about how he responded verbally. He was also reserved about his own body, almost as if he'd been brought up being ashamed of it, as if he placed no worth on it. Kate had wanted to cry when she had realized that, but she had gone slowly and carefully and very, very gently. And he had responded with such a fervor of need.

His frankness now was a giant step for him, and she rewarded him with a hard hug. "Well," she responded, her voice catching on laughter, "I guess we can't have that."

There was the slam of a vehicle door outside, and Tanner ran his hand up her back, then reluctantly eased his hold. "I've got to go, Kate," he said, his tone husky with regret.

Wanting to get another smile out of him before he left, Kate gave him a light kiss, smiling as she whispered against his mouth, "Try to take good care of those blue jeans, McCall. They're particular favorites of mine."

He laughed against her mouth and gave her a quick, hard hug. "I'll keep that in mind."

Sighing her own reluctance, Kate let him go, taking some satisfaction in the fact that when he gave her one final look from the door, there was a hell of a lot more in his eyes than just amusement.

Feeling light and effervescent inside, Kate entered the kitchen, her bubble bursting abruptly when a loud crash came from Burt's room. Alarmed, she dashed into his room, closing her eyes in relief when she realized he'd knocked over the lamp on his bedside table, which in turn had knocked the thermal water jug onto the floor. Nothing serious, except that he looked like he was fit to be tied.

The boys came scrambling into the room right behind her, their eyes wide with alarm. "What happened? Did Burt hurt himself?"

Kicking the lid of the jug out of the way, Kate set the lamp back in place. "No, he's fine." She glanced at Mark. "Would you get a towel from the laundry so we can wipe this up? And, Scotty, take the jug to the kitchen, please." She turned to look at Burt, her mood somber. God, it had to be so frustrating for him. She took both of his hands to stop their agitated fumbling. "It's okay," she said, her tone calm. "It was only a jug of water."

His mouth trembled, but he used anger as a vent. "Damned table. I need a damned ladder to get to it. Damned thing."

Lord, but she did like the cantankerous spirit of this old man. Smiling a little, she gave his hands a small shake. "There, now. Are you all damned out?"

He glared at her, his eyes fierce. "Don't you take that tone with me, missy. Just remember who signs your checks."

She gave him a level look and answered, her tone pointed. "Tanner signs my checks." Which wasn't exactly true. Because she didn't want to open a bank account, he paid her in cash. But Burt didn't know that.

His chin set at a pugnacious angle, he stared at her, at a total loss for words. She watched him, admiring the fight in him. After a moment she saw a familiar glint appear in his eyes. "I should have known you were trouble, with all that whiskey hair and them damn green eyes."

Amused by his tenacity, Kate brushed back the wisp of hair on top of his head. Deciding now was as good a time as any to plant an idea, she stared at him. "Now watch it, Burton. If you weren't such a stubborn, bullheaded man and would ask for a little help now and again, you wouldn't get yourself into these wrecks. And if you don't like your situation, you better start thinking about changing it. Like going back to the hospital for some physical therapy."

He narrowed his eyes at her, a conniving gleam appearing in them. "That's what we hired *you* for."

Releasing her hold on his hands, she adjusted the pillows under his head, her amusement intensifying. You had to get up very early in the morning to keep ahead of Burton Shaw. She kept her tone crisp. "No, you didn't. You hired me to look after you. The few exercises I do with you are to keep your muscles from cramping. I'm not trained to do therapy, and I have no idea what they do to get a stroke victim back on his feet."

His tone was blunt. "You think they could get me back on my feet?"

She looked at him, surprised by his response. "With work, yes, I do—at least with a walker. But the longer you lie here, the more your muscles are going to deteriorate."

He stared at her. "You think I could get myself back on a horse?"

She grinned at him. "Providing it's not a bucking bronc or a steeplechaser, it's a possibility." She gave him a long look, doing a little conniving herself. "Depending on how much you really want to get back on one."

Scotty came in, carefully carrying a full jug of water. Mark came in right behind him. "We got you some more cold water, Burt. We even put some ice in it."

Kate took the towel from Mark, then crouched down and began wiping up the water. "You boys had better go down and make sure Bess has been fed and watered. Most of the men left this morning, so Cyrus might not have had time to do it."

The boys left, and Kate finished wiping up the floor. Wadding up the towel, she rose, glancing at Burt. "Are you ready for some breakfast, or do you want to go back to sleep?"

He fixed his sharp blue eyes on her, his expression as innocent as a babe's. "Tanner's looking a mite more relaxed the past couple of days," he said, his tone a little too guileless. "Like somebody took a burr out from under his saddle."

Kate shot him a startled look, then began tidying his bedside table, feeling a fine flush creep up her neck. It took her a second to think of an appropriate response. "I suspect it's because it's finally quit raining. It was beginning to get on everyone's nerves."

He eyed her with that same sly look. "I expect sunshine will do that all right—ease a man's nerves."

Kate wasn't sure she trusted that glint in his eyes. She gave him a dubious glance, then picked up the wet towel and an empty glass. "Breakfast, then?"

He tipped his head in assent, then gave her another sly look. Kate gave him another skeptical one, then turned. She was two feet from the door when he began humming "You Are My Sunshine" in a surprisingly strong voice.

Kate nearly dropped the glass. Not sure whether to laugh or strangle him, she left the room. There was certainly nothing wrong with Burt Shaw's eyes.

Chapter 10

Kate sat on the back step, her arms crisscrossed on her thighs, the wind in her hair, watching the boys romp with the puppies and Bess, making sure they didn't wake up Burt, who was napping in a new chaise longue under the big old poplar, the spare sheepskin beneath him. It had been ten days since her trip to Pincher Creek, ten days since that first unbelievable night with Tanner. Ten days of sunshine and brightness and spring. Not since childhood could she remember feeling so happy inside.

It wasn't as if it was perfect. It wasn't. She'd had nightmares two nights in a row over something dark and sinister. And there were times when she got such anxiety attacks about her dwindling time on the Circle S that her heart felt as if it might explode. And she and Tanner didn't have enough time alone together—not nearly enough time.

All they had together were the nights, and for Kate, those were almost enough. They were the source of that well of contentment deep inside her. She knew with every touch that he found enormous pleasure in her, but what filled up her heart and made her soul sing was how, in a hundred ways, he let her know how much he wanted and needed her. He hadn't said it in words; she didn't want him to. Not yet. There was too much wrong in their lives right now. But she knew, deep down in her heart, that she *was* a ray of sunshine for him, and that made her happy, down-deep-in-the-soul happy. And God, he was such a rock for her. Such a solid, steady rock.

The sound of a vehicle approaching interrupted her musings, and Kate turned, watching as a black dual-wheeled three-quarter truck with tinted windows, loaded with chrome and lights, appeared over the rise, taking the turnoff for the house. With a brashness and flash that made her smile, the driver whipped the vehicle onto the gravel pad and was out of the truck before the vehicle stopped rocking, a cloud of dust rolling in around him.

He was tall and lanky, with dark, curly hair under his pro-rodeo Stetson, and he moved with the cocky swagger of a man who liked living on the edge. He had sin and danger written all over him, and his grin was enough to stop every heart between the Circle S and Texas. Kate knew who he was before he ever opened his mouth.

He came through the gate, his eyes glinting as he came toward her. "Well, if this isn't enough to blow warts off a hog. Ol' Tanner's been holding out on me." Bracing his foot on the bottom step, he stretched out his hand. "Chase McCall. I'm Tanner's little ol' baby brother."

Taking his hand, she gave him a smile. "Kate Quinn." Scotty and Mark stopped playing and stood staring at this new arrival. She had drilled them about good manners often enough that she didn't dare ignore them now. But in spite of good manners, she couldn't resist letting him know she was on to him. "These are Mark and Scotty, my little ol' sons."

Chase shot her a sharp, almost surprised look, then nodded to the boys, a deep grin creasing his face. Propping her chin in her hand, she studied him as he reached down to scratch Bess's ears. His skin wasn't as dark as Tanner's, and his cheekbones weren't quite as high, and there was, of course, a complete absence of Tanner's native heritage, but the resemblance was startling. Only Chase had had the benefit of a privileged, affluent and indulged childhood; Kate could see it in the way he carried himself, in the way he walked. Bruce McCall's legitimate son.

Kate realized that Chase was assessing her, as well, and she felt a blush creep up her cheeks. The glint in Chase's dark hazel eyes intensified. "So, Kate Quinn. Is my brother around?" He spoke in a lazy, Colorado drawl, and Kate guessed that more than one woman had fallen victim to his smoky, lazy voice. The kind of come-to-bed voice that mothers had nightmares about.

But in spite of his blatant sexuality and unchecked virility, Kate knew she was going to like this man. And it had nothing to do with the husky sensuality in his voice. It had everything to do with the expression in his eyes and the way he said "my brother." He had disclosed more than he realized about how he felt about his older brother. And from the cocky swagger and the aggressive set of his jaw, Kate was willing to bet that there wasn't another man alive or dead whom Chase looked up to.

Experiencing a funny little cramp in her throat, Kate rested her arms on her knees and met his gaze, amused by his blatant use of charm. He was as bad as Cyrus. Restraining a smile, she finally answered, her tone dry. "I expect so. He often is."

Bracing one foot on the riser, Chase draped his arm across his knee, the gleam in his eyes full of hell, his drawl deliberate. "I was hoping for something a little more specific. Like a location, maybe even some directions."

Managing not to laugh, she held his gaze. "You might," she said, her tone pointedly patient, "try the barn." Then, unable to resist, she gave him an impish grin. "That's the big red building at the bottom of the hill."

There was a flash of perfect white teeth, but Chase continued to watch her with an unnerving degree of steadiness, his eyes narrowed, the glint becoming more and more speculative. Finally he spoke, his tone soft and seductive, almost as if he were speculating aloud. "So, Kate Quinn. I guess I'm at a disadvantage here. I wasn't expecting to find a pretty lady sitting on my brother's doorstep, or two small boys playing with his prize pups. Seems like some changes have been taking place."

Determined not to squirm under his scrutiny, Kate let her gaze drift to the boys, trying to ignore the butterflies in her stomach. Clearing away the nervous catch in her voice, she responded, hoping she wouldn't do something foolish, like blush. "Tanner hired me to look after Burt when they brought him home from the hospital. I've been here not quite a month."

He continued to watch her, amusement flirting around his mouth. "Seems like a plausible explanation. If I was looking for plausible." Kate shot him a startled look, and he grinned at her, tipping his hat lower over his eyes. "Bet you set ol' Tanner back a space or two."

Kate was scrambling for some kind of response when she heard the distinctive sound of a horse approaching, and Tanner, astride the bay gelding, appeared on the path leading up from the barn. He rode toward them at an easy lope, and Chase straightened, his hands on his hips as he watched his brother approach.

Tanner reined in the horse and dismounted on the other side of the fence, wrapping the reins around the top rail. Sweeping off his hat, he wiped his forehead with the sleeve of his shirt, resettling his hat as he came through the gate.

Chase straightened, a wide, wicked grin appearing. "Well, hell. Things are looking up around here. A personal welcome from the boss." Chase folded his arms and stared at his brother, his grin deepening. "You wouldn't be checking up on me, would you?"

Amusement deepening the creases around his eyes, Tanner gave his brother a warped grin, but there was something in his eyes that was oddly sober, and Kate frowned. He had his doubts about Chase being there—and she had a strange feeling that his uncertainty had something to do with her. It was almost as though he expected Chase to ride in and sweep her off her feet. Not sure whether to be amused or insulted, Kate stared back at him, deliberately running her finger slowly up and down the deep V of her blouse. He held her gaze for an instant, then raised one eyebrow, genuine amusement flickering in his eyes. Chase, realizing something was going on behind him, turned and looked at her, and Kate gave him a wide-eyed innocent look, serenely fingering the point of her collar. Watching her play out her little game, Tanner shook his head, the twinkle in his eyes intensifying. Reaching the step, he took Chase's outstretched hand, his tone underscored with amusement when he greeted his brother. "I don't recall anyone being too successful in checking up on you, Chase. Always struck me as a monumental waste of time."

Chase grinned and firmly gripped his brother's hand, then clapped Tanner on the shoulder. "Things change, big brother. Things change." His expression sobering, he met his brother's gaze. "I just heard about Burt. And I figured I'd better get my butt up here."

One of the dogs started barking, and a cranky voice interrupted from under the tree. "It took you long enough. A two-legged steer could have crawled up here faster." Burt swung his eyes to her. "And don't you start on them boys for making the dog bark. That Mac hasn't got an ounce of sense."

Knowing exactly what he was up to, Kate met his fierce gaze with a level look. "That kind of tone won't get you a piece of fresh peach pie, Burt," she said, her own tone mildly chastising.

He stuck his chin out at her and glared. There was a deep chuckle behind Tanner, and Chase brushed by. "Well, you old dog. How the hell are you? I thought there was nothing here but a wadded-up blanket."

There was a bright glint in Burt's eyes, but he managed to maintain his glower. "Might as well be a blanket for all the good it does me." He stretched out his bony hand, a telltale glitter suddenly appearing in his eyes. "You're a sight for sore eyes, boy. A sight for sore eyes."

Taking the old man's hand, Chase crouched down beside him, and Kate glanced up at Tanner, watching his face. He stood with one foot on the bottom stair, his forearm resting on the banister of the steps, his hat low over his eyes. Kate's own throat closed up when she saw his jaw tense and the muscles in his throat contract. Shifting closer to the railing, she reached down and laced her fingers through the backs of his. She saw him swallow again; then he tightened his fingers around hers, his grip almost painful as he rubbed her thumb. He didn't say anything; he just continued to watch the two men under the tree, and Kate knew he was struggling with something very big.

It wasn't until later that night, after she'd got Burt settled and the boys into bed, that Kate found herself alone with Chase. He and Tanner had spent the day together, then had left again after supper to check one of the pastures that had been flooded during the rains. When she came downstairs after tucking the boys in, she found him seated at the kitchen table, a cup of coffee by his elbow, a newspaper spread out in front of him. He looked up, humor glinting in his eyes. "Damn, don't you make any noise? I thought you'd gone to bed."

Kate gave him a wry smile. "And miss the only quiet time in the entire day? Not a chance." She picked up some comics Mark had left scattered on the table, stacked them, then placed them on the end of the counter. "Where's Tanner?"

Chase leaned back in his chair and stretched his legs out in front of him, hooking his thumbs in the front pockets of his jeans. "He had some things to go over with Ross, and he wanted to check a horse that came up lame today."

She motioned to the coffee. "Would you like a piece of pie or muffin to go with that?"

He gave her an almost sheepish grin. "I must admit, I've been sitting here thinking about that pie. Except I know Burt will nail my hide to the door if I eat it on him."

Kate smiled. "There's more in the freezer. And Burt loves having something to get in a huff about."

Rocking back in his chair, Chase hooked one ankle across his knee and crossed his arms, studying her with a mix of amusement and intentness. "He's a cantankerous old devil. He used to scare the hell out of me when I was a kid, but by the looks of it, it didn't take you long to get a twitch on him. He's downright docile now."

Kate laughed. "'Docile' seems a little extreme. 'Almost manageable' might be closer to the truth."

Amusement dancing in his eyes, Chase met her gaze. "Might be at that."

Kate opened the cupboard and got out the pie. She cut him a thick wedge and put it on a plate, then turned to ask him if he wanted whipped cream. He was still sitting with his arms folded, his chair rocked back, but he was watching her with a hard, unsmiling look that made her insides drop. Chase McCall, she realized with a start, was a presence to be reckoned with. He might be reckless, and he might have a daredevil attitude, but this man was no pushover. Trying to contain the nervous flutter in her middle, she placed a fork on the plate and took the pie over to the table.

He carefully aligned the fork, as if he were considering something, then he looked up at her. "Don't ever start jerking Tanner around, Kate," he said, his voice dangerously quiet. There was a taut silence; then he exhaled heavily and let his chair slam down. He massaged his eyes and released another sigh. His voice was strained when he spoke. "I'm sorry. That was out of line."

Not sure how to handle the situation, Kate stepped back and stuck her hands in her pockets. Something happened in that instant, and she wasn't quite sure what it was, but it was a kind of releasing sensation in her midriff, as if some sort of tension had let go.

Deciding that maybe Chase deserved a little honesty, she tried to clear away the funny feeling in her chest, then spoke, her voice unsteady. "Your brother is the best thing that's happened to me in a long, long time, Chase, but I can't promise that he won't get hurt." Feeling suddenly chilled, she folded her arms and huddled in their warmth, trying to find the words to make him understand. "I can't even be sure *I* won't get hurt." Struggling with a wealth of feelings, she managed a wobbly smile. "We're just sort of feeling our way along."

Chase looked up at her, his gaze solemn and unwavering. He didn't say anything for a while, but finally he spoke, his tone quiet. "In other words, one day at a time."

Kate looked away. "Yes."

There was a long silence, then Chase spoke again. "What has he told you?"

Kate pulled out the chair across from him and sat down, her expression solemn as she turned one of the tulips in the butter crock. Finally she inhaled heavily and shook her head.

Chase abruptly pushed his chair back and stood up, then walked to the window. Bracing his hand on the frame, he stood staring out at the fading twilight. His tone was flat and bitter when he finally spoke. "So you don't know what a rotten deal he got from our old man."

Kate rubbed her thumb along the broad leaf of one of the flowers, then looked up at him. "Rita told me a bit—I wanted to know about the Bruce McCall Arena in Bolton, so I asked her."

Chase stood staring out the window for several moments, then he turned, giving her a humorless smile. "Hell of a family I come from, isn't it?"

She smiled and shrugged. "I don't know. You and Tanner turned out all right."

Chase sighed and came back to the table. Swinging the chair around, he straddled it, hooking his arms over the back. There was a glimmer of real humor in his eyes when he looked at her. "If it hadn't been for Tanner, I probably would have spent my formative years in juvenile detention. I was determined to make my old man's life a living hell."

Kate folded her arms and leaned back in her chair, watching him with interest. "How formative?"

He shot her an amused look. "Most people want to know what I did to make my old man's life hell."

Kate gave him a lopsided grin. "I don't want to know. I'm a mother of sons."

He chuckled, then gave a small shrug. "I used to spend a lot of time out at the family ranch when I was a kid. My father was still pretty involved back then, and he used to take me with him quite a bit. I was about four when Cyrus and Millie brought Tanner to live with them." He ran his thumbnail along the edge of the table, the expression in his eyes altering, becoming more solemn and reminiscent. Finally he looked up at her, a wry smile tugging at the corner of his mouth. "I followed Tanner around like a second shadow—dogged his every step. Asked him a million questions. He was always so damned patient, and I thought he could spit gold. Then something happened when he was about fourteen—Cyrus would never tell me what it was—but it must have been bad, because Tanner disappeared, and so did Cyrus. I guess I must have been eight or nine before I found out he was my half brother. My father and mother were having a hell of a row late one night, and I woke up. She was yelling at him about Tanner. It was that same night I found out he was working for Burt Shaw."

Her gaze fixed on him, Kate assimilated all his information, trying to suppress the churning in her stomach. She didn't dare think about what could have happened to drive Tanner away from the Bar M. Knowing what kind of a childhood he'd had was bad enough.

Chase lifted his head and looked at her, the glimmer of humor back in his eyes. "So the next time we went out to the Bar M, I saddled up my horse and rode over to Burt's—he was still living on the original Shaw homestead then, so it was only a couple of miles across country. Anyhow, I was going to enlighten Tanner about this new discovery. I was pretty ticked off when I found out he already knew—tried to beat him up, as I recall." He paused, his expression softened by the recollection. "That was one thing my old man never did figure out— why I'd ride over to Burt's every chance I got."

Kate watched him, absorbed by his recounting of Tanner's role in his life, touched by his openness. Crossing her legs at the ankles, she tipped her head to one side. "So you're eight years younger?"

"Yeah. Which means—hell, he'll be turning forty-two this fall."

"Rita said you came to work for Burt when you left high school."

He grinned, shaking his head. "Which probably saved my butt. I was pretty wild back then—did my fair share of hell-raising. But nobody messed with Tanner in those days, not even me, so I kept my nose pretty clean." His grin broadened, and he looked up at her. "Burt taught him the fine art of knife throwing right after he came here, and he could spike a dime at fifty paces—never missed, and faster than lightning. He used to wear a buck knife back then—kept it in a sheath on his belt whenever he was in rough country. Old Tommy Brown saw him use it once, and after that, everyone was real careful what they said around Tanner.''

Intent on his story, Chase shook his head over some recollection, amusement glinting in his eyes. "Cyrus always figured Tanner could have been a legend in his own time. Swore all he needed was a knife, a bullwhip and a good horse, and he could have tamed the old West all by himself." He looked at Kate, the glint intensifying. "I figured there was a certain amount of truth in that. So I sure in hell wasn't going to tangle with him."

Kate heard the screen door open, and she glanced at the clock over the cupboard. Another sixteen-hour day. She glanced at Chase as she got up, giving him fair warning. "You'd better eat that pie, or you *will* be in big trouble with Burt."

Tanner had his back to her and was prying off one boot in a bootjack when Kate paused in the doorway. Resting her shoulder against the frame, she watched him. She couldn't see his face, but she could tell by the set of his shoulders that he was dead tired. Realizing that he didn't know she was there, she spoke, her voice husky. "Hi. I was beginning to think you were going to spend the night in the barn."

He finished drawing off the boot, then gave her a quick glance, his half smile not quite reaching his eyes. "Hi. I thought you'd be in bed by now."

Disquieted by the somberness in his voice, she folded her arms and watched as he hooked his other boot in the bootjack, wondering what was wrong. "A bad day?" she asked softly.

He drew his foot from the boot, then straightened. "Yeah," he responded, his voice gruff. "It was."

Troubled by the fact that he wouldn't quite meet her gaze, and even more troubled by the vulnerability she sensed in him, she tried to think of some possible reason for the sudden change from that morning. And the only thing that had changed since that morning was his brother's arrival. His handsome, daredevil, charming-as-hell brother. His father's son.

It was in that instant that Kate understood fully just how badly she could hurt him, how unsure he was of her, how little he expected for himself. Angry at those who had done this to him, wishing she could make it better, she went to him and took his weary face between her hands, then stretched up and gave him a soft kiss.

He stopped breathing and went very still. Kate could feel the need in him, the lonely, lonely need, and she put her heart and soul into that kiss, wordlessly telling him things she couldn't say aloud. A shudder coursed through him, and he drew a ragged breath, catching her by the back of the head, his jaw flexing beneath her hand as he responded. He moved his mouth slowly against hers, tasting her, savoring her, drawing her breath from her and leaving her weak.

It went on and on and on, until Kate felt as if she were suffocating from all the sensations pouring in on her, and she flattened her hand against his chest. Tanner tensed and dragged his mouth away from hers. His heart was slamming in his chest, and his breathing was harsh and uneven, but he gathered her up in a cuddling embrace, and Kate hung on to him, needing him—needing his strength around her. Finally she was able to get a breath past the frenzy in her chest, and Tanner ran his hand up her back, pressing her to him. He turned his head, pressing an unsteady kiss against the curve of her neck, then nestled her closer. "Ah, Katie," he whispered unevenly. "I shouldn't even be touching you, I'm so damned filthy."

Kate closed her eyes and hugged him hard, moved by his husky admission. He was fastidious in his personal grooming—always neat, always clean, always washed his hands before sitting down at the table—a holdover from his twisted, sick childhood, no doubt. She had a mental picture of a small, somber half-breed boy, his hands being roughly scrubbed with a stiff brush and harsh soap because he hadn't got them perfectly clean. That image was bad enough, but what upset her was that he felt he didn't have the right to hold her, the right to any kind of comfort, unless he was clean. That made her feel so sad.

Struggling against the feelings he'd created in her, she tightened her arms around him when she felt him ease away. "I don't care," she said in a fiercely defensive whisper, "if you've been dipped in the septic tank and rolled down the manure pile. I just want you to hold me."

She was rewarded with a husky chuckle and a hard hug. There was an undercurrent of amusement in his voice when he finally responded. "The manure pile I can handle. The septic tank is a bit much."

Unaccountably moved by the hug, even more moved by the protective way he tucked her head against his shoulder, Kate shut her eyes and struggled against the sudden threat of tears. Lord, but this man deserved some joy in his life.

Resting his cheek against her hair, Tanner continued to rub her back, and Kate turned her face against his neck, saturating herself in his touch. Finally Tanner released a long sigh, running his hand up the full length of her back. "Chase usually sleeps at the house when he's here," he said, his voice heavy with regret. Kate opened her eyes, considering his comment, then smiled to herself when she figured out what he was really saying. She caressed the side of his neck. "That's fine. I figured he would, so I fixed my bed for him. I put Scotty in with Mark, so I can move into the boys' room—whenever."

Tanner raised his head and looked at her, his gaze solemn. "You don't have to do anything you're uncomfortable with, Kate." He shifted his gaze as he smoothed his thumb along her eyebrow, then looked at her, his eyes dark and solemn. "Believe me, I'd understand if you wanted to keep all this quiet."

It had cost him a lot to make such an open admission. Kate could see it in his eyes, and it was all she could do to keep from letting her feelings get the upper hand. "I don't care if the whole world knows," she responded softly, holding his gaze. "And I don't care who finds out about us. I'd just like to keep the boys out of it if I can."

He stared down at her, his gaze troubled. He lifted a wisp of hair off her face and carefully tucked it behind her ear; then he looked at her again. "And I don't want you feeling uncomfortable because Chase is here," he said huskily.

She met his gaze and grimaced, then grinned. "Just in case, I'll go up first."

It was late when she finally went upstairs, and it was even later when Tanner came up. She'd indulged herself in a long, relaxing soak in the Jacuzzi in Tanner's bathroom and was just zipping up the front of her housecoat when he entered the bedroom. Securing a towel around her wet hair, she hung up the other towel, then turned toward the bedroom. He was standing by his dresser, emptying his pockets, when she entered the room. He glanced up, indicating the bathroom with a lift of his chin. "Are you finished?"

She nodded, noticing again how exhausted he looked. He undid his belt and pulled it free of his jeans, then folded it up and laid it on the dresser. He turned toward the bathroom, stiffly rolling one shoulder, and Kate watched him go. She knew from Chase's comments that he'd been slammed into a cattle feeder by a rank steer earlier that day, and the shoulder was obviously bothering him now.

"Why don't you let me give you a back rub?" she said softly. "It would help work out that stiffness."

He shook his head. "All I need is a hot shower and bed."

Kate stared after him, the funny churning in the pit of her stomach very disquieting. She had yet to see him naked. In fact, she had yet to see him with his shirt off. It was almost as though he didn't want to acknowledge his own body—except at night, in total darkness; then his barriers would come down. Releasing a resigned sigh, she pulled the towel off her head, then sat cross-legged on the bed and began drying her hair. She wasn't sure she ever wanted to know the whole story of Tanner's childhood. She suspected she might try to kill someone if she ever found out the whole truth.

She was already in bed when Tanner came back into the room. His shirt was open, and his jeans weren't done up, but that was as far as his comfort zone extended. He switched off the bedside light, then began removing his clothes. Kate waited for him, emotion thick inside her, profound tenderness making her heart ache. When he finally stretched out beside her, she rose to her knees beside him, her voice husky and gently prodding when she spoke. "Come on, Tanner," she whispered. "Roll over and let me give you a back rub. It'll make you feel better."

He hesitated, then rolled onto his stomach, turning his face away and resting his head on his folded arms. There was a reserve about him, yet he sought out her touch—as if he'd been deprived of it for so long that he couldn't get enough of it now. And she was going to touch him—stroke after stroke. She would replenish him.

Straddling his hips, she slowly smoothed her hands up the muscled length of his back, her fingers skimming over the puckered scar on his right shoulder, a weakening flutter unfolding in her middle. She was going to give him a back rub that eased his soreness and soothed his aching muscles, and she would slowly, thoroughly massage away his weariness. She was going to caress and stroke every inch of him, telling him through touch alone just how beautiful she thought he was.

Dragging her hands down his back, she aligned the heels of her hands along the base of his spine, then moved them in a slow, massaging tempo, the movement dragging a low groan from him. She closed her eyes and began slowly, sensually, seductively kneading his flesh, her pulse growing thick and heavy. It was going to be a long, long night.

Chapter 11

Burt was adamant. For the past hundred years, from the time the first Circle S brand was hammered into shape at a blacksmith's forge, branding day had always taken place the second week of June. And damn it, they weren't breaking with tradition because of a little rain. But because of the heavy rainfall, the preparations were behind schedule.

Cyrus told Kate that branding day was something of a tradition in the community, with neighboring ranchers pitching in. Ross had hired on extra hands, and some of the young men from the Hutterite colony had come over three days in a row to help, but even so, with over six hundred cows and their calves to round up and separate, it meant long, exhausting days in the saddle for all of them. And in June, the days were already at their longest. Tanner usually left the house at dawn and often didn't return until well after last light. It helped that Chase stayed on, and just from the little Kate saw, it was clear that Tanner's brother knew the Circle S operation inside out. Kate wasn't sure how Tanner would have managed without him.

Because of Burt, she was removed from most of the action, but she did what she could. Cyrus told her that, come branding day, there would be upward of fifty people, some just there to hang on the corral and give advice, but most of them there to work. Three meals, two lunches and grab-as-you-go snacks—multiplied by fifty or more—meant a mountain of food preparation. She baked pies until she never wanted to see another crust and made enough muffins to stop a stampede, and Cyrus praised her cooking with his considerable cowpoke charm.

Kate didn't think it would ever end, but two days before, everything fell into place. Cyrus stopped by the house with a bouquet of irises that he claimed came from the same neglected garden, but Kate knew enough about flowers to recognize some very exotic specimens among them. They were beautiful, and she told him so. She didn't, however, say anything about his blatant deceit.

He stood at the end of the counter, chewing on a toothpick, watching her arrange them in the crock. "If you get a snatch of time tomorrow, you should take them young ones over to where we've got the cattle mustered. It's something to see if you ain't ever had the opportunity. Branding itself might upset 'em some, but tomorrow they'll jest be sortin' the herd."

Kate shifted some of the blossoms to better display their colors, then stood back to view her handiwork. "I can't leave Burt, and with everyone so busy, there won't be any spare help here."

His eyes narrowed in contemplation, Cyrus smoothed down his mustache and moved the toothpick to the other side of his mouth. "I expect it would do Ol' Burt some good to get out there hisself."

Kate shot him a slightly startled look. "I'd take him in a minute, Cyrus, but I can't get him in and out of the truck by myself. And I expect everyone will be leaving first thing."

Cyrus nodded, thoughtfully stroking his mustache. "Well, I've been thinking. Since we already fixed up that ramp off the veranda so you can wheel him right outside, we could rig something on top of that so you could jest roll him right up to the truck. 'Course, you'd have to shift him from the wheelchair to the front seat, but he's stronger than he was. He should just about manage that on his own."

She stared at him, suddenly hopeful. "Could we rig something before tomorrow?"

He gave her a wide grin, rolled his toothpick to the other side, then nodded. "Yes, ma'am. I think we jest might."

Kate didn't say anything to Scotty and Mark. Nor did she say anything to Burt. The boys were bad enough, but she couldn't bear to disappoint the old man. But when she came downstairs the next morning, a second ramp had been inverted on the first, making a straight loading platform. Before she said anything to anyone, she brought the truck around the house and backed up so the passenger door was aligned with the ramp. She wanted to hug Cyrus when she saw how easy it was going to be. At least this end was going to be easy. She would worry about the other end when she got there.

When she rolled Burt out onto the veranda, telling him that they were going to take a little trip, he said that sitting under a tree, watching grass grow, was no damned trip. But when he saw the Bronco parked there, with the passenger door already open and the chaise longue in the back, his mouth started to tremble and tears welled up in his eyes. She had trouble keeping her own eyes dry.

The sun was high over the horizon by the time they got to the mustering area, and heat and dust hung in the air, the din of hundreds of bawling, milling cows creating a pandemonium of noise. Burt, his eyes bright and sharp, explained the network of corrals and holding pens, and how the calves would be separated from the cows.

They bounced along a narrow prairie trail toward a stand of trees overlooking the largest corral, where all the other rigs were parked. Kate parked under a huge old poplar on the side of the hill, then draped her arms over the wheel, watching the action below. The dogs, their tongues hanging out, lay in the grass along the rail fence, intently watching what was going on, waiting for a signal to go to work. Kate reached behind Burt's seat and extracted a container of water. "Why don't you boys take some water down to the dogs? There's an empty ice-cream pail in the back you can use."

Scotty was in such a hurry to get out that he practically fell out of the truck, and Cyrus, who'd appeared between two trucks when they pulled up, picked him up and dusted him off. "Slow down there, sprout. You're going to be here a spell." Handing the water to Mark, he rested his arms on Burt's open window and grinned at Kate. "So you managed to drag this tough old carcass out here after all. You've got grit and fortitude, Miz Quinn. I'll give you that."

She gave him a dry look. "I had a little help from my friends."

He pretended he didn't hear, directing his comment to Burt. "Do you want to stay sitting in there, or do you want to set a spell out here?" He grinned, a twinkle appearing in his eyes. "A little dust on your teeth is probably jest what you need."

Burt opted to sit outside, and Cyrus set up the lounge chair under the tree, covered it with a sheepskin, then helped Kate get him settled. Dragging up an old stump, he sat down beside his old friend, then proceeded to start an argument. Smiling to herself, Kate found a vantage point in the sun that was upwind from the dust. They could squabble and spar all they wanted to; she had come here to watch.

It was powerful country, this open rangeland. Off in the distance the mountains rose up gray and rugged, their peaks still outlined with snow. The past few days of sunshine had transformed the countryside, and the usually barren hills were lush green, the foliage on the trees thick and verdant. Spring flowers bloomed among the prairie grasses, and the smell of silver willow carried sweetly on the light breeze. Just below her a hardy bramble of wild roses showed the first deep pink buds, and she could detect the scent of a few open flowers. There was no scent on earth like it: sunshine, silver willow and roses. She wished she could bottle it and take it home.

The light wind feathered some curls across her face, and Kate turned her face into the breeze and shook her hair back to clear it away. Her gaze landed on a horse and rider entering the corral, and her heart stalled in her chest, the sensation making her go all weak inside. He wasn't riding the bay gelding but sat astride a muscled buckskin stallion.

He rode deep in the saddle, moving to the rhythm of the horse's gait with an easy grace, his shoulders twisted to the side as he rewound his rope. The reins were looped over the horn, and he was guiding his mount with his thighs, and Kate had to close her eyes against the sudden rush of heat that made her lungs seize up and her whole body pulse.

Images and sensations from very, very early that morning skittered through her mind, images of Tanner, hard and aroused against her back, sensations of his fingers massaging her breast, of his hand stroking between her thighs, of pleasure, slow and erotic and consuming, of him slowly, slowly entering her, his hand cupped hard against her when everything exploded into a shattering release. And how hard it had been to leave him, to ease away from him and out of his hold when he drifted back to sleep, how much she missed him when she crept into the empty bed in the boys' room. It was getting harder and harder to go. It didn't matter whether they made love or not—it felt as if she were stripping half of herself away every time she had to leave his bed and go back to her own.

Feeling as if she'd just got off some wild ride at the fair, she expelled all the air in her lungs and lifted her head, half expecting everything around her to be spinning. A flicker of amusement worked its way free; obviously thinking about Tanner's thighs was out of the question.

Making herself relax, she tightened her grip on her legs, then turned to check on the boys. Mark had found an old piece of rotted rope and was on top of the hill, swinging it over his head. Kate grinned. He'd barely known what a cowboy was until a few weeks ago, and now he was one. The boy stopped and dropped his arm, staring intently at the corral; then he turned and started coming back toward her, still watching the action below. Kate got a funny feeling in her middle when she realized he was trying to copy the actions of one of the riders. It took only one glance to identify who.

The sensation in her middle intensified, and she looked away, her throat suddenly tight. She'd caught glimpses of it before, of her son's quiet, unobtrusive attempts to copy Tanner's actions and mannerisms—to try to be like him. It broke her heart, watching one small boy trying to covertly model himself after the man. Tanner's relationship with the boys was the only dark spot in her life right now. Tanner pretty much ignored them, although she'd caught him smiling a couple of times over their pranks with Burt. And even though Mark might mimic him from a distance, both he and Scott were pretty much intimidated by Tanner. He was just too big a presence for them.

One of the men standing by the corral swung open the front gate, and Tanner rode through, pausing to speak to Ross, who had dismounted to tighten the cinch on his saddle. With a parting comment, Tanner turned his horse toward the parked vehicles and cued him into an easy canter. She watched him ride toward her, and she stood up and stuck her hands in the back pockets of her jeans, shaking her windblown hair out of her face. He was magnificent on a horse—effortless, smooth, commanding. He belonged there, just like he belonged on the open range. Both by right of his mother's people, and by right of his McCall heritage. She wondered if he realized that.

He reined his mount down to a walk as he neared, and it wasn't until he got closer that Kate realized the horse was testing Tanner's authority with every step. She started toward him, shading her eyes against the bright morning sunlight. She grinned as he stopped beside her. "I like your horse. He looks like he has a mind of his own."

The creases around his eyes deepened as he stared down at her, crisscrossing his arms on the horn. He gave her a warped half smile and answered, his tone dry, "He's Burt's."

Kate broke out in unrestrained laughter. She couldn't believe it. That explained everything.

He continued to watch her, amusement deepening his smile and making his eyes glint. "I'm glad you think it's so funny. I'd like to geld him right about now, except he's the best cow pony on the place."

Expelling the last of her amusement, Kate wiped her eyes, then reached out and stroked the stallion's muzzle. "So you've got a streak of ornery in you, too, huh, fella?"

Tanner spoke, his tone laced with dry humor. "Watch it. He'll bite you if he gets the chance."

Straightening the horse's forelock, Kate looked up at Tanner, a sweet sensation unfolding in her when she saw the way he was looking at her. It wasn't sexual. It was warmth she saw in his eyes—a warmth that was a mixture of amusement and tolerance and affection. That look created such a response in her that it was almost more than she could handle. And she wanted to touch him so badly that it was all she could do to keep her hands on the horse.

A strand of hair blew across her mouth, and Tanner leaned over and lifted it away. Kate's breath caught on a wave of sensations, and she closed her eyes and grasped his wrist.

He rubbed his knuckle along her jaw, then reluctantly pulled free of her grasp and straightened. Kate briefly rested her forehead against his knee; then, drawing a shaky breath, she looked up at him. "I wish," she said, trying to sound cross, "that you would quit doing that to me."

He gazed down at her, that same mixture of warmth and amusement and tolerance lighting up his eyes. "Sounds like you got your tail in a knot this morning. Kinda like old Buck here."

Hooking her thumbs in her pockets, she grinned up at him. "Kinda," she agreed.

He chuckled and straightened, picking up the reins. "I think maybe I'd better go talk to Burt. I could end up digging myself into a lot of trouble around you."

She walked beside him, dragging her feet through the thick tufts of grass. "Just don't let him talk you into sticking him on a horse." She glanced up at him, giving him a rueful smile. "He's going to try, you know."

His mouth quirked. "I know."

Burt was full of orders and opinions and bluster, but Kate could tell by the way he kept wiping his eyes that he was glad to be there, and even more pleased to see his horse. Kate sat on the ground at the foot of Burt's lounge, her elbow braced on the chair, her head propped on her hand. Scotty was throwing sticks for Mac to fetch farther up the hill, but Mark came and sat by his mother, intent on every word. Kate smoothed his sweat-dampened hair back from his forehead, then brushed a smudge from his cheek. Mark fidgeted uncomfortably over her mothering, and Kate smiled to herself. None of that baby stuff here.

Tanner never dismounted. He sat hunched in the saddle, his arms resting on the horn, constantly monitoring what was happening below. They were discussing the plans for the following day when Chase rode up, lather dripping off the haunches of the palomino he rode. He grinned down at Burt. "Well, hell, you're here. I was planning on slapping my brand on some of those black calves of yours."

Burt scowled. "Keep your irons to yourself, Chase McCall, or I'll do some branding of my own."

Mark giggled, and Burt shot him a sly look. Kate rolled her eyes. She might as well have three kids. Chase swung down from his horse, lifting off a second rope that had been tied to the back skirt of his saddle. "I saw you up there watching Tanner and trying to get the hang of roping, sport. Figured if you were trying so hard to throw a loop like he does, you need a real rope to practice with."

Mark's face turned pink, and he took the rope without meeting Chase's gaze, his voice barely above a whisper as he thanked him. Kate wanted to hug her son, to shield him from his discomfort, but she knew that would only make matters worse. Needing to give him some reassurance and an avenue of escape, she pulled his hair back from his face. "Why don't you go show Scotty? Maybe there's something up there on top of the hill that you could practice on." Keeping his gaze averted, the boy scrambled up, and Kate watched him go, hurting for him.

She glanced at Chase. He was standing with one foot braced on the edge of Burt's lounge, his arms folded on his knee, the reins held loosely in his hand. He was studying the toe of his boot with a solemn intentness. Experiencing a funny feeling in the pit of her stomach, she glanced at Tanner, and her stomach dropped to her shoes. He was staring at the horizon, his face set in grim lines, and Kate experienced an awful sinking sensation. As if sensing her watching him, he straightened in the saddle, giving her a chilling glance before wheeling his horse around and heading toward the corrals.

A strained silence remained, and Kate glanced back at Chase, who was still standing with one foot cocked on the edge of the lounge, his arms folded across his knee. Only now he was watching his brother ride away, his expression unsmiling, his eyes solemn. Burt clutched at the light blanket covering him, obviously distressed. "You spurred him pretty hard, boy," he said, his voice quavering.

Chase watched the horse and rider, his face set in sober lines. Then he clenched his jaw in a grimace of self-disgust and abruptly straightened, looking like he wanted to hit something. Swearing, he turned, caught the horn and swung into the saddle, then turned. Something let loose in Kate, and she went after him. The lush grass was slick beneath her feet, the slope of the hill threatening her footing, but she finally caught up to him. Stumbling against the horse, she grabbed the bridle. "Chase, please," she pleaded, her voice breaking.

Swearing under his breath, he reined in, then exhaled heavily. Nearly sick with alarm, she touched his hand. "Please, Chase," she whispered unevenly. "What was that all about?"

Finally he looked down at her. He didn't say anything for the longest time, then he sighed heavily and looked away. "Tanner's mother was a trick rider before she hooked up with our old man. She used to perform at some of the smaller rodeos." He paused, the muscles in his jaw flexing; then he continued, his tone harsh. "When Tanner left the Bar M, the only thing he took with him was a lasso that she used in her act. Cyrus told me about it once a long time ago, when he was falling-down drunk."

She stared up at him, the sick feeling turning to horror. "Oh, God," she whispered, the full impact hitting home. "How could you?"

He held her gaze for an instant, then looked away. "Because I'm a bastard." He paused, then continued, his voice turning gruff. "And because I saw what young Mark was doing up on that hill."

Before Kate had time to respond, Chase rode off, and Kate tipped her head back, her vision suddenly blurring. He had seen Mark up on the hill. He had also seen himself, as he had been so many years before.

Tanner didn't come home that night. Cyrus phoned up to the house when he got back to the ranch, telling her not to expect him, that he and Ross were spending the night at the camp to keep an eye on the herd. Feeling Tanner's absence like a constant weight, Kate acknowledged Cyrus's message. She was just about to hang up when he cleared his throat, hesitated, then told her that Chase wouldn't be up, either, that he was in the bunkhouse getting rip-roaring drunk.

Unable to sleep, she spent most of the night in the living room, staring at Tanner's books. She finally went to bed at two in the morning, then was up again at five, when the first of the neighbors rolled in. She knew that Cyrus was feeding everyone breakfast, and she stood at Tanner's bedroom window, hoping she would see his truck among the others that arrived. Ross showed up, but Tanner didn't. And Kate couldn't get that last image out of her mind, when he'd given her that hard, cold glance and ridden off.

The only thing that provided her any kind of respite was that Burt was worn out from his outing the day before and slept most of the day. And the boys seemed content to build roads for their Dinky toys in the old garden.

It was nearly ten o'clock in the evening when the Circle S rigs started pulling into the yard. Kate had a sickening feeling that Tanner's wasn't going to be among them, and she was right. She finally went to bed at midnight, listening to the boys' even breathing in the other bed, wondering where the two McCall men were, wishing that Tanner would come home. Feeling miserable and alone and very, very guilty, she finally fell asleep.

The sound of a vehicle rolling to a halt on gravel brought her sharply awake, and she stared into the darkness, her heart suddenly pounding frantically in her chest. *Let it be Tanner,* she prayed silently. *God, please let it be Tanner.* The sound of a truck door opening came in through the open window, then she heard a quiet command to one of the dogs, and the door closed.

Closing her eyes in a rush of relief, she tried to conquer the wild flutter in her midriff, then threw back the bedclothes. Fumbling to do up the buttons that had come loose on her nightshirt, she slipped from the room, closing the door silently behind her; then, just as soundlessly, she went down the stairs.

Her heart hammering with dread and her insides in knots, she entered the kitchen.

He was at the fridge, drinking straight from a container of juice, the fluorescent light on the back of the stove and the light inside the fridge the only illumination. Worrying the top button of her nightshirt, she watched him, not knowing what to say.

Tanner turned slightly and put the carton back in the fridge, his expression altering when he saw her. He stared at her for a moment, then shut the door. The rectangle of brightness gone, Kate could no longer see his face clearly, but the way he was holding his body told her more than she wanted to know. She rubbed her thumb over the surface of the button, then folded her arms, feeling alone and vulnerable. She didn't know what to say to bridge the silence. And the last thing she wanted to do was betray Chase's confidence. Feeling as if her heart were stuck in her throat, she took a shaky breath and spoke. "I missed you last night."

Tanner held her gaze for a split second, then stared at the floor. There was something about the set of his shoulders, about the tight lines around his mouth, that made her want to cry, and she looked up at the ceiling and swallowed hard.

The ache finally eased, and she looked at him. "Please, Tanner," she pleaded softly. "Talk to me."

His face contorting in a fury of pent-up feelings, he hit the fridge with the side of his fist, then abruptly turned away. He raised his hand for a second blow, but Kate was across the kitchen before he could act. Shaken by his uncharacteristic display of anger, she seized him by the wrist, then slid her free arm around his rigid shoulders. Grasping him by the back of the neck, she used all her strength to hold him against her. "Don't," she whispered brokenly. "Please, don't." He tried to pull away, but she refused to let him go. Closing her eyes against the feelings that washed through her, she tried to soothe him with the sound of her voice. "Shh, shh," she crooned softly. "It's okay. It's okay."

He shuddered and turned his face against her neck, then dragged in a deep, ragged breath and caught her in a crushing embrace. Cradling the back of his head, Kate pressed her whole body tight against him, trying to physically give comfort, trying to wordlessly let him know that it was okay. His hand tangled in her hair as he shifted his hold, locking her flush against him. He inhaled raggedly and turned his face against her neck. "I feel like such a bastard. But I don't know how to be around kids, Kate. I never have. And I didn't realize what was happening with Mark."

Letting go of his head, Kate quickly wiped her eyes, then hugged him hard. She didn't want Tanner to know that she and Chase had talked, but she could do something he would understand. "Yes, you do," she said, her voice softly chastising. "They're just little people, that's all. You treat them how you would've liked to be treated when you were that age." She brushed back his hair, then rubbed the back of his neck. "That's all you have to do." She continued to caress him, giving him time to think about it.

After a while he released a heavy sigh, and Kate raised her head and looked at him. His expression drawn and sober, he touched her cheek. "I don't know how good I'll be at this," he said, his voice strained.

She rubbed a trace of juice from the corner of his mouth and gave him a soft, reassuring smile. "You don't have to change, Tanner. They don't want you to be anyone else."

"God, I hope you're right."

She hesitated, then spoke, her tone quiet. "Have you talked to Chase yet?"

Tanner dropped his gaze. "Yeah," he said gruffly. "I talked to him tonight."

"Good," she whispered.

Tanner caressed her hip, then eased his hold. "Why don't you go check on Burt, and I'll take a shower."

Kate placed her hands along his jaw and began stroking his mouth with her thumbs, rising up on tiptoe. "Burt doesn't need to be checked."

Tanner's pulse leapt beneath her touch, and his breath caught sharply. "Katie, I—"

Tightening her hold on his face, Kate closed her eyes and brushed her mouth against his. "Shut up, Tanner," she murmured against his lips.

He hesitated, then he whispered her name and gathered her up against him. Holding her fast, he shifted against her, and Kate gave a soft cry and opened her mouth against his. It was like touching fire to tinder, and a fury of want, a frenzy of need ignited between them, and Kate made a helpless sound against his mouth. Angling his arm across her back, he lifted her higher and caught her behind one knee, dragging her leg around him. Then he continued, sliding his hand up her thigh, his breathing fracturing when he encountered nothing but bare skin. Securing both legs around him, Kate tipped her head back and rolled her pelvis against his groin, and Tanner grasped her by the hips and held her still. "Katie—not here. I—" As if unable to control himself, he thrust up against her, then locked her against him in a savage hold. "Kate, I don't have anything with me."

Forcing her head down against his shoulder, he tightened his arms around her, his breathing harsh and labored. "Just hold on." He hauled in a deep, jagged breath, then turned toward the doorway. "And for God's sake, don't move."

Kate woke up in Tanner's bed the next morning—naked, boneless, weighted with a delicious heaviness. God, but she felt wonderful. And happy. And light—as if she could almost float. Stretching out on her stomach, she rested her head on her folded arms, listening to the sounds from outside. She wished she could stay in bed all day.

She heard the back door slam, and she sighed. Rolling over onto her back, she looked at the digital readout on the clock by the bed. Six-thirty. She sighed again. If she was going to be up before the boys, she had to get moving.

It wasn't until Kate got out of the shower in Tanner's bathroom that it hit her; she had nothing to wear. Putting her nightshirt back on, she slipped out into the hallway, her stomach dropping when she saw that her bedroom door was shut—which meant Chase had returned late last night, or Tanner had closed it when he'd gotten up. And the boys' door was still shut, as well—which meant at least one of them was still asleep. Feeling like a fool and praying that the room was empty, she eased open the door to her room, closing her eyes in relief when she saw the empty bed. The empty unslept-in bed. She grinned to herself. Somehow she didn't think Chase had spend another night on the bunkhouse floor.

By the time Kate finished dressing and was ready to go downstairs, there was a different set of sounds outside, and in the clear morning air she heard the cook house door slam. When she passed the window on the way out of the room, she heard Mark talking to someone outside. Holding back the curtain, she looked out. Mark was talking to himself. She'd seen him put the rotted rope in the truck yesterday, after he returned Chase's rope to him. Now he was out in the side yard, the end knotted in a loop, trying to rope a fence post. Experiencing a familiar tightness in her chest, she watched her small son, wishing things could be different for him.

She was about to turn away when a movement along the fence caught her eye, and she lifted the curtain farther away from the window. The ache in her chest was abruptly replaced by a different sensation. Tanner, dressed in new blue jeans, a gray suede, Western-cut sports jacket and his best gray Stetson, opened the gate and came through. He was obviously dressed for town, and he was obviously about to leave. But her heart nearly stopped altogether when she saw the coiled rope he had in his hand.

At the sound of the gate, Mark turned, and Kate could see the color drain from his face. As if he'd been caught doing something he shouldn't, he stuck the rope behind his back.

Resting his hand on his hip, Tanner looked down and worked a clod of dirt with the side of his boot. Finally he looked at the boy and spoke, his tone quiet. "I was watching you rope yesterday, Mark. I found this rope in the tack room, and I thought you might like to have it."

Mark looked from Tanner to the rope, then back to Tanner. Then Kate saw him let go of the rope behind his back. "Wow," he said, his voice quavery. "Thank you."

Kate could tell by the way Tanner looked down that he hadn't missed the little subterfuge that had taken place behind her son's back. His guilty conscience obviously getting the best of him, Mark rubbed his hands against his jeans, then bent over and picked up the rope he'd been using. "I was practicing with this," he said, shamefaced.

Tanner crouched down in front of the boy, laying down the coil of rope he'd brought and taking the frayed piece. He fingered the knot, then handed the makeshift lariat back to the boy. "Maybe we could fix this for Scott instead. You need to practice with something longer."

Mark looked up, meeting Tanner's solemn gaze. He stared into the man's eyes with the unwavering intentness of a child, then managed a wobbly smile. "Okay. We'll give it to Scott."

Tanner handed him the new rope, then got to his feet. "I have an appointment in town this morning, but maybe we can work on it later. Okay?"

Mark hugged the gift to his chest and looked up at Tanner, his eyes wide with awe, as if he'd just been handed the world. All he could do was nod and hold his rope. Tanner stared at him for a moment, then gave him a little flip on the end of his nose. "Tell your mom I'll be back later, okay?"

Mark nodded again, so much wonder on his face that he seemed to vibrate with it. "Thank you, Tanner," he said fervently, looking up at the man who stood before him. "I'll take good care of it."

Tanner stared down at him, then responded, his voice gruff. "I know you will." Squeezing the boy's shoulder, he turned and walked away.

Clutching her hands against her breastbone, Kate watched him disappear from sight, her vision blurred, so many emotions breaking loose inside her that she couldn't distinguish one from another. She wondered if Mark would ever know the significance of that gift. Or its ties to the past.

Realization dawning on her, she bolted for the door and out into the hallway, flying down the stairs two at a time. She had to catch him before he left. She just had to.

Mark was coming into the kitchen just as she was making for the door. His face still awash with wonder, he held up the rope and started to speak, but she brushed past. "Just hold on a minute, sweetheart. I've got to catch Tanner before he leaves."

She stumbled and nearly lost her balance on the last step, then caught herself on the rail. Realizing that he was about to climb into the truck, she called to him, and he turned, one hand on the open door, the other resting on his hip, the brim of his hat shading his face. Her mind was a jumble of thoughts as she went toward him. She was caught, she knew. What she had overheard was between Mark and Tanner, and she couldn't interfere in that, but there was no way she could let him leave with disquieting memories from the past foremost in his mind. Not after what he had just done for her small son.

Reaching him, she held her wind-whipped hair back from her face and squinted up at him, the sun directly in her eyes. Nearly overwhelmed by feelings too great to express, she gazed up at him, her smile not quite steady, her voice catching when she spoke. Lied, actually. "Mark said you were going to town."

The solemn expression in his eyes altered, changing to a heart-stopping look that made Kate's heart roll over. "Yeah. To Pincher," he answered, his tone husky. "Did you want me to pick up something?"

Something sweet and wonderful washed through Kate, something that made her feel light and happy. She shook her head and smiled into his eyes. "I just wanted to say goodbye."

He pulled back a wisp of hair, his touch soft and sensual, but the glint in his eyes was mostly amusement. "Saying goodbye to you is not good for my health, Kate," he responded dryly. "I tend to suffer a lot afterward."

Loving his lopsided smile, delighted that he had made such a remark and happy that the shadows were gone from his eyes, she braced her hand on his chest and kissed him.

Without touching her anywhere else, he opened his mouth and kissed her in return, his lips pliant and moist and tasting of coffee. Then, on an uneven intake of air, he broke off the kiss, his heart pounding beneath her hand. He stared down at her, one hand still slung on his hip, then he bent his head, drew his hand across his eyes and exhaled sharply. Kate, feeling unaccountably pleased with herself, straightened the lapel of his jacket. He caught her hand and held it tight, then lifted his head and looked at her, a gleam of rebuke in his eyes, amusement lurking around his mouth. "I knew you were trouble the minute I laid eyes on you in Rita's café," he said, rubbing his thumb across her palm, the very male glint in his eyes making her knees want to buckle. "And you're trouble this morning. I should have locked you in the closet." He gave her one final amused look, then climbed into the truck.

Kate remained rooted to the ground long after he had disappeared, feeling as if all her insides might disintegrate, not sure who had distracted whom.

Chapter 12

Kate finally had to forbid the boys from bringing their lariats in the house. At first it amused her when they both insisted on eating with them, sleeping with them, even going to the bathroom with them. Tanner had fixed the short, softer rope for Scotty—the ends properly taped, the frayed parts singed off—and he had shortened the one he'd brought for Mark. She thought it cute, the way they lugged those ropes around. That lasted two days. By the third day, nothing was safe. Anything that moved, and anything that didn't, was a fair target, and she was getting damned tired of being ambushed at every turn, cooking supper, hanging clothes outside, ironing, coming out of the bathroom—it didn't matter.

So she outlawed the *throwing* of ropes in the house. Burt said he would keep them in his room. Then she caught her sons taking turns trying to rope Burt's feet, with him giving instructions, so ropes were banned from the house. Period. Privately she had to admit that Mark was getting pretty good.

It was Sunday morning, four days after branding, and Kate had made blueberry waffles and whipped cream for breakfast. Everyone was at the table, even Burt, and the others had just finished eating when Chase casually mentioned that he'd talked to his business partner early that morning. Kate knew his timing wasn't casual at all; she could tell by the tautness in his jaw and the way he avoided looking at anyone.

There was a strained silence; then he told them that there were problems with supplying stock to a major rodeo, and he was going to have to roll out that morning. Kate, who hadn't finished eating yet because she'd been feeding Burt, laid her fork on her plate, then looked at Tanner. He was sitting with his forearms resting on the table, his gaze averted, rolling a fallen iris petal between his fingers. He had that same tight, impassive expression on his face that she'd seen when she'd first arrived, and it tore her apart.

Burt fumbled with the paper napkin tucked in the front of his shirt, his mouth trembling. She wanted to comfort him, as if he were a small child, but instead she tried to bridge the silence. "We're going to miss you, Chase."

He rubbed his thumbnail along the rim of his mug; then he looked up and met her gaze, his eyes stark. He started to say something, but instead he shook his head and shoved his chair back, getting to his feet. "I have to make a quick trip down to the bunkhouse before I go. I'll wheel up this way before I pull out." He left the kitchen, and Tanner shoved his chair back and got up, following his brother out of the room.

Burt muttered and looked ferocious, wiping roughly at his eyes with the napkin. "Damn fool. He should come back here where he belongs. He don't belong on some ranch in Colorado. He belongs on the Bar M—like his granddaddy before him."

Kate's own throat closed up, and she leaned over and gave the old man a tight hug, careful of his fragile old bones. "You did a fine job with the pair of them, Burt Shaw. You truly did."

He didn't answer, so she took his cold, blue-veined hand between hers to stop the trembling, and he clutched at her fingers. He stuck out his chin at her and gave her a fierce, defiant look. "I know prime stock when I see it." But then his eyes got all watery again, and he clawed at the napkin and blotted his eyes. "Damn it, woman. You must have burned something. I got smoke in my eyes."

* * *

Chase McCall knew a lot about saying goodbye. He made it quick. He made it short. But nothing he could have done would have made it painless. There were fresh tears in Burt's eyes when the black truck headed down the road, and Scott had refused to come out of his room. As soon as Chase pulled away, Mark ran along the path leading to a low hill overlooking the lane and stood there watching for the vehicle to turn onto the main road.

Tanner didn't show any emotion at all. His expression completely closed down, he took Burt into the house and put him to bed, then turned around and strode out of the room. Before Kate could even get the guardrail up on Burt's bed, she heard the back door slam. Burt closed his eyes, his face sunken with exhaustion, and Kate glanced anxiously at the door, then turned back to her patient. He opened his eyes and looked at her, then closed his eyes again and let out a sigh. "Don't forget to put a light in the window," he said, his voice thick.

Kate wasn't sure whether he meant it literally, or if the past and the present had gotten muddled in his mind. She gently wiped some moisture from the corner of his eye, then leaned over and kissed his forehead. "I won't," she said softly.

Changing the angle of the venetian blinds, she quietly left the room, pulling the door partially closed behind her. Cyrus was standing at the kitchen window, his arms folded. He turned and looked at her. "I don't usually jest bust in, Miz Quinn. But I thought you might want me to stay with Burt and the sprouts. It ain't always good when Chase leaves. 'Course, I don't think Chase is over fond of it hisself. Too much water under the bridge."

Grateful for his offer, she started for the door. "Mark's east of the house on—"

"Well, no, ma'am, he ain't. He's gone upstairs to get his brother. Figured we might try a game of Snakes and Ladders."

"I won't be—"

"Now don't go worrying about time, Miz Quinn. You'll likely find the boss saddling up that bay of his. He usually heads out to the back country for a spell after his brother leaves.''

Kate ran all the way to the barn. Between the awful feeling building in her chest and the downhill sprint, she was out of breath and flushed by the time she reached the open door. Tanner was standing with his back to her, his blue chambray shirt pulled taut across it, his horse already saddled and bridled.

The stirrup was hooked on the horn, and Tanner was making some final adjustments to the cinch. Kate gave herself a moment to catch her breath and for her pulse to settle. She couldn't even guess what was going through his mind, and she didn't know what to say, but she knew that if she didn't say something, she would have failed not only him, but herself, as well. Bracing herself with a deep breath, she stepped from the brightness into the shadowed interior, her voice not quite steady when she spoke. "Tanner?"

He stuck the end of the latigo into a slit in the saddle, then dropped the stirrup. "What?"

She folded her arms and looked at him. "I think we should talk."

He straightened the brow band of the bridle and pulled the horse's forelock free. "It has nothing to do with you."

Kate felt something slip inside her, and she started to tremble. She clutched her arms tighter and looked at him. "Who, exactly, does it have to do with?"

Tanner finally looked at her, the muscles in his jaw flexing and his eyes stony. "Just what is it you want to know, Kate?"

It was as if she'd experienced an internal avalanche—cold, fast, leveling. She hadn't known anything could hurt like that remote, icy look in his eyes. She dropped her arms and nearly turned away, but then she turned back to him, deciding to put everything on the line. "You won't give me a chance, Tanner. You know everything about me, about my family, about my marriage. I've kept nothing from you. But you hold everything back. I know bits and pieces, but I don't know the most important part—and that's how those things affected you. I don't know what it was like for you after your mother died, and I don't know how you felt when you found out about

Chase. You don't even trust me enough to tell me why you left the Bar M—or how you ended up here.''

She paused for a moment, then tightly folded her arms, her whole body trembling. "This is about trust, Tanner. About trusting me with all the really awful stuff that's happened to you.'' Suddenly unable to see, she roughly wiped at her face, desperate to make him understand. Swallowing hard, she went on, her voice trembling with emotion. "Don't you know I'd never betray anything you shared with me? Don't you *know* that?''

The back door of the barn slid open, and Ross entered, leading a saddled horse and two others with just halters on. He looked at Tanner. "You riding out?''

"Yeah, I am.'' Without looking at Kate, Tanner flipped the reins over the gelding's neck, then swung into the saddle, turning the horse toward Ross. Realizing she'd lost whatever advantage she had, Kate turned and walked quickly out the front door, struggling with the anger and the terrible hurt. What was she doing here? She already had one mess in her own life that she couldn't manage. And now she was in another one—only, this one hurt like hell.

Kate sat on the back step, watching the vibrant sunset colors change, the last rays painting the clouds caught against the mountains with hues of purple and flame and gold. She braced her elbow on her knee and propped her head on her hand, a knot of desolation catching in her throat. God, she felt miserable. And dishonest.

She'd been so wrong, so damned wrong. She'd been pretty self-righteous saying what she had to Tanner. It had taken her all afternoon to work through it, but she'd finally figured it out. His unwillingness to talk about his past was his way of surviving. And who was she to make judgments on how he dealt with his life? She hardly had an unblemished track record herself. She'd said some truly stupid, stupid things—about his trusting her with the awful stuff. That was her own insecurity talking. Trust had nothing to do with sharing pain; trust was about unconditional acceptance. He had unconditionally accepted her—and then she'd let him down. God, how she'd let him down.

The colors in the sky blurred together, and Kate hooked her heels on the edge of the step and drew up her legs, locking her arms around them. Lord, she had screwed things up. All because she'd wanted to play mother when he needed to go back into the hills and lick his wounds.

Releasing a heavy sigh, she resisted the urge to look at her watch again. It had been quarter to ten the last time she'd looked, and that had been only moments ago. He had been gone hours and hours—twelve, to be exact—and there wasn't that much light left. He hadn't had any lunch or any supper, and for all she knew, he didn't even have any water with him.

Anxiety twisting her insides into knots, she got up and entered the house, careful not to let the screen door slam behind her. The house was dark, except for the fading light coming in through the kitchen windows, and she went to the stove and turned on the fluorescent light, then went into Burt's room. She could tell by the angle of his head that he'd fallen asleep watching the sunset, and that made her feel even worse.

She pulled the covers up, careful not to disturb him, knowing how cold his hands got if they weren't covered. He opened his eyes and looked at her. "Is he home yet?"

She shook her head.

Burt continued to watch her, and Kate sat down on the edge of the bed. "What is it?" she queried softly.

She saw him fumble beneath the quilt, and she pushed the blanket down and took his hand. He made a gruff sound, then looked up at her. "Were you pulling my leg about that rehabilitation thing, or were you speaking fact?"

Kate rubbed her thumb across his knuckles, her expression sober. "So much depends on you, Burt. But if you make up your mind you're going to give it your best shot and really work with the therapist instead of against her, I think you can improve your situation a lot. You might need a cane or a walker to get around, but that's better than this. And the longer you lie here, the harder it's going to be to recover that lost ground."

He tightened his bony fingers around hers and closed his eyes. After a moment, he spoke. "So you don't think I'm on my last legs here?"

The thought of Burt dying was almost too much for Kate to cope with right then, but she somehow managed to keep her voice steady. "I don't know the answer to that. But I do know you're strong, and you have a stubborn streak a mile wide, and I also know if you make up your mind to do something, nothing on earth is going to stop you."

He looked at her, his eyes suspiciously wet as he scowled. "I ain't afraid of dying, if that's what you're driving at." He closed his eyes, and Kate heard him try to swallow as moisture seeped out from beneath his lids. "It's just that I don't want to die and leave that boy alone," he said gruffly, his mouth trembling. "I just can't abide the thought."

Her own eyes suddenly stinging, Kate swallowed and tightened her hold on his hand. He drew his good hand from beneath the blanket and awkwardly patted her arm. "You're a good woman, Kate Quinn."

"And you're a good man, Burt Shaw," she whispered unevenly.

He tightened his fingers around her hand, his tone cross. "And I can't abide tears, either."

Kate gave a shaky smile and squeezed his hand, then wiped her face with the inside of her wrist. Tucking the blanket up around him, she sat beside him until he went back to sleep, wishing her grandfather could have met him. They would have been cronies right from the start.

It was going on eleven when Kate finally went up to bed. She had planned on finding a book to keep her mind off Tanner's absence, but she couldn't focus on anything. She kept checking to see if there were any lights on in the barn, but it finally hit her that he was probably avoiding her. Dispirited beyond words, she checked Burt one last time, turned out all the lights except the control panel one on the stove, then went upstairs. She collected her nightshirt and the mobile monitor for Burt, then went into the bathroom and started running the tub. Maybe a hot bath would help.

When she came out of the bathroom twenty minutes later, there was a light on in Tanner's room. Her heart lurching, she stood there in the darkened hallway, hugging her clothes to her chest, trying to decide what to do.

Almost too ashamed to face him, she collected every bit of courage she had and approached his open door. He was standing by the dresser, the light from the bathroom the only illumination, and she realized he'd just come in. She wondered why she hadn't heard him—unless, of course, he hadn't wanted to be heard. Depressed by that thought, she pushed the door open wider, trying to ignore the frenzy in her chest. "I owe you an apology, Tanner," she said, her voice quavering. "I said some really stupid things. And you have every right to be ticked off with me."

He tossed his pocketknife on the dresser, then reached for the buttons of his shirt. The way he was standing, Kate couldn't see his face, but she could see the rigid set of his shoulders, and her stomach plummeted. There was no leniency there. Yet she couldn't blame him if he didn't want to talk to her; she'd said some pretty thoughtless things. Experiencing an awful feeling in the pit of her stomach, she tightened her grip on her clothes. Her pulse thick with dread, she spoke, her voice just above a whisper. "I just wanted you to know how sorry I am. I was way out of line." She hesitated, hoping for some response, but when she got none, she turned and started back to her room.

She was halfway across the hall when there was a movement behind her and Tanner spoke, his voice strained. "I think we need to talk, Kate."

A sudden sweep of dread made her whole body tense, and she closed her eyes, feeling sick and shaky. Lord, but that subdued tone scared her to death. Bracing herself, she turned. Tanner was standing framed in the doorway, the faint light from his bathroom casting him in silhouette, his face obscured by shadows. Kate stared at him for a moment, then retraced her steps. He stood aside, and she entered the room, her heart skipping a beat when he closed the door behind her. Unnerved by the silence, she placed her clothes on the old trunk, then stuck her hands up the wide sleeves of her nightshirt, suddenly cold. Deep in thought, Tanner stood at the end of the bed, absently tracing the grain on the bedpost, his face unreadable. Finally he dropped his hand and turned, going over to the windows. Bracing his hand on the frame, he stood staring out at the lighted yard, and Kate experienced a disquieting chill.

Rubbing her arms against it, she watched him, not knowing what to say, or if she should say anything at all. She had done so much damage already.

His hand on his hip, Tanner continued to stare out the window. After a long pause, he spoke, his voice strained. "What do you know about me, Kate?"

Her knees suddenly unsteady, she sat down on the bed, the flutter in her chest expanding. "I know that your mother died when you were six, and I know you spent the next six years in a foster home, and I know that you went to live with Cyrus and his wife on your father's ranch when you were twelve." Feeling as if she'd betrayed him in the most unforgivable way, Kate made a helpless gesture with her hand. "Tanner, please," she whispered. "You don't have to do this. I was wrong."

Tanner remained motionless at the window, not saying anything for a long time. Finally he spoke, his voice strained. "You asked me today why I left the Bar M."

Kate stared at him, her heart suddenly hammering, a sense of foreboding settling heavily in her. And she knew—just knew by the tightness in his voice, by the rigidity of his body—that this was not going to be about neglect or abuse. This was going to be about stripping away a person's pride and dignity. And she wasn't sure she wanted to hear about it. She hugged herself, her insides shaky. "You don't have to do this, Tanner," she repeated, her voice wobbling. "It's not important."

He straightened, touching the hardware on the window. "You're wrong, Kate," he answered roughly. "I do have to do this." He bent his head and rubbed his eyes, then stuck his hand in his back pocket and stared out the window. "I was not quite twelve when Cyrus and his wife took me back to the Bar M to live with him. He was the ranch foreman at the time, and probably the only person in the entire county who wasn't intimidated by my father. I guess there was hell to pay when

Chase's mother found out I was living with them. She tried to get my father to fire Cyrus, but Millie squared off with her—told her that trouble could go both ways, and if Ellie decided to kick up a stink, she and Cyrus would go to the child welfare authorities about me. My old man was being considered for a senate appointment, and Ellie was shrewd enough to know what publicity like that would do to his chances. So Ellie backed off." Tanner paused, his voice soft with recollection as he added quietly, "Those were two of the best years of my life."

Kate watched him, feeling as if he had gone somewhere she couldn't follow. Unsettled, she shivered against a sudden chill and used the sound of her voice to draw him back. "What changed it?"

Tanner gave another little shrug. "Millie died of a cerebral hemorrhage. Cyrus started drinking. I hit high school." He drew his hand out of his pocket and stilled the blind pull that was swinging in the breeze coming through the open window. He fingered the weight, then stuck his hand back in his pocket. "It was my first year of high school, and I got mixed up with a girl who was two years older. Her father had a long-standing feud with the McCalls, and he raised holy hell when he found out she was hanging around with me. Not only was I Bruce McCall's bastard, I was a half-breed to boot. Needless to say, it didn't go down well."

The heaviness in Kate's chest increased as dread settled in, and she felt as if she were at the edge of a dark, deep hole. He hadn't brought her in here to tell her about some adolescent involvement with a sixteen-year-old girl. Something much worse had happened—much, much worse. Her stomach suddenly churning, she watched him, knowing he was going to tell her, knowing he was going to be forced to relive it all over again. All because of the stupid, thoughtless things she'd said.

Tanner straightened the blind pull again, then tapped the weight, sending it swinging. He watched it for a moment, then stopped the movement. Kate could sense the avoidance in him from all the way across the room. When he finally continued, his voice was barely audible. "Every fall, a group of Bruce's political back-room buddies would come out to the ranch, supposedly to plan party strategy and get in a little hunting. A couple of them always brought women along, and things usually got pretty rowdy. I'd gotten to know the back country pretty well, so if anyone wanted to go hunting, Bruce had me go along as a guide. Cyrus dealt with them, mostly, but one night he got into a bottle, and I had to go into the house to find out what was planned for the next day. I could tell some heavy partying had been going on, and everyone was pretty drunk.''

As if getting too close to the edge of a precipice, he fell silent. Tension filled the room, and Kate's insides shrank into a hard, cold knot. Experiencing the almost strangling sensation of dread unfolding in her, she clenched her arms around her knees and watched him, every muscle in her body braced for a blow.

It felt like drowning, that awful silence, then he spoke, not a trace of inflection in his voice. ''Bruce started telling them about the trouble I'd landed myself in with the girl. He went on about how I was definitely his son, saying that he'd seen stallions who weren't as well-hung as his young buck. Everybody laughed, and he staggered off somewhere. One of the women said she wondered if it was true what they said about Indians, and she'd sure like to have a look at Bruce's young stud.'' Tanner's voice was so strained, so raw with the shame of remembering, that it was an agony to hear him, and Kate had to swallow to keep from getting sick. She let the words wash over her, not wanting to absorb their full meaning, knowing there was no way she could avoid it.

Tanner shifted, bracing his forearm on the jutting corner of the alcove, his hand resting across his mouth as he stared out into the night. Kate could see part of his face—the hard, drawn angles speaking of his pain.

He remained immobile for a moment; then he made a small, abrupt gesture with his hand. ''One of the men decided that she deserved a bonus, and the next thing I knew, they had me pinned to the floor. The men held me down, and the women stripped off my clothes, deciding they were entitled to a little fun.''

For an instant Kate thought she was going to lose her supper, and she had to close her eyes and rest her head against her knees so the churning sensation would pass, a different kind of sickness washing through her. If she could have gotten her hands on Bruce McCall right then, she would have drawn and quartered him. Without a second thought.

Feeling as if every bit of warmth had been sucked out of her, Kate lifted her head and looked at him, her stomach in knots. He was standing as he was before, his arm on the corner, his hand resting across his mouth, but now his face was like stone. But what wrenched at her heart was that beneath that rigidly controlled surface, she saw the absolute humiliation of that fourteen-year-old boy. Experiencing such a rush of feeling for that youth, and for the man he had become, Kate slipped from the bed and crossed to him. Her throat so full she didn't dare unlock her jaws, she put her arms around him, pulling his head against her shoulder, easing in a careful, constricted breath so he wouldn't know she was crying.

For an instant he simply stood there in her arms, then he let his breath go and put his arms around her. Kate closed her eyes and cradled his head against her, tears slipping relentlessly down her face.

Sensing how raw and stripped he felt, knowing without a doubt that he'd never told another living soul about what had happened, she hung on to him, finally, finally understanding the source of his reserve, his wariness, his aloofness from people. She wished she could take him right inside her and keep him safe.

Surreptitiously wiping her face with the heel of her hand, Kate swallowed hard, struggling to achieve a degree of self-control, an outward calm. It wasn't finished. Somehow she had to find the resources, the composure, to see this through to the end.

Stroking his head, she closed her eyes and forced herself to speak. "Tell me the rest, Tanner," she whispered, her voice breaking. "Finish it."

She felt his chest expand, then he tried to pull away, but she simply tightened her arms around him, determined not to let him go. Waiting for another contraction in her throat to ease, she cupped the back of his head, pressing her face against his. "Tell me," she whispered.

He remained rigid and silent in her arms, then he took a deep jagged breath and started talking. Kate wanted to kill them all. The humiliation they had inflicted on that boy, the sick degradation they had forced upon him, held down by five drunken men and explicitly fondled by two crude, equally drunk women, filled her with cold, killing rage. God, it was so twisted and sick. It made her want to tear them apart, piece by piece.

Tightening her arms around him, Kate forced herself to keep the fury out of her voice. She spoke, her tone quiet. "Your father—where was he while all this was going on?"

Easing his hold on her, Tanner fingered the collar of her nightshirt. "I don't know. It was Cyrus who broke it up. When he came in a few minutes later and saw what they were doing, he went a little crazy. He threw one of the women against the wall, then went after the others with the bullwhip Bruce used to keep on his desk. Bruce came in then, but he was pretty much out of it..." His voice trailed off, and Kate knew he was recalling everything that had happened that night. Finally he continued. "Cyrus took me to Burt's. Then he went back the next day and beat the hell out of my father. Put him in the hospital for a few days."

Kate didn't want to ask the next question, but she had to— it was part of the unfinished business. She looked at his face. "Did any of this ever get out?"

Avoiding her gaze, he toyed with her hair, straightening a curl between his fingers, his expression drawn. He shook his head. "No. Cyrus warned them that if one word was said, he'd do some talking of his own. I never went back to school—I finished high school by correspondence."

Even in the faint light, Kate could see the effect that telling had had on him. And his eyes—oh, God, his eyes. Refusing to give in to the feelings churning inside her, she freed her arms, then took his face between her hands, wanting him to look at her. "And Burt?" she queried softly.

For the first time since she had come into his room, he met her gaze. And she could have wept when she caught a tiny glimmer of humor in his eyes. "Burt was Burt." Shifting his gaze, he caught one of her hands, then carefully laced his fingers through hers. His voice was husky and a little unsteady when he went on. "He thought the world of my mother—that's one reason why Cyrus took me there. Cyrus told him a bit about what had happened, and Burt flew into a rage—said it would be a cold day in hell before Bruce McCall ever got his hands on me again." His voice wavered, and he stopped and rubbed at his eyes; then Kate felt him try to swallow. It took a while before he was able to continue. "She's buried in a little country cemetery, so he took me to her grave—my mother's grave—the next day. He told her that she could rest easy now, that he'd take good care of me."

Kate had been fighting the good fight; she'd thought she had everything under control, but that roughly spoken admission, that statement of commitment, completely did her in. Unable to see, unable to speak, she clenched her arms around his shoulders, and Tanner held her hard, his face turned against her neck.

It was a long, long time before Kate could ease her hold. She felt as if she'd been mauled, wrung out and stomped on, but there was one last thing she had to say that might offer him some solace, that might change things just a little. Rubbing the back of his neck, she turned her face against his. "I know it's not going to change anything," she whispered unevenly. "But if things hadn't happened the way they did, you might never have ended up on the Circle S with Burt Shaw."

She felt his chest expand sharply; then he hugged her so hard that she couldn't breathe, and she hugged him back, knowing that if Tanner McCall had ever needed anyone, he needed her right then. She held him until she felt the awful tension ease; then she shifted her head, smoothing her hand up his neck. He needed her. He needed sweetness and solace. And soft, soft loving. "Let's go to bed," she whispered. He went still; then he inhaled sharply and gathered her up in a hard, enveloping embrace.

Kate awoke at dawn, tucked into the curve of Tanner's body, his arm secure around her waist, his breath warm against her neck, and she let her eyes drift shut, loving the feel of waking up in his arms. She couldn't have had more than three hours' sleep, but she was feeling surprisingly rested. They had ended up talking into the night—not about his childhood or what had happened that awful night, or even about his father. Instead, Tanner had told her about Burt, about Cyrus going on the wagon and coming to work at the Circle S.

But now it was morning, and the sun was coming up. Softly rubbing the back of his hand, Kate shifted and looked at the clock. Deciding it was just too risky to stay there any longer, she lifted his arm and eased away from him. As soon as she moved, Tanner rolled over onto his stomach. Smiling down at him, she pulled the sheet up to cover him, and her stomach dropped. It was the first time she'd had a chance to see his back in any kind of light, and it was the first time she'd seen the scar. It was a long, puckered wound just on his shoulder. Her expression sober and her stomach rebelling, she dragged her gaze away and covered him, then leaned down and lightly kissed his temple. Lord, she hoped she could make things better for him. Picking up her clothes, she went to the windows and pulled the blinds all the way down, leaving the room in total darkness. Maybe, just maybe, he would sleep in.

By the time the boys got up at seven, she had fresh cinnamon buns coming out of the oven and had done two loads of laundry. She took the laundry outside to hang it on the line, the grass still dewy beneath her feet. After jamming her hair back with two combs to keep it out of her eyes, she shook the top towel out and pinned it to the line, savoring the clean, fresh mountain air.

"You've been goin' a spell, I see."

Kate turned, squinting at Cyrus. "Good morning, Cyrus. Yes, I have."

He fiddled with the brim of his hat, then cleared his throat. "Did Tanner make it back last night?"

She let the next towel sag in her hand, and she felt her throat start to tighten. Cyrus and Burt might have been the most unlikely pair ever to parent an adolescent boy, but they had done a damned fine job. Clearing her own throat, she met his worried gaze. "He got home about eleven. He's still in bed."

He gave a relieved nod. "Good. Good." He smacked his hat against his leg, then gestured to the south. "I have to head over to George Riddlestone's this morning. His missus butchered a bunch of stewin' hens for me, and he phoned—said we could pick 'em up this morning. Figured maybe them boys of yours might like an outing.'' He grinned, tipped his chin toward the house. ''Could haul Ol' Burt along. He could do with another airing.''

God, it sounded like heaven. It also sounded impossible. Jamming down that spurt of excitement, she managed a smile. ''It would be too much—''

''Won't be too much,'' he interjected firmly. Then he grinned again. ''One can't move a-tall, and the other two are halter-broke. I can manage jest fine.''

Burt was so anxious to go that he wouldn't eat breakfast, so Kate sent along a thermos of juice and a big bag of cinnamon buns, with strict instructions to Mark on how to feed Burt. Burt told her to mind her own business, that he'd been chewing his food on his own since before she was born. Kate hoped that Mrs. Riddlestone had a supply of patience and a sense of humor.

Feeling almost giddy over having some time alone with Tanner, she waved them off. She fixed a basket of cinnamon buns, two large mugs of coffee and a large bowl of fresh strawberries, then placed everything on a tray. Tanner McCall was going to get breakfast in bed.

She eased into his room, then crossed to the bed and set the tray on the floor. She was on her way to open the blinds when he spoke from behind her. ''Don't, Kate.''

She was about to tease him about still being in bed, but she stopped, remembering the look on his face when he'd told her about being stripped. Ignoring the ache around her heart, she went back to the bed. Bracing her arms on either side of his head, she leaned down and brushed a kiss along his jaw. ''I brought you breakfast in bed,'' she said softly.

Kate felt him smile as he ran his hand under her T-shirt and up her rib cage. ''Is this breakfast on the hoof?''

Grinning, she nipped his bottom lip, then looked down at him, the heavy shadows in the room tinged with a sepia tone from the blinds. "Not that kind of breakfast, Tanner. Real breakfast. Cinnamon buns, coffee, fresh strawberries."

He rubbed his hand up and down her rib cage, then stroked the indentation between two ribs with his thumb, amusement glinting in his eyes. "The real thing, huh?"

Kate kissed the corner of his mouth, a sudden frenzy in her chest leaving her breathless. "The real thing," she whispered.

His breathing faltered, and he caught a handful of hair and pulled her head down, then kissed the side of her neck, his mouth hot and moist and erotically searching.

"Tanner," she whispered, her tone a little breathless, a little urgent.

Releasing a long, tremulous sigh, he pulled one of her arms free, then drew her down on top of him, dragging her hair back from her neck before giving her another wet kiss. "The door's wide open, Katie," he said gruffly.

Weakness flooded through her, and Kate rolled her head, the feel of his mouth against her neck sending shivers up and down her spine. Barely coherent, she told him about Cyrus taking the boys and Burt. He went still, then exhaled in a rush, catching her under the jaw and holding her head as he nuzzled the taut muscle in her neck. Kate quit breathing altogether.

Hauling in a deep breath of air, he forced her head against his shoulder, holding her still. "Katie," he whispered, his voice unsteady. "I need to use the bathroom. And it might be a good idea if you went downstairs and locked the back door."

Kate knew what he was doing, and the last thing she wanted to do was leave him, but Tanner was still Tanner, and the reserve was still there. Only now she understood it. Feeling as if every muscle in her body had turned to jelly, she levered herself off the bed and left the room, having to stop and lean against the wall after she closed the door.

She did go downstairs and lock the door, then went to her room and stripped off her clothes, putting on her short cotton robe. She heard the shower running when she entered the bedroom, and she closed her eyes and leaned back against the door, her heart thundering in her chest, the thought of him touching her, stroking her, making her breathless and weak.

"Kate."

She opened her eyes and looked at him, saturated in sensation, her pulse thick and heavy. He was staring at her from the open bathroom door, his wrist braced high on the frame, his face taut. His jeans were unsnapped, and his shirt hung open, and he looked male, aroused, restrained—and hot. He stared at her, and Kate's knees went weaker and weaker; then he spoke, his voice low and strained. "Have a shower with me, Katie."

The intent was clear, but so was the fact that he was willing to let her see him at his most vulnerable. Unbearable feelings swelling up in her chest, she moved away from the door and reached for her belt. Without breaking eye contact with him, she put her own vulnerability on the line and undid her robe, then let it slide from her shoulders.

A muscle jerked in Tanner's jaw, and he came toward her, his hot gaze drilling into her. Reaching her, he gripped the back of her neck, taking her mouth in a kiss that paralyzed her and made her knees buckle. Expelling a ragged breath into her mouth, he swept her up, then turned toward the bathroom. The room was full of steam, the water from the shower running down the opaque glass in the shower stall, and Kate hung on to him with a desperate grip. The calluses on his hands were rough against her skin as he dragged his hand across her buttocks, then let her slide down his body, a spasm coursing through him as she turned flush against him. Taking her mouth in another hot, deep, wet kiss, he rubbed his hands over her hips, his breathing arrested as she pushed his arms away, then slid her hands down his shoulders and arms, stripping his shirt from his body. Breathing raggedly against her mouth, he reached for the front of his jeans, but Kate brushed his hands away, needing to do this for him. Needing to create new, untainted memories.

Opening her mouth wide against his and drinking in his taste, his need, she slid her hands under the fabric and down his buttocks, then dragged her mouth down his neck, down his chest, stopping to lick his hard male nipples. Slowly, so slowly, she settled to her knees. He made a low, guttural sound and grasped her head, his fingers snagging in her hair, holding her immobile. Sliding her hands down the backs of his thighs, she slowly licked his navel, and Tanner ground out her name and flattened himself against the wall, his hands clutching her head. She wanted to touch him everywhere, to erase the memories of those other humiliating, shaming, touches. She wanted to give him such pleasure that he would forget; she wanted to paralyze him with need. Caressing the backs of his knees, she pressed her mouth lower, then lower still, dragging her hands up and up, until her thumbs stroked the soft flesh of his inner thighs, and Tanner jerked and groaned her name. But he didn't pull her head away, and sensations piled in on her. "Look at me, Tanner," she whispered brokenly. "Please look." Then, on a soft moan, she took him into her mouth.

Lying with her head on Tanner's shoulder, Kate shifted, drawing her leg up over his, lazily stroking his ribs as she watched the blinds move in and out in the breeze. Tanner kissed the top of her head, then continued combing his fingers through her wet hair, gently easing out the tangles. He adjusted his other arm around her and stroked her hip, then spoke, his voice husky with amusement. "We're going to have to get some snorkels if we take any more showers like that."

Kate laughed softly and pinched him. "You could have just shut off the water, you know."

He found another knot in her hair and worked it loose. She could tell he was smiling when he answered. "It wouldn't have been the same, somehow."

Kate gave him a little hug, then shifted her head and looked at him, loving the warm glimmer in his eyes. She wasn't sure when or how they actually got into the shower, but by the time he backed her up against the wall and slipped into her, she'd been nearly out of her mind. And she hadn't quite recovered from it yet. Cupping his jaw, she stretched up and kissed him, loving the way his mouth went soft and pliant beneath hers. Drawing away, he released a long sigh and smoothed his hand across her hip, reluctance darkening his eyes. "It's nearly eleven, Kate," he said huskily. "Cyrus will be rolling in anytime now."

Kate heaved a sigh, as well. She wished she could stretch this morning out forever. She wiped the moisture off his mouth, then met his gaze. "Can you stay for a while?"

He smoothed her hair back, then lifted her chin and kissed her again. "I thought I'd make a day of it."

His answer filled her with happiness, and she cupped his jaw and kissed him, then reluctantly drew away. She did not want to get out of that bed. But Tanner was right; the others would be back any time. Extracting herself from his hold, she sat up, clutching the sheet against her. All at once she was faced with a new dilemma. Her robe was on the floor by the door, and she was very naked in bed. She felt suddenly shy and very awkward. Taking it off was one thing; getting out of bed and going to get it was something else altogether.

Shifting beside her, Tanner braced himself on one elbow, then turned her to look at him, his expression unsmiling. "Don't," he said softly. "Don't ever feel that way with me." Pulling the sheet from her hand, he gently, so gently, caressed the swell of her breast with the backs of his fingers; then he shifted closer and covered the nipple in a soft, wet, open-mouthed kiss. Kate couldn't breathe, and she closed her eyes and gripped his shoulder. He drew away, then pulled her head down, kissing her with immeasurable care. "You taste so damned good," he whispered huskily, and Kate wanted to dissolve.

"Tanner," she said, her tone breathless and eloquent.

She felt him smile against her mouth; then he abruptly rolled away, and she drew up her knees and weakly rested her head against them, her pulse in a frenzy. God, the things he could do to her.

She heard a dresser door open, then the rustle of clothing. When she opened her eyes, he was zipping up a clean pair of jeans. He picked up the quilt off the floor and dropped it on the bed, then crossed the room and swept up her robe. Kate experienced a sobering sensation in her midriff when she saw the scar. He brought her robe to her, a definite smile in his eyes, but Kate couldn't smile back. Suddenly she had to know.

"How did you get that scar, Tanner?" she asked softly.

He shot her a startled glance; then, much to her amazement, she saw a flush creep up his cheeks. And it wasn't shame; it was simple embarrassment. The knot of disquiet eased, replaced by curiosity. "Tanner?" she prodded.

He sat down on the edge of the bed, avoiding her gaze, straightening the empty mugs on the tray. Kate poked him in the ribs.

He exhaled and looked at the ceiling; then he turned and met her gaze. "It's not what you think."

Suddenly Kate wanted to smile. "Then what is it?"

He gave her a long look; then a small smile appeared, and he shook his head at her tenacity. Finally he gave in. "I told you about getting mixed up with a girl my first year of high school." She nodded, and Tanner gave her another long look, and she could tell he was trying to make up his mind whether to tell her or not. After a moment of consideration, he gave her a warped grin. "When her father caught us, he had a dinner fork in his hand. I ended up wearing it."

Repressing a grin, she said solemnly, "I see."

The twinkle in his eyes intensified. "I thought you would."

Clutching her robe against her, Kate leaned over and kissed him, feeling almost indestructible. Life didn't get any better than this.

Chapter 13

It lasted three days, that feeling of absolute security. But then Kate got a phone call from the hospital in Calgary, informing her that Burt had been selected as a candidate for a provincially-funded geriatric rehabilitation program.

A strange, gnawing feeling unfolded in her, and her chest tightened up, as if she couldn't get a full breath. She took down the information and verified—twice—that his personal doctor had registered him for the program. But knowing that didn't stop the gnawing feeling; it got worse.

After she hung up, she stood staring out the window for a very long time, then went into Burt's bedroom. He and the boys were watching cartoons on TV, and she picked up the remote control and shut off the set. Three pairs of hostile eyes turned her way. She indicated Mark and Scotty. "Out," she said, using the tone of voice they knew better than to argue with.

Scotty scrambled off the bed, casting a worried look at Burt. "We were being good. Honest."

She managed a small smile. "I need to talk to Burt."

Scotty looked even more worried. "But he didn't do anything."

Genuine amusement surfaced, and she straightened his hair. "I know. I just need to talk to him about something." Both boys cast dubious looks at their cohort, then reluctantly headed toward the door. Kate gave them a stern look. "And I do mean out. Like right out the back door."

Kate expected Burt to give her a hard time, so he caught her off guard when he said gruffly, "You boys go down and make sure those pups have water. And you better check and see if that old gray cat has had her kittens yet. She usually hides them in the tack room."

She waited until she heard the back door close; then she sat on the edge of the bed and looked at him. "I got a call about a rehabilitation program for disabled seniors, Burt."

He shot her a wary glance, then looked away and fumbled with his cane. Kate studied him, assessing his reaction. "What's this all about?"

Burt looked at her, then his gaze shifted away again. He tried to bluff her with belligerence. "I ain't dead yet, you know."

Folding her arms, she stared right back at him, another twinge of amusement working loose. "I know. Now, what's this all about?"

He gave her an irritated glare. "Well, if you must know, I called Doc and asked him about it."

"*You* called the doctor?"

The scowl deepened. "I can still think for myself, you know. I had Mark bring the phone in here—"

"You had Mark *sneak* the phone in here," she qualified.

"Well, you were upstairs making that damned racket with the vacuum," he retorted, as if it was all her fault. "He did what I told him and hit the numbers for me. Then I talked to Doc." He gave her a fierce look. "I told the boy not to say anything. I knew you'd get your tail in a knot."

Maybe it was a good thing, she thought wryly, that her grandfather wasn't around. Three were bad enough. Four of them colluding against her would have made her life impossible. She stared at him for a moment, then spoke. "Are you sure this is what you want?"

He gave her a disgusted look. "Hell, no. It's not what I *want*, woman. It's what I'm going to *have* to do if I want to get the hell out of this bed."

Kate's mouth lifted. Two "hells" in three sentences; he had to be aggravated. The flicker of amusement faded, and she experienced an unnerving rush in her middle, as if she'd just stepped into a rapidly descending elevator. The sensation faded, and she made herself meet Burt's gaze. "If you're going to sign up for the program, we have to let them know by tomorrow morning—and if you do go, you have to be there a week from Monday."

Looking as ill-tempered as possible, he made an impatient gesture with his hand. "Well, then, what are you sitting here for? Phone 'em and tell 'em."

"Aren't you going to talk it over with Tanner?"

"No, I *ain't* going to talk it over with Tanner."

Feeling totally unprepared for all of this, Kate rubbed her thumb over an old cut, unease spreading through her. She'd thought it would take weeks to talk him into this. Weeks. Trying not to let her uncertainty show, she looked up at him. "Are you sure you don't want to talk to him?"

Burt shook his head and made a clumsy, dismissive gesture. "I make my own road, missy. Now go phone."

She hesitated, and he waved his hand at her again. "Go on. Don't just sit there looking at me like that. I said I was going, so I'm going."

Filled with misgivings, she left his bedroom. Once back in the kitchen, she checked the number on the pad and picked up the phone, an unnerving rush hitting her. A rush that was closely related to panic. When she made the call, she would be effectively putting herself out of a job. Blocking out that unsettling thought, she took a deep breath and dialed the number. The decision was out of her hands.

For the rest of the day Kate didn't give herself any time to consider Burt's decision. Every time she thought about it, her stomach would drop and tentacles of dread would begin unfurling in her, and she would close them out and find something else to do. She polished all the furniture, she vacuumed and she collected every shred of dirty laundry she could find, but the feeling persisted.

She knew that going to Calgary was the very best thing for him. In fact, if she'd had any say in the matter, she would have had him in some kind of program weeks ago. There was no reason why, with proper retraining, he couldn't recover some mobility, some level of independence. Yes, his program technically left her unemployed, and that realization set off a host of anxious butterflies in her stomach. But until the program checked out, and until it was absolutely certain that Burt could cope with it, she would stay here.

By early afternoon she had done everything that needed doing and a dozen things that didn't. She took the last of the laundry off the line and folded it, then took everything upstairs. When she came back down, Tanner was at his desk, his back to the stairs, leafing through the mail that Cyrus had dropped off earlier. Letting the laundry basket rest against her legs, she paused halfway down the stairs. "Hi. I didn't think you'd be back until suppertime."

He shuffled through the remaining stack, then tossed everything in the basket and turned, not a trace of expression on his face. Resting his hand on his hip, he stared at her, his eyes reminding her of an eagle's eyes—haughty and unblinking—and unfeeling, so unfeeling. He didn't say anything for a moment, then he answered, his tone blunt. "I got a message from Cyrus to call Doc Casey."

Her insides dropping away to nothing, Kate stared back, feeling suddenly trapped. She made a motion with her hand, then nervously stuck it in her pocket. "You're going to have to talk to Burt, Tanner—"

"I've already talked to Burt," he interjected flatly. He stared at her for a second longer, his expression cold, then strode out of the room. Paralyzed by the sickening sensation sweeping through her, she stared at the empty archway, her heart pounding with alarm. God, what had Burt told him?

She heard the back door slam, the sound somehow releasing her, and she dropped the laundry basket and went after him. But by the time she got to the back door, his truck was turning onto the lane, and for one desperate instant she considered getting the Bronco and going after him.

Upset over his reaction, her whole system fizzling with dread, she headed for Burt's room. God, what had happened?

Not sure what she would find, she entered the room, her heart lurching to a stop when Burt looked up at her, his expression irritable. "Don't anyone know how to shut a door proper around here? Enough slamming to wake the dead."

Kate stared at him, her legs suddenly too shaky to hold her, and she abruptly sat down on the end of the cot, clamping her trembling hands between her thighs. She didn't understand. He looked as he always did. Taking a shaky breath, she spoke, her voice trembling. "Did Tanner talk to you about going in for rehab?"

Burt glared at her. "Doc had to poke his nose in. Called him and told him. You'd think I didn't have the sense of a mule, the way he keeps checking up on me."

A terrible sensation unfolding in her, Kate clamped her thighs tighter together, her pulse turning heavy. "What did Tanner say, Burt? Why is he upset?"

The old man looked at her for a moment, then started fumbling with the controls for the bed. He elevated his shoulders a little, and Kate knew he was stalling. She went cold inside. "Burt?" she queried urgently. "What's going on?"

He set the controls aside, then looked at her, his expression solemn. "He's not having any trouble with me going back to the hospital. He sees it needs doing." He turned his head against the pillow and stared off into space. "But I figure he ain't too happy about how it was done. How nothing was said to him." He awkwardly dragged his thumb across his eye, the tremor in his hand noticeably worse, and Kate saw the muscles in his throat contract. Finally he continued, his voice gruff and quavery. "Tanner don't like to get caught unawares. Makes him skittish."

Kate closed her eyes and rubbed her forehead, a chill of comprehension making her insides shrink. It wasn't skittishness she'd seen in Tanner. It was anger. And it had been aimed directly at her.

Kate could barely function after she left Burt's room. She felt like a bomb ready to explode. Every sound sent her heart into overdrive, and all she could think about was the look in Tanner's eyes.

Minutes dragged into hours, and the afternoon seemed endless. She must have gone to the window a thousand times to see if there was any sign of him. She waited supper for over an hour, then finally fed Burt and the boys, her stomach in such turmoil that she couldn't eat anything herself. Her anxiety got worse and worse, until she couldn't even sit still.

Out of desperation, she finally phoned down to the cook house at eight o'clock, her voice uneven as she asked Cyrus if Tanner had shown up there for supper. There was a long hesitation, then he said that he hadn't seen Tanner since he'd given him the message to call Doc Casey.

At a loss and needing an excuse to get out of the house, she took the garbage that could be burned out to the burning barrel, folding her arms and watching the light breeze fan the flames, sending a spiral of sparks skyward. Her nerves felt as jumpy as the flames, as unpredictable. Hugging herself tighter, she looked away, feeling as if she had nowhere to turn.

As she turned to go back to the house, she noticed that the big overhead door on the Quonset hut was open, and that the lights were on inside. The structure, which was used as a shop, was situated in a stand of trees along the road leading down to the barn, and she realized there was a vehicle up on the hoist. A funny feeling stirred in her belly, and she went down the path until she could see which vehicle it was. Her knees went weak, and she closed her eyes, waiting for the rush to pass. It was unquestionably Tanner's truck. He drove the only supercab on the place.

Kate finally lifted her head and stared at the structure, feeling what little hope she had fade away to nothing. Her vision blurring, she turned and started back toward the house, unhappiness flooding through her. She didn't know why he was so angry at her—it had to be more than her suggesting treatment for Burt—but it hurt that he was.

When Kate reentered the house, dusk had infiltrated the kitchen, and the muted sound of the TV in Burt's room was the only indication that anyone was there. Wearily raking her hair back, she stopped in the doorway, resting her shoulder against the frame. The blinds on the west window had been closed to block out the afternoon heat, but tinges of sunset crept in through the unobstructed north window. Dusk had also claimed this room, the light from the big screen creating a blue aura. Scotty was asleep on the cot, and Burt was dozing. Only Mark was awake, sitting cross-legged at the foot of the bed, the remote control in his hand, the sound low. He was watching something about volcanoes, unaware that she was there.

"Mark?"

He turned and looked at her, the light from the TV tinting the side of his face. "What?" he whispered.

Entering the room, Kate stopped at the end of the bed. "Do you think you could watch Burt and Scotty for a few minutes—I have to go over to the shop."

He nodded and turned his attention back to the TV.

Kate knew that Mark at nine was more responsible than most thirteen-year-olds, but he was still only nine. "If you need me, you blow twice on the whistle Cyrus gave you, okay?"

He nodded again. Kate wanted him to look at her, to acknowledge her instructions, but he'd done this before, staying in the house if she had to run down to the cook house for something. He could manage. She knew he could; she just didn't feel right about it.

Burt spoke from the bed. "Go and quit yapping. And put something over the young one. It's cooling off outside, and the window's open."

Feeling almost mechanical, Kate covered Scott with an extra blanket off Burt's bed, then turned and looked at the old man. "I'll be right back, okay?"

Burt made a shooing gesture with his hand.

Kate collected a jacket in the utility room and went outside, easing the screen door shut behind her. Burt was right. It was cooling off, as it did nearly every night this close to the mountains. Slipping the jacket on, she stuck her hands in the pockets and started toward the Quonset, stirrings of dread springing to life. She didn't know what she was going to say to Tanner. She didn't know what was wrong.

Reaching the shop, she paused in the doorway, the sound of a country station coming from somewhere. The truck was no longer up on the hoist, but its hood was raised, and Kate caught the distinct smell of oil. She entered, her insides clumping together into a knot. "Tanner?"

A voice came from under the hood. "He ain't here."

Kate recognized Barney Shortt's voice, and she stepped around the back of the truck. Barney did all the vehicle maintenance for the Circle S, and he showed up every two weeks to take care of things. As Kate approached, he stuck his head out from under the hood, his grubby ball cap on backward, his overalls dark with oil and grease. Kate gave him a weak smile. "Do you know where he is?"

Barney waved toward the barn with the container of motor oil he was holding. "Think he headed down to the barn—either there or the cook house."

By the time Kate left Barney, her insides were in such a ball that she felt almost sick, and she briefly considered returning to the house. But she went down the hill toward the barn instead, her heart in her throat, her hands like ice. She had never been good at confrontations. Never. But this one scared her to death.

The barn was dark, but there was a light coming from the tack room midway along the aisle, and she walked down the dark alleyway, the open doorway at the other end framing the last vibrant rays of the setting sun. Swallowing against the flutter of nerves, she stopped at the tack room door, panic grabbing at her when she saw Tanner straddling a shoemaker's bench, a bridle lying on the raised work area. Folding her arms tightly under her breasts, she spoke, her voice shaking. "Tanner."

He glanced up, his face expressionless, his eyes revealing nothing. "What?"

Kate realized he'd heard her coming and had all his defenses up and armed. She entered, closing the door behind her, then huddled in the warmth of her jacket. "I wanted to talk to you about Burt going back to the hospital."

He shot her another cold glance, then answered, his tone flat. "A little late for that, isn't it?"

Feeling her throat closing up, she gave a tense shrug. "I didn't think he'd act on his own. I just made a couple of comments about how much he'd benefit from a good therapy program. I never once dreamed he'd arrange it himself."

His hair gleaming blue-black in the overhead light, Tanner took two leather screws out of the headstall and set them on the scarred wood, then threw the broken cheek strap in a metal pail sitting in the corner. He didn't even look at her.

Desperation gripping her, Kate stared at him, needing some response from him. Something. "Tanner, please," she pleaded. "I wasn't going behind your back. I wasn't manipulating him. I just wanted what was best for him, that's all."

Twisting at the waist, Tanner reached back for the replacement strap, then turned, fixing it in place.

"Don't do this to me, Tanner," she whispered urgently.

He finally looked up at her, his face cast in harsh lines, his expression glacial. "Just drop it, Kate."

Starting to tremble, Kate hugged herself. "I can't drop it. I don't know what's wrong."

It was as if those few words uncorked his temper, and anger flared in his eyes, the muscles in his neck suddenly taut. "This has nothing to do with Burt checking into a rehabilitation program, and you know it." He slammed the leather punch down on the bench and stood up, swinging his leg over the seat. "So what are *you* going to do, Kate? Have you made other arrangements?"

Her pulse heavy with uncertainty and confusion, she stared at him, not knowing how to respond. "Of course not. I was just—"

"Of course not," he responded, his tone cold. "What *are* your plans? Or is that up for grabs?"

Feeling as if she'd been blindsided, Kate faced him, confusion mixing with dread. "Tanner, I don't know what you're talking about."

He stared at her, his face like granite. "Yes, you do. What were you planning on doing? Just disappearing one day after

Burt went into the hospital? Or were you planning on sticking around for a while?''

Kate didn't know what to say, and she stuffed her hands in her pockets and forced herself to meet his gaze. Her own defenses were under attack, and fear began to unfold in her. "I wouldn't do that to you—"

"Wouldn't you? Do you want to know something very interesting, very revealing, about you? Not once—not once in the whole time you've been here—have you ever made any kind of reference to a future here, not even casually. Not even a reference about next week, about any plans for the boys for school—or even something as insignificant as wondering what it's like here in the middle of winter. Nothing. You don't make plans, Kate. You haven't even made one offhand comment about us going somewhere or doing something in the future. *Never*—because you never intended on staying here."

An unnerving cold started deep inside her, and Kate stared at him, trying to grasp even one solid denial. But there was nothing, nothing, just a sickening feeling.

His hand on his hip, Tanner clenched his jaw and stared at the wall, visibly trying to check his fury. He didn't say anything for the longest time, then he looked at her, his expression cold and controlled, his eyes even colder. "You choose to live your life one day at time—I knew that right from the beginning. I tried like hell not to crowd you. But I can't live like that—never knowing if you're going to cut and run. You can live your life in some kind of limbo, but I can't."

He snapped up his hat and and turned toward the door. "I wish to God I'd never laid eyes on you. It wasn't worth it." He jerked open the door, giving her one final glare. "Let me know what you decide."

Feeling as if the bones had been stripped from her body, Kate numbly sat down on the bench, her whole body trembling. She didn't understand why he had attacked her that way. Locking one arm around her middle, she covered her eyes, despair washing over her. She had to be honest. She *did* know why. Because she realized what he'd said was absolutely true. She was still running. Maybe she'd been running all her life.

* * *

Kate didn't go to bed at all that night. She'd remained in the tack room for a long time after Tanner left, too fragmented to pull herself together. By the time she made the long walk back up the hill, the sky had lost its color and the stars were starting to poke through. She found a note from Mark, explaining that Tanner had told him it was all right to go to bed, that Tanner would check Burt.

Kate checked on Burt and Scott, then went upstairs to kiss Mark good-night. Tanner's door was closed, and there was no light under it. Kate peeled the quilt off her own bed and went back downstairs. She curled up in the corner of the sofa, feeling raw, as if some protective outer layer had just been peeled away. She had challenged Tanner about not sharing himself with her, but what she'd been doing was even worse. She'd skirted the truth. She'd never been forced to recognize that, but she'd been doing it for a long time, skirting the truth about herself. The truth was that she was a coward. She had never seen herself in that light before. Because of the way she'd grown up and the things she'd done with her father and grandfather, she'd always thought she had a fair amount of backbone. But she had let Roger bully her because she was afraid of the consequences if she fought back. She'd convinced herself that she'd come to the Circle S so she would have time to get herself together, but the truth was that hiding from him was easier than confronting him.

And Tanner was right: she hadn't made even the most casual reference to the future, not even once. Nor had she ever once indicated that she planned on staying. She hadn't even told him that she loved him. It was her way of being cautious. But it wasn't being cautious. It was her way of skirting the truth. No wonder Tanner expected her to walk. She'd given him nothing to indicate otherwise.

But then, Tanner hadn't mentioned love either—or anything about the future. Except with Tanner, it was different. He had told her about his past, and for him to do that, he would have had to see their future as a given. And she knew he loved her—and she also knew that he would never put those feelings into words until he was absolutely sure of her.

Feeling alone and more miserable than she had ever thought possible, she couldn't stop the tears. Finally she developed such a headache that she couldn't have slept if she'd wanted to. She watched the first fingers of dawn creep above the eastern horizon.

The sky turned from midnight blue to flame and coral, the bellies of the clouds brushed with indigo and pink. It was so beautiful—and after a little over a week, she might never see it again. That thought set off a new rush of tears, and she brushed them away with the side of her hand. Her eyes nearly swollen shut and her nose plugged solid, she pulled another tissue from the box, then tugged the quilt back around her shoulders. God, but she had royally screwed up—and she had no one to blame but herself. And she didn't have a clue how to fix it.

"It's five o'clock. Why aren't you in bed?"

Her heart lurching in fright, Kate whirled, her stomach dropping like a rock when she saw Tanner standing at the bottom of the stairs. She hadn't heard a sound. Not a single sound. Remembering the mess her face was in, she turned back and faced the windows, quickly wiping her nose. She was afraid that if she tried to say anything, she would start crying again, and that would only make matters worse. If they could get worse. Swallowing the clog in her throat, she made a motion toward the windows. "I was just watching the sunrise," she said, her voice thick.

He came over and lifted the corner of the quilt, then released it and dragged his hand down his face. Jamming his hands on his hips, he stared out one of the windows; then with a heavy sigh, he sat down on the coffee table and hunched over, his forearms resting across his thighs. Finally he raised his head. "You haven't been to bed, have you?" he asked gruffly.

Unable to meet his gaze, Kate shook her head.

He fingered the edge of the quilt, his expression somber; then he reached out and took her hand.

Grateful for that one small gesture, Kate locked her jaw against the intense ache filling her chest, her eyes welling up again. Tightening her fingers around his in a death grip, she nearly broke down when he folded her hand between both of his. His head bent, he rubbed his thumb across her nails in solemn preoccupation. "I don't know what to say, Kate," he said, his voice uneven.

Kate wiped her face with the heel of her hand, knowing she was only going to get one chance to make things right. Struggling against the unrelenting cramp in her throat, she tightened her grip on his hand and spoke, her voice shaking. "You were right, Tanner," she whispered brokenly. "I haven't talked about us or the future. I didn't realize until last night that that's my defense mechanism, just like aloofness is yours." Afraid she was going to start crying in earnest, she forced down a deep breath, fresh tears slipping down her face. She balled up the damp tissue in her free hand, then looked up at the ceiling, reaching deep down for control. Finally she was able to will away the awful constriction. "I never told you how much this means to me. And I never told you how much I never want to leave here." Her voice broke, and she waited for a moment, waited until she knew she could get the words out without coming completely apart. Tightening her fingers around his, she took a tremulous breath and continued, her voice fragmenting. "And I never told you how much I love you. But that was also part of my defense mechanism." She squeezed his hand, silently imploring him to look at her, and when he raised his head, she could barely see him. "I can't promise you much," she whispered unevenly. "But one thing I can promise you is that I will never just disappear. When I get my life figured out, you will be the first to know."

The need to cry disabling her, and unable to see, Kate started to wipe her face on her sleeve, but Tanner brushed her hand away, wiping away her tears with his hand. That almost finished her off, and a sob nearly escaped, but she clenched her jaw, swearing she would suffocate before she broke down in front of him. He leaned over and pulled another tissue from the box, then caught her nose. "Blow," he commanded gruffly.

Caught completely off guard by his actions, she gave a surprised little laugh and caught at his wrist. "Tanner—"

"Blow," he instructed again. He met her gaze, a tiny flicker of humor appearing in his eyes, and her heart lifted just a fraction. Feeling a little foolish and a little bit forgiven, she complied. He dropped the tissue on the pile at her elbow, then brushed the tangle of hair back off her face. "Better?" he asked, his tone still gruff.

It *was* better—not because she'd blown her nose, but because he was there, and because he was being kind to her. But she couldn't tell him that.

He rose, pulling her upward. "Come on."

Kate shed the blanket and untangled her feet, giving him a bewildered look.

He waited until she was standing, then he swept up the quilt. "You're going to bed," he said in response to her silent query.

She resisted the tug of his hand. "I can't, Tanner. The boys and Burt—"

"I can take care of Burt and the boys. You're going to bed."

He went with her upstairs, and Kate fought more tears with every step. He was being kind. But he didn't look at her, and she knew just how far he'd withdrawn when he didn't stop at his door but led her across to her room. He closed the blind and pulled the quilt over her, then went to the bathroom and got a cold compress for her face.

His expression drawn, he crouched down by the bed and pulled her hair out of the way, then wiped her face. Another huge wave of despair rolled through her. Her vision blurring, she caught his hand. "I'm so sorry, Tanner," she whispered, her voice breaking. "I didn't see what I was doing."

He finally met her gaze, his expression solemn. "I know you didn't." He leaned over and pulled the quilt over her shoulders. "Now go to sleep," he said, his voice strained.

Feeling as if her heart were in tatters, Kate closed her eyes, more tears seeping out from beneath her lashes. She heard the door close behind him, and she pressed the cold compress over her face. God, she didn't know what she would do if he shut her out.

Chapter 14

The next week was a bad one for Kate. Tanner remained distant, almost as though he had physically separated himself from everyone, but in other ways there was a new level of carefulness between them. As if they both recognized the fact that they were on shaky ground, with neither of them wanting to cause any more damage. Kate couldn't define it, really, but it showed up in a dozen little ways, like when she'd mended several of his shirts, and he made a point of thanking her. And when he took a basket of laundry upstairs, she made sure she let him know she appreciated it.

But their conversation was always strained and meager, as if they were skirting a danger zone—and Kate had slept alone ever since the phone call. She often lay awake, listening for sounds from his room, hoping that something, anything, would bring him to her. But she knew that wouldn't happen, and she missed him so much that she felt as if someone had torn her heart out. But then she would catch him watching her, his eyes so stark and somber, and she would have to go upstairs and lock herself in the bathroom. She hadn't cried as many tears in her whole life as she cried in that one week.

She stood at the kitchen sink, scrubbing new potatoes that Cyrus had got from the Hutterites, her expression pensive. It was Friday, exactly one week since the hospital had phoned, but it felt like an eternity. She hadn't been sleeping that well, and even scrubbing potatoes seemed to take an enormous amount of effort. And she hadn't even thought about what she was going to do now. Burt had made it plain that he expected her to be there when he came home, and Kate wanted to be there. But she didn't know how to undo the damage she'd done without it seeming like a blatant attempt to do just that. It had to be honest. . . .

"Cyrus is cheating at cards."

Kate looked down at Scott, who was standing watching her. "Pardon?"

He reached into the sink and took one of the carrots she'd already cleaned. "Cyrus is cheating at cards."

Kate dropped the potato she'd just cleaned in the pot, then gave him a scolding look. "Who told you that?"

"Burt." He took a bite, then connected drops of water on the counter. He didn't say anything for the longest time; then he spoke, his voice uneven. "Will Burt be scared in the hospital?"

Kate dried her hands, then crouched down in front of him, taking him by the shoulders. "No, honey," she said quietly. "He's not going to be scared. He might get lonely, and there will be times when he'll be discouraged, but he won't be scared."

"Will we be able to go see him?"

She wiped a smudge of dirt off his cheek. "I don't know if we'll be able to go see him or not, but we'll be able to phone him." She lifted his chin and made him look at her. "He's going to be fine, Scotty. Honest. He might even make some new friends."

He looked at his mother, his small face solemn. Then his eyes filled up, and his mouth started to tremble. "I just wouldn't want him to be sad," he whispered.

Kate hugged him, cuddling him close, not wanting to break down in front of her small son. She couldn't do that to him. Struggling against the awful pressure in her chest, she smoothed down his hair. "I think you need to talk to Burt about this, Scott," she said, her voice unsteady. "It'll make you feel better. Honest."

She felt him dash away his tears; then he pulled out of her arms. Wiping away a smear of moisture on his cheek, she lifted his face again. "Okay?"

He nodded.

Kate watched him return to Burt's room; then she turned and headed for the stairs, unable to hold back the tears. God, she wished she would quit feeling so damned wretched. She locked herself in the bathroom and had a good cry, then used the toilet, giving a sigh of resignation when she saw the dime-size stain in her panties. No wonder she was feeling so moody. She reached for the supplies under the vanity, then went stock-still, a fizzling sensation coursing through her. She counted back in her head, then closed her eyes, the fizzling sensation turning into a cold rush. Tired. Tears. A rusty colored stain. She should have known.

She numbly attended to herself, suddenly so shaky, she wasn't sure her legs were going to hold her. She was pregnant. As sure as anything, she was pregnant. Suddenly too shaky to stand, she sat down on the edge of the tub, trying to remain rational. Except for that very first time, he had always been adamant about using something. But obviously something had gone wrong at least once. Lord, she couldn't believe it. She was going to have Tanner McCall's baby. Elation washed through her in one fantastic rush, and she started to tremble all over. Sliding to the floor, she drew up her knees and rested her forehead against them, so weak from shock that she felt light-headed. A baby. She couldn't be more thrilled—or more scared. She couldn't tell Tanner—not now. Not after this past week. Not until she put her own life in order. Which meant she was going to have to deal with Roger, and she was going to have to face him soon. Locking her arms tighter around her legs, she raised her head and stared into space, wondering how Tanner would react when she told him she would be leaving, that she was going back to settle her life.

Kate stopped, a shock of realization blossoming in her.

That was what he'd needed her to do all along. He needed her to make the conscious decision to shed her past, to get on with her life. More than that, he needed to know that she was here not by accident, but by choice.

At first it was all so simple, but the more Kate thought about it, the more complex it became. And by late that afternoon she was having such an attack of self-doubt that she changed her mind a dozen times about what to do. The only thing she was sure of was that whatever action she took, it was going to have to be quick. She could not continue to do this to him, keeping him hanging the way she had.

When he came in for supper, his expression strained, she felt even worse. She had been so unfair to him. Somehow she got through the meal and the rest of the evening, but as soon as it was humanly possible, she went to bed, feeling wretched and miserable and unhappy, and like such a traitor. She'd been so blind to what she'd been doing to him. So blind.

She spent most of that night worrying about it, but by morning she'd come to at least one decision. She was not going to tell Tanner that she was certain she was pregnant—not before she dealt with Roger. If Tanner knew, he would insist on going with her. Without question, his presence would make things a hundred times easier for her, but for her own self-respect, she had to do this on her own. No one else could do it for her.

But that wasn't the only reason why she didn't want to tell him. She wanted to wait until she had absolute medical confirmation that she was pregnant. But more importantly, she wanted to tell him when all this was behind them, when they were able to go on without looking back.

She knew it was going to be hard to face him, so she put it off until Saturday night. She probably would have put it off longer, but Tanner had made arrangements to check Burt into the hospital on Sunday evening, which meant they would be leaving the Circle S sometime the next afternoon.

Finally it was time to talk to him alone. She put the boys in bed and got Burt settled for the night, then she stood out in the kitchen, her heart hammering and her stomach in a mess. All she had to do was explain that she was going back to B.C., and that she wanted to go, while Burt was in the hospital, when she wasn't needed here. It was straightforward and direct, and it shouldn't have scared her to death. But it did. God, but it did.

Tanner was at his desk going over a long column of figures, a cold cup of coffee by his elbow, the angle of the banker's lamp obscuring his face in shadows. She paused, nearly paralyzed with doubt. Knowing she could not put this off any longer, she spoke, her voice unnatural. "I need to talk to you, Tanner."

He glanced up, stared at her for an instant, then looked back down. "Then talk."

Not sure how long she could keep herself together, she reached down and touched the base of the lamp, then folded her arms. "I think I'd better go back to B.C. while Burt's gone. I've got to put an end to this mess with the boys' father."

Tanner didn't even look up. His voice had a hard edge of finality to it when he responded. "Fine."

Feeling as if solid ground was slipping away from beneath her, Kate hugged herself and swallowed hard, knowing she had to reach him, to make him understand—or she wouldn't be coming back at all. "I know I let you down," she whispered, her voice breaking. "And I know you don't have a whole lot of faith in me, but I'm trying, Tanner. You've got to believe I'm trying." She looked away, clenching her jaw until the awful contraction eased, trying to will away the swell of tears. There was a long strained silence, then she quickly wiped her face and huddled in the warmth of her arms. "I've got to go back and do this. I've got to deal with Roger, and I've got to make sure my divorce gets finalized. I've got to settle it once and for all."

He didn't respond. He continued to check figures on the list as if he hadn't heard her, and fear swept through her. Nothing. God, nothing. Her breath jammed up in her throat. "Or don't you care?" she whispered, fear making her voice tremble.

He didn't move; then he slammed the pencil down and rose abruptly from his chair, his sudden action making her heart lurch. He went over to the door leading to the veranda and braced his hand on the frame, staring out through the screen. He didn't say anything for a moment, then he spoke, his tone low and vehement. "After you settle all this, are you coming back here, or is that up for grabs, too?"

He had never seemed farther away, and Kate struggled to bring everything under control, to fight her way through this. When she finally was able to speak, she looked up at him, her voice breaking with unhappiness. "I love you, Tanner. You may not believe that right now, but I do. And if you want me back, I'll be back."

There was a long pause; then he spoke, the harshness gone from his voice. "Why are you doing this, Kate?"

"Because," she whispered unevenly, "I want us to have a life together. I want us to be a family."

He dropped his hand and turned, staring at her across the semidark room; then he exhaled roughly and rubbed at his eyes. When he raised his head, some of the tension had left his face. He met her gaze, his voice quiet when he asked, "How long will you be gone?"

The rush of relief made her weak, and she started to tremble. "I don't know." She took a steadying breath, the effort making her chest hurt; then she spoke again, her voice soft and beseeching. "Just know that I *am* coming back. But I've got to get rid of all the other garbage before we can go forward. You know that, don't you?"

He stared at her for a long time, then turned and stuck his hands in the back pockets of his jeans. "Yeah," he said quietly. "I know that."

Kate watched him, not sure what to say, what to do. But when the silence stretched out, she realized there really wasn't anything more to say. Giving him one last glance, she turned toward the stairs, suddenly so drained that she could barely move. She was partway up the stairs when Tanner spoke. "Kate."

She stopped and looked back, and he turned from the window. He stared at her, a somber expression in his eyes. There was a strained pause; then he spoke, his voice gruff. "No trips downstairs tonight, all right?" The corner of his mouth lifted a little. "If you keep it up, Burt's going to start expecting regular visits at two in the morning."

Kate had to fight back another wave of tears. It made her heart ache, knowing he'd been aware of her middle-of-the-night rambles. It meant that he'd been sleepless, too. She managed a small smile in return, not sure how she was going to get through the next few minutes. "I don't think I'll have to worry about that tonight." She gazed at him, wanting so much to touch him, but she forced another smile instead. "Good night."

He tipped his head. "Good night."

Kate was just about to close her bedroom door when she heard the screen door onto the veranda squeak open; then she heard his footsteps on the board floor. She closed her eyes and wrestled with a dozen emotions, then shut her door. She was going to have to make do with the fact that he could have let her go up to bed without saying anything at all. But he hadn't. And she had to believe that one small gesture meant something.

Kate awoke very early the next morning. The room was darkened and the door closed, and for one disjointed instant she thought she was in Tanner's room. Then she realized where she was. Except she hadn't remembered pulling the blind the night before, and she distinctly remembered lying down on top of her quilt. Not wanting to think about Tanner or the fact that he might have been in her room sometime during the night, she thought about getting up and slipping downstairs to watch the sunrise, but she closed her eyes instead. She was just too tired, too miserable, to face anything.

The next time she awoke it was nearly eleven o'clock, and she came out of bed in such a rush that she had to grab the bedpost and wait for her head to clear. When she opened her eyes, the first thing she saw was the quilt, and her stomach dropped away to nothing. It wasn't her quilt that had covered her. It was Tanner's. Gathering it up, she closed her eyes and hugged it against her, knowing that if she started crying, she would never stop. He had come. In the night and silently—but he had still come, and that gave her one small ray of hope.

Everyone was in the kitchen when she went downstairs, and Burt glared at her. "Well, where have you been? We're going to be leaving in a few hours, and you're lollygagging around."

For the first time in days Kate experienced a genuine flicker of humor, but before she had a chance to respond, Tanner interjected, his tone abrupt, "She hasn't had a day off since she got here. I think we can spare her a few hours."

His response had a devastating effect on her, and she felt dangerously close to tears. The fact that he'd come to her defense over such a little thing meant the world to her—Lord, she wanted to hang on to it just as she had the quilt—but somehow she had to get things back on track, or everyone would end up feeling miserable.

She had to dig for it, but she finally managed to come up with a smile. "Nice to see you this morning, too, Burt. Tanner must have fed you porridge for breakfast."

Burt snorted. "Porridge? I've tasted better wallpaper paste."

It wasn't much, but it was enough to ease the tension, and Kate took the rest of the day hour by hour, knowing that if she let herself think beyond that she would be a mess. She held it all together really well until they loaded Burt in the Bronco and she had to help the boys up to say goodbye. Scotty was first, and Kate saw him push his green dinosaur into Burt's hand, then he gave the old man a hug. The glimmer of tears in Burt's eyes was more than Kate could handle, and her throat started to close up. But when Mark climbed up and hugged the old man, and the tears slipped down his cheeks, Kate's own vision blurred. Fifteen minutes. Fifteen minutes. Somehow she had to get through the next fifteen minutes.

It was her turn, and she nearly lost it when he put his frail arms around her. "Take care," she whispered brokenly. Then she looked across the cab at Tanner, knowing this was goodbye to him, as well, remembering something Burt had said to her once. "Keep a light in the window."

His face like granite, he stared at her, then abruptly looked away and nodded. She wanted to say so much more to him—that she would be back, that she wanted him to take them on a trail ride in the mountains, that she wanted to plant tulips

along the east side of the house in the fall. But it was too late
for that. So she gave Burt another hug, then closed the door—
hanging on, hanging on until they pulled out of the yard. She
stood at the gate, unable to hold back the tears any longer,
watching the truck turn onto the main road. Then she turned
and went into the house, wishing she could have found some
way to make him understand what she'd been trying to say.

She entered the kitchen, overcome with the nearly irrational urge to throw something on the floor. Then an idea hit
her—like a flash of light, and she turned, prepared to go after
them, knowing she would never catch them. Dragging her hair
back off her face with both hands, she tried to stop crying,
tried to think; then she made a beeline for the phone.

Her hands shaking so much she could barely press the but-
tons, she entered the numbers for the cellular phone in the
Bronco. It rang twice; then his voice came across the distance.
"Tanner."

She wiped her face on her sleeve, struggling for just a small
piece of composure. "I just wanted you to know," she said,
her voice thick with tears and misery and hope, "that I've always hated this awful gray linoleum."

There was an electric pause, then he answered, his voice
gruff. "Is that so?"

Relief rushing through her, she wiped her face again. "Yes,
and it's going to be the first thing to go when I get back." Not
expecting him to answer, not even wanting him to, she gripped
the receiver and tried to will away the ache. "Take care, love,"
she whispered, then hung up the phone.

The next morning Cyrus drove her to Pincher Creek, where
she and the boys caught the first bus heading west. It was July
20, the hottest day of the summer, and Kate had never felt so
cold in her life.

Five weeks. Thirty-five days. And they were some of the
longest days Kate had ever lived through. Fear, uncertainty,
loneliness, self-doubt, mental exhaustion and, toward the end,
morning sickness. It was something she never wanted to go
through again. But she survived it.

She had left the boys with her parents, then gone on to confront their father alone. She had been terrified, knowing what was ahead of her, but she was met with one piece of good news: her lawyer had pushed the divorce through, and it would be final at the end of September. The bad news was that Roger was threatening legal action over the boys and was getting nasty about it.

It was one night a little over three weeks after she'd left the Circle S—a night when everything piled in on her, and she felt as if she had her back to the wall, the night she'd come within an inch of calling Tanner—that inspiration struck. The thought of acting on it scared her to death, but the alternatives were even worse, so she had no choice but to follow through.

Roger had his own plumbing business—a very successful and profitable plumbing business—and Kate knew he gave discounts to customers who paid cash—cash that she strongly suspected was never included on his income tax returns. She also knew that he kept records of those cash transactions in the safe behind his credenza. If she could get her hands on those, they would be her ticket out of a very nasty mess.

She'd never once expected her keys to still open the shop. But they had. What had changed was the combination on the safe, and she'd nearly panicked. But the old combination had been the day, month and year he'd incorporated the business. So in a darkened office at three in the morning she had gone through all the dates that had been significant to him—the safe opened on the day, month and year the chamber of commerce had named him businessman of the year.

Once the safe was open, she'd taken the papers out of the thick file folder, replacing them with old invoices, and reset the lock. Then she reset the burglary alarm, locked the door and drove away. She made it two blocks before she started to shake, and she hadn't stopped shaking for two hours after. But for the first time she felt totally empowered, and she knew, *knew*, that she had secured control. She had photocopies made of all the records she'd taken, sent the originals to herself at the Circle S, gave a set to her lawyer, and she kept a second set with her.

And when she walked into his lawyer's posh office, it felt so good, knowing she had the upper hand.

Roger tried to bully her, to intimidate her—and his lawyer tried to threaten her with frightening legal action. Her response was to push the bundle of copies across the conference table to Roger; then she smiled and told them exactly what she wanted. She would retain full custody of the boys, Roger could have limited visitation privileges providing the boys wanted to see him, and she wanted education trust funds set up for each of them, which she would administer. He could have the house, his business and any other assets. She didn't want them. And she didn't want child support. But if he ever tried to intimidate her again, or if he ever made any more threats concerning the boys, she would send the file where it would do the most damage. And then he wouldn't be seeing anyone for a very long time. Roger had looked as if he'd been poleaxed.

She met with Roger and the two attorneys one more time after that, the day she was to sign the necessary papers for the transfer of ownership and guardianship of the boys' trust fund. Roger tried to bully her again, saying he could have her charged with breaking and entering. Her lawyer pointed out that since she was still listed as a shareholder, that would be pretty foolish. Kate's response was to take the shop keys off her key ring and lay them on the table in front of her. Roger got the message. He withdrew his threat, Kate signed her shares of the business over to him and he got his keys and signed documents.

She spent the last week with her parents, making arrangements to ship the few things of the boys' that she was taking with her, and it was there that she went to the doctor and had her pregnancy confirmed. Due date: the first part of April. For some reason the night of her appointment was when everything caught up to her—the stress, the worry, the awful anxiety—and she went to bed at seven and slept for twenty hours straight. It was as if knowing that she had that tiny being growing inside her was a signal for her body to simply shut down.

She borrowed her mother's car for the return trip. She couldn't handle another bus ride, and she needed to make the transition from one life to another with just her and the boys. She would get the car back to her mother somehow. She just wasn't up to worrying about it at the moment.

It was a long trip—a long, tiring trip. And after nearly two days with nothing to do but think and drive and referee fights, Kate's nerves had worn thin. And they got worse the farther south she went.

When they drove through Bolton, she got such an anxiety attack that she started to tremble, and when she reached the turnoff for the gravel road, she had to stop until she quit shaking. It seemed to take forever, that last seven miles, and with each mile her heart beat a little harder and the butterflies got a little bigger. It wasn't until she pulled up to the house and parked by the gate that she realized there wasn't another vehicle in sight.

Not wanting anyone to know she was back until she saw Tanner, she unloaded the car, then parked it in the garage beside the Bronco. She was halfway between the garage and the house when the boys came flying out.

"Mom! Mom! Come see! You've got to come see."

Without giving her a chance even to think, they started dragging her up the walk. Scotty pulled at her hand, urging her to hurry. "Are you ever going to be surprised, Mom. Boy, are you ever."

"Don't tell," ordered his brother. "It'll spoil it if you tell."

They dragged her through the kitchen and up the stairs, and, not sure what to expect, she went along with them. She reached the top of the stairs and stopped dead in her tracks.

The gray linoleum was gone. In the hallway. In the bathroom. In the boys' bedroom. There was only beautiful bare wood—freshly stripped and sanded. Her room had been started, but not completed, and the fourth bedroom, the one full of old furniture, hadn't been touched. But the rest—ah, God, the rest. It was enough to leave her reeling. She sat down in the hall, so many emotions cartwheeling through her that she couldn't tell one from the other. The gray linoleum was gone. She tipped her head back against the wall and closed her eyes, giving way to overwhelming relief.

"Why are you crying, Mom? Don't you like it?"

Kate opened her eyes and looked at her sons' worried faces, and she laughed through her tears. "I love it."

Mark answered. "Me too."

Wiping her eyes with the side of her hand, Kate gazed at him, knowing she was going to have to make some explanations. She knew they understood about the divorce, and she'd told them that they were coming back here to live—that this was going to be their home—but she wasn't sure if they understood what that meant exactly. Now seemed like the right time to make those explanations. She lifted Scotty onto her lap, then drew Mark up against her. "There are going to be some changes now that we're back," she said, her voice soft. "You guys understand that, don't you?"

Mark looked at her, his gaze open and direct. "You mean like you and Tanner getting married?"

An hour ago Kate wouldn't have been sure how to answer that, but sitting here on the bare wooden floor, she had no doubts at all. "Yes, but not for a while. Not until your dad's and my divorce is final."

They both accepted it as if it was old news, and Scotty, who was obviously bored with all this, started picking at a scab. Amusement flickered, and Kate caught his hand. Screwing up her courage, she forged on. "That means that I'm going to be sleeping in Tanner's room from now on."

Scotty looked at her and frowned. "You mean like on TV?" Kate prayed that Burt had been censoring the program content when they'd watched TV together. "Yes, like that."

He made a face. "Yuck." He scrambled off her lap. "I got to go to the bathroom."

Kate wanted to smile, but she glanced down at Mark. "Is that okay with you?"

He gave her a confused look. "If Scotty goes to the bathroom?"

She did smile then. "No. If I sleep with Tanner."

He gave her a skeptical look. "I don't have to sleep with anyone, do I?"

Kate laughed and ruffled his hair. "No, not until you want to. Then we'll talk." She got to her feet. "Let's get things put away, okay?"

* * *

Kate hadn't known one compact car could hold so much, so by the time they got everything put away, it was well after six. She made the boys some supper, sent them up for a bath, then let them watch some TV in Burt's room. Scott crashed almost immediately, but she let Mark stay up until eight, then carried Scott up. She had a bath herself, trying to will away the butterflies that kept springing to life. She was just so damned nervous.

It occurred to her that he might be in Calgary with Burt, but she didn't even want to consider it. He had to come home tonight. He just had to. She paced from room to room, the butterflies getting bigger, anxiety making her restless, every minute longer than the last. She didn't turn on any lights, partly because she didn't want Cyrus walking up to to see what was going on, and partly because she knew she couldn't stand the brightness. She finally made herself sit at the kitchen table and watch the light fade from the western sky, nervous tension building in her. It felt as if she'd been waiting a lifetime for him to walk in that door. A lifetime.

It was nine when she heard a vehicle drive in, and she went absolutely still, listening for some sound from outside. She heard the gate creak, and she closed her eyes, her heart suddenly clamoring in her chest. Then she waited for the back door to open, and it struck her what it must have been like for him night after night, coming home to an empty, dark house. There was the sound of him removing his boots, and she stood up, compelled by the frenzy inside her, immobilized by anxiety, her pulse so labored that she could feel it all the way down to her fingertips. She waited, waited, her gaze riveted on the door; then a dark shape appeared, and the light flashed on.

He went absolutely still when he saw her. Not a trace of anything on his face. He just stood there, staring at her. Then he clenched his jaw and bent his head, gouging at his eyes with his thumb and forefinger, his face twisting with emotion.

Kate was so shaky, she wasn't sure how she made it across the room and into his arms, but she did, and Tanner made a choked sound and crushed her roughly against him, holding on to her as if she were his next breath. His chest heaved, and he clutched her tighter, his voice raw and shaking. "Ah—God, Katie," he whispered raggedly. "What took you so long?"

Burying her face against his neck, Kate clung to him with every ounce of strength she had, holding on to him like salvation. She had come home. God, she had finally come home.

Night sounds filtered in through the open windows, and the clock on the bedside table changed from 11:04 to 11:05. Kate shifted her head on Tanner's shoulder, then slowly smoothed her hand up the thick wall of his chest. He trapped her wandering hand beneath his, and she smiled, finding it incongruous that someone as big and as male as Tanner should be ticklish. He caressed her hand, then raised it to his mouth and kissed her fingertips. "What are you smiling about?"

Rising up on one elbow, she looked down at him, glad that she could see his face in the muted illumination from the yard light. "I'm smiling because I'm happy, and I'm smiling because I'm glad to be home. And I'm smiling because that awful gray linoleum is gone." She leaned down and kissed him on the mouth, running her freed hand back up his rib cage. "And I'm smiling because you're ticklish," she whispered against his mouth.

He gave a huff of laughter and caught her hand again, holding it secure against his chest. "Stop it, or I'll throw you on the floor."

Shaking back her hair, she grinned down at him. "No, you won't." They had made love three times in the past three hours, but they had also talked. He'd told her about Burt's amazing progress, about how he'd felt when he got the package she'd sent herself in the mail, about starting on the floor the night he got back from Calgary.

She'd told him everything that had happened while she was gone, told him that her divorce was final—she'd also told him about the talks she'd had with the boys, including the one about them sleeping together. The only thing she hadn't told him was that she was pregnant. And there had been a reason for that. She'd wanted everything else out of the way. She wanted that bit of news to be the beginning of their new life together, not tied in with the finalization of her old. She wanted it to be special, and it seemed right that she should tell him here in this bed.

Her expression growing sober, she stroked his cheekbone with her thumb, a funny little flutter unfolding in her chest. "How do you feel about being a father, Tanner?" she asked quietly.

He smoothed back her hair, then met her gaze, his expression solemn. "I'll do my best, Kate," he answered, his tone husky. "It might take us a while to sort things out, but we'll make it work."

Kate smiled; she knew that he would do his best for the boys. She'd seen that already. She leaned down and kissed him again. "That's not what I meant," she chastised gently. "I mean as in baby. Like around the first part of April."

He didn't move a muscle. He stared up at her, and when she smiled, he closed his eyes and hugged her fiercely against him. She felt his chest expand, and he tightened his arms even more. "Are you sure?"

She chuckled. "Dead sure. And I've got the morning sickness to prove it."

He didn't say anything; he just held her like that, and Kate could feel his heart hammering beneath her hand. She knew he needed time to assimilate the news, to digest it. She gave him a few moments, then she kissed the curve of his neck, and Tanner inhaled deeply. Catching her under the chin, he lifted her head and stared into her eyes. "Are you okay with this?" he whispered, his gaze solemn.

She smiled and touched his mouth. "Thrilled to bits is more like it."

He closed his eyes and drew her head back down against his shoulder, his fingers tangled in her hair. She felt him swallow; then he pressed a kiss against her forehead. "So am I," he whispered huskily. "God, so am I." His chest expanded again, and he tightened his hold on her. He held her for a long, long time—just holding her, as if he couldn't let go, as if he needed to hold her more than he needed anything else.

Finally he eased his hold and raised her face, giving her a soft searching kiss. Releasing his breath in a long sigh, he looked up at her, the expression in his eyes making her heart contract.

"I love you, Katie," he whispered, his voice uneven.

Kate held his solemn gaze for a moment, her heart so full that it was almost too much to contain, the last knot of uncertainty unfolding in her in a joyous rush. Closing her eyes against the sudden swell of emotion, she hugged him hard, her happiness absolute and complete. Swallowing against the ache in her throat, she cradled his head tightly against her. "God, but I love you, Tanner. So much."

He hugged her back, his hand buried deep in the tangle of her hair. He didn't say anything for the longest time; then he raised his head and looked at her, his eyes dark with emotion. "We're going to have a good life together, Katie," he said, his voice uneven. "I'm going to do everything in my power to see that we do."

Kate smiled and took his face between her hands, lightly stroking his high cheekbones with her thumbs. Then she lifted her head and brushed a soft kiss against his lips. "I know we are," she whispered against his mouth. And she did.

In fact, she was beginning to think she'd known it right from the very first.

Epilogue

Kate sat on the top step of the veranda, her knees drawn up, watching the sunrise unfold in the eastern sky. It had been a year ago today that she had come to the Circle S. A year of changes, a year of new beginnings, a year of putting down roots.

Resting her chin on her knees, she looked out across the yard, smiling to herself. She and Cyrus had practically torn it apart last fall, with considerable help from Rita, and he had done an enormous amount of work in it this year, thanks to an early spring. It was going to be beautiful, providing they could keep Burt away from the flower beds with the riding lawn mower.

Everything had been mowed to within an inch of its life since Tanner had brought the machine home. Along the lane, around the outbuildings, between the trees—there wasn't a blade of grass that got longer than four inches before Burt was out there roaring around. Cyrus said he was worse than a flock of sheep. And the boys were right there with him, finding new vistas for him to mow.

She grinned to herself, thinking about Cyrus and Burt. She hoped that they would behave themselves when her parents came for spring branding, but she didn't hold out much hope of that. Her mother laughed at everything they did, which made them worse, and her father was just as bad as they were.

She'd found that out at Christmas. They'd had a heavy snowfall a week before, just after her folks and Chase had arrived, and Burt had suddenly got it in his head that it would be a terrible, terrible thing if the boys couldn't have a Christmas hayride. So he'd bought a matched set of champion Clydesdales off a neighbor who bred them, along with the show harnesses and bells, an old-fashioned sleigh and a hayrack, then insisted she invite some of the neighbors over for Boxing Day. Midway through the afternoon, Chase and Rita found some old inner tubes in the shop, which they inflated and tied on behind the sleigh. The trick was to ride them standing up— waterskiing-style—and Kate couldn't remember laughing as much as she had that afternoon. It had been the best Christmas.

Of course, now they were stuck with the team of Clydesdales. Now Burt and Cyrus were dropping hints about the big draft horses, arguing about heavy horse pulls, and Kate had found a breeder's catalog in Burt's room. Burt told her to mind her own business, saying it was for the boys. Tanner just smiled, shook his head and wrote out the checks for their follies.

But the biggest change of all had taken place between Tanner and the boys. Mark was practically his shadow, and Kate had yet to see Tanner lose his patience with either one of them. She knew it had been hard for him when they'd started school in the fall—the same school that he'd attended, the same place that held such humiliating memories for him—but he had gone with her when she'd enrolled them, and he'd gone again for parent-teacher interviews.

But the thing that had been most difficult for him was the school Christmas concert. It was a small town and a big public event, and Tanner was, by nature, a very private person. Kate suspected there had been a fair amount of speculation about Tanner McCall's new wife, so she wasn't surprised when several heads turned their way when they all walked in. But what created a stir was the fact that Chase McCall was there with his half brother's family.

It wasn't until after the concert, when several people made a point of stopping to speak to Tanner and Chase, that Kate realized just how highly he was regarded by other ranchers, and when the new bank manager found he *was* the Circle S Ranch, he all but slavered at Tanner's feet.

The thing with the bank manager had struck her as so immensely funny that every time she looked at Tanner after that, her shoulders would start to shake. Tanner finally hooked his arm around her neck, threatening that if she didn't quit it, he would make her walk home. That set her off all over again, and Tanner stood there in the middle of the school library, staring at her with that half-disgusted, half-amused expression in his eyes, as if he couldn't quite make up his mind whether to strangle her or kiss her, and she knew, from somewhere deep inside her, that they had just turned a major corner.

She heard the screen door open behind her, and she turned. It was Tanner, his jeans unsnapped and his shirt unbuttoned, his four-week-old daughter cuddled against his shoulder. Allison Dawn. Allison for Tanner's mother. Dawn because Kate thought it was appropriate. And Kate's insides turned to mush every time she saw him with her.

He grinned down at her. "Our star boarder is complaining."

Kate gave him a dry look. "Then our star boarder shouldn't have fallen asleep at two this morning." She took her daughter, then moved down a step. Tanner sat down behind her, pulling her back between his thighs. She unzipped the front of her sweat suit and undid her nursing bra, and the baby rooted hungrily against her breast, then found the nipple and latched on. Tanner loosely looped his arms around Kate, then rested his head alongside hers. He slipped his finger beneath his daughter's hand where it lay against Kate's breast, and the baby gripped it, continuing to suckle. Tanner spoke, his tone amused. "At least nothing is going to distract her from breakfast."

Kate's tone was dry. "She must be related to Burt."

Tanner chuckled and kissed the curve of her neck, then continued to watch his daughter feed, and Kate leaned back against his chest, loving the feel of his warmth around her. It was so rare that they got any time alone during the day, so she'd learned to value times like this—quiet, private times with no interruptions.

Tanner snuggled her closer and rubbed her arm. "Do you know what day this is?"

For an instant Kate considered stringing him along, but this was too important, too personal, to treat lightly. She turned and rubbed her forehead against his jaw. "A year ago today, a man walked into a roadside café and my life changed."

He laced his fingers through hers. "A year ago today I walked into a roadside café and knew my life would never be the same."

Kate's vision blurred, and she closed her eyes, resting her head against his. She was under no illusions. It was Saturday. The boys were likely already downstairs cooking up something with Burt. The baby would decide that now would be a good time to get fussy. And Cyrus would almost certainly show up for coffee. So the private part would have to wait until later that night—when she'd made arrangements to take him back to that roadside café.

Turning in his arms, she kissed his neck, then grinned up at him. "I *thought* I recognized you from somewhere."

Holding her gaze, he stared down at her, amusement appearing in his eyes, then he smiled that slow, sensual, intimate smile that made her go weak inside. But it was the glint of amusement making her heart falter. "You're nothing but trouble, do you know that?"

Supporting the baby, she reached up and kissed him, loving the way he opened his mouth and kissed her right back. "You like it," she whispered against his mouth.

He chuckled, then lightly brushed her bottom lip. "You're right. I do."

* * * * *